Rosebush

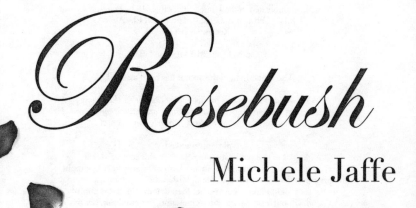

Rosebush

Michele Jaffe

www.atombooks.net

ATOM

First published in the United States in 2010 by Penguin
First published in Great Britain in 2011 by Atom
Reprinted 2011

A CIP catalogue record for this book
is available from the British Library.

ISBN 978-1-907410-38-3

Printed in Great Britain by Clays Ltd, St Ives plc

Atom
An imprint of
Little, Brown Book Group
100 Victoria Embankment
London EC4Y 0DY

An Hachette UK Company
www.hachette.co.uk

www.atombooks.net

For Heather, Lila, and Elle Vandenberghe
I am so grateful to have all three of you

Acknowledgements

Writing a book is always a thorny proposition, and I was beyond lucky to have the guidance, support, help, and patience of—

Meg Cabot

Susan Ginsberg

Lexa Hillyer

Peter Jaffe

Princesses of Apt 11D

Laura Rosenbury

Ben Schrank

Bethany Strout

Jennifer Sturman

Anna Webman

Whole Foods biscuits

the marvelous people of Writers House and Razorbill

everyone who tolerated me when I was pretty intolerable

—in cajoling the manuscript into blossom. Thank you all immensely.

Anything that came out smelling like a rose is because of them. Everything else is my doing alone.

Prologue

*T*he image is stark yet beautiful.

It's just before dawn, at that moment when the world turns monochrome and everything is subsumed under a blanket of blue-gray light. The streetlights have gone off, the street is a still gray ribbon scarred with two black marks trailing from the upper left of the picture to the lower right. In the background, blurry, large houses hunker down, streaked dark from rain. In the foreground and slightly to the right, set in blue-gray grass, is a fantastic bush. It looks like something from a fairy tale, a witch cursed into an alternate form, gnarled fingers reaching for the sky. At the center lies a girl.

Shreds of her tulle skirt are tangled among the branches blowing in the morning breeze like tiny flags. A ceramic rabbit, a mother duck followed by five tiny ducklings, and a squirrel playing the flute stand silent guard around her. One of her legs is bent up; the other juts out of the bush dangling a platform shoe, Cinderella after the ball gone bad. Her left hand is under her and the right one, with a friendship ring on the index finger, reaches up as though to pluck the single deep-red rose that hangs above her—the only spot of color in the image. Her face is lovely, dark hair feathering over half of it. Her body is covered with angry gashes and a magenta river of blood trickles from her head. Her lips part, as though she's about to say something.

But then you see her eyes and know it's impossible. They are wide open, pupils fully dilated. And sightless.

It looks like any one of a dozen photos I've taken for my Dead Princesses series, with two crucial differences.

The girl in this photo should have been dead. And I didn't take it.

I'm in it. I'm the girl.

It was the police who shot it, responding to the 911 call from Mrs. Doyle reporting a dead body in her front yard on Dove Street. They arrived three minutes after the call. It took them five minutes to stabilize my breathing and thirty-two minutes to cut me out of the bush.

When I woke up, I had no memory of how I got there or what led up to it, which is apparently normal. All I remembered was pain and the single thought *I must not let go*.

But slowly pieces of it have been coming back. An intensive care unit is a good place to do a lot of deep thinking—or a bad one, depending on what you're thinking about. I stare at the photo in my hand trying to see myself as an object, another clue. In the past three days, much of the puzzle has been filled in and I'm not sure I like the picture that is emerging.

"Hello, princess," says a cheery voice from the door of my room.

I look up and see an unfamiliar man in scrubs walking in. I miss Loretta.

Loretta's the regular nurse in the ICU, the one I was used to seeing. Plus she was on duty when I first opened my eyes, and even though I was only in the ICU three days, I felt like she and I knew each other well. Time passes in strange ways in the ICU, allowing you to form unusual relationships.

"Oh, that's ICU time," Loretta had explained to me.

"ICU time?"

"It's like how they say dogs age seven years for every one of ours? Well, every minute in the ICU feels about an hour long. Time here either crawls or flashes by, and let me tell you, sweetheart, you'd rather it was crawling. Flash-forwards never mean anything good."

The new guy is now saying, "I'm Ruben. And from the looks of this room, you're Little Miss Popular."

Ruben, I repeat, mentally cataloging the name. One thing Loretta likes to do is gossip, but I can't remember her saying anything about him.

He fingers several bouquets on the windowsill, ending up with the two dozen red roses. "This must have set someone back plenty. I wish I could find a boyfriend as generous."

"They're not from my boyfriend," I tell him.

"*Woo-hoo,* then you're doing something right. What about this guy?" He picks up a teddy bear wearing a muscle shirt that says GET WELL BEARY SOON! "Not sure if that's from a friend or an enemy."

"Me either." I'm thinking about how that's true in more ways than one as he moves on to study the rest of the get-well presents covering every surface of my room, so I only half pay attention as he asks about the card with the puppies on it playing instruments from David and the balloon bouquet from Nikki with the card that says CHEERS.

Now Ruben is standing in front of a heart-shaped wreath of roses that's flanked by a figurine and a doll. "What are all these over here? 'From your secret admirer,'" he reads aloud from one of the cards. "All this?" He gestures. I nod. "So let me see—you've got a boyfriend, a *not* boyfriend, and a secret admirer." He shakes his head at me.

"Girl, no wonder someone tried to run you down."

He's right. I have a lot of presents because somehow—unaccountably—I'm actually popular. And most of the "We miss you!" and "Get well soon" messages are lies—*because* I'm very popular.

That's the irony, isn't it? The cruel lesson I've learned. In movies everyone loves the princess, but in reality it's different. Popularity isn't a double-edged sword; it has only one edge—kill or be killed. There's a finite amount of space at the top of the social pyramid and once you've reached it, there's only one direction to go and no shortage of people who want to push you there.

I know now who tried to kill me, but I don't want to believe it. Every part of my mind seeks out other solutions, any other possible explanation, because the truth is too horrifying. I've had every clue I needed to figure it out in front of me all along, but I've been willfully blind. It's like that moment when you're framing a shot and what was blurry comes finally and acutely into focus. Only in this case I don't want it to.

"I'll be back to check on you in a tic, princess," Ruben says.

I could try to stop him, but it won't change anything. This killer can get at me anywhere.

My gaze returns to the photo of me in the rosebush and it's all completely clear. There is only one person who could have done all of this. One person to whom everything points. The drink. The slammed door. The kiss. The car. The ring.

The eyes.

I've seen the writing on the wall. I know what has to come next.

"Hi, Jane," the male voice says from the door.

Thursday

Chapter 1

*I*t's hard to talk when you're being kissed. I experienced that for the first time with Liam Marsh when I was in ninth grade. I was experiencing it again with my boyfriend, David Tisch, as a junior in front of Livingston Senior High School at two forty-five on the Thursday before Memorial Day weekend.

Which was why I had planned a surprise for that night. Because as much as I loved the Flintstone-vitamin-plus-pot flavor of David's kisses and the way he used his tongue to nudge my lips apart while he held my shoulders in his big hands, I had something important to talk to him about.

I pulled away now. His eyes opened halfway, slowly, and focused on me. "What are you doing, babe?"

"I told you, I'm saving up. For tonight."

"Right. For the surprise." He twisted a piece of my long dark hair between his fingers. "I wish you wouldn't go to all that trouble. We can just be together like we always are." His fingers moved to knead the muscles in my neck, almost too hard. He didn't realize how strong they were from all his drum practice. "Why do we have to drive all the way out to the shore and go to some stupid party?"

"It will be worth it," I said, giving him a look I hoped was at once cute and suggestive. "I promise."

He shook his head but seemed more amused than annoyed. "You and your plans."

It had rained almost continuously for the past week, but today was clear and fine and blazed with sun so bright that the white trim on the brick face of the main building shimmered. The big elm tree above us moved lazily in the breeze, the leaves rich spring green. Shadows fell like puddles around us. It was the kind of day, the kind of moment, when anything can happen.

The seniors had planned to make the long weekend even longer by ditching Friday and naturally we juniors were going to stand in solidarity with them, so everyone who was anyone was headed to Jocelyn Gunter's party in Deal on the Jersey shore that night.

The sun picked out the golden highlights in David's brown-sort-of-long-sort-of-curly sort of hair, framing his face, making him look like a cross between Jesus and Jim Morrison, a comparison I knew he'd like.

David's hand was on my chin, tilting it toward him, looking into my eyes over the top of his glasses. "Hey babe, where'd you go?"

"I'm right here," I said, and brushed my hip against him.

But the truth was, I hadn't been listening. Not because I wanted to avoid something, which was what my mother would say. I was trying to think about how I would capture the shot, what it would look like framed by my camera lens, and half wishing that David hadn't set down his drumstick bag because the tilt of his shoulder would have made a more interesting picture. I'm a photographer; I can't help it if my mind wanders to how things would look from the outside.

Besides, if I was avoiding something, would I have organized a whole special dinner to talk about it?

"I can't wait until we're on our camping trip, babe," he said, smiling lazily. I saw myself reflected in the lenses of his glasses, a distorted fuzzy image. "Just you and me and the wilderness. None of these other people, no distractions, no—"

I stood on my tiptoes now and kissed him on the lips. He took it as me agreeing with him, not me wanting to change the subject. "Hold that thought until tonight," I said.

He sighed and tucked a piece of hair behind my right ear. "Temptress. I don't know how long I can control myself around you. I'd better go."

I laughed. He gave me a goofy grin, said, "Stay soft" (his version of goodbye), then lumbered off.

I loved the way he moved, smooth and relaxed, his fingers drumming on his leg. He high-fived Dom, the guitarist in the band, and put his arm around Chelsea, their lead singer. I might have been a little jealous if he hadn't turned around at that moment and shot me a smile and a peace sign over her shoulder.

God, I was lucky.

He disappeared into the crowd and I turned and spotted Langley and Kate already in Langley's five-and-a-half-month-old red BMW convertible. I was about to walk over when I noticed Ollie leaning against the passenger-side door. Maybe I should take a sec and do a few shots of the facade of the school, I thought. The light really was perfect and it hardly ever—

"Jelly bean," Langley said as I was reaching for my camera. She waved at me. "Come on, we've got so much to do." I slid the camera back into my bag and started toward the car. As I walked over, Ollie's olive-green eyes raked me up and down lazily.

Oliver "Ollie" Montero was David's best friend and his complete opposite. While David wore James Brown Loves Y'all T-shirts and Chuck Taylors, Ollie wore button-downs and Gucci loafers. Where David liked me, Ollie didn't. Talking to him always made me feel insecure, like he'd ordered filet mignon and someone brought him a burger instead.

Now he was blocking my access to Langley's backseat. "Will we see you at Joss's party tonight?" I asked, just to be saying something. I also always had the sense that, like a dog, Ollie could smell my fear and it amused him.

He looked at me two beats longer than he needed to. "I never went to Livingston High School parties before, why would I start now?" According to rumor, Ollie only dated girls from the fancy schools in New York City like Chapin and Spence, girls whose last names were almost as long as the strings of zeros on their trust funds.

"Can a girl ask who your date is tonight, Mr. Montero?" Kate drawled from the passenger seat, giving Ollie a sugary smile and batting her eyelids. She was doing her Scarlet O'Hara imitation, which was one of her best and usually had a subtle barb at the end. "Blair? Muffy? Brent?"

Unlike me, Kate had no problem dealing with Ollie. With long-lidded gray eyes edged with a dark blue ring and wavy golden-brown hair, Kate was pretty much drop-dead gorgeous. She ruled the drama program at Livingston High, getting every lead since her first day on campus. She also had what my political-consultant mother described wistfully as perfect political-wife manners, a way of looking at you like she cared about what you said, like you were the only person she wanted to talk to in the room. Her style was slightly bohemian. She never rushed, never seemed concerned about anything and yet always looked perfect, unsmudged, unchipped, un-covered-with-crumbs-from-the-cupcake-she-scarfed-before-English. Unlike me, the mess magnet.

Kate also had a wild streak that I didn't exactly advertise to my mother. It came out onstage, in her laugh, and when operating motor vehicles.

Which was why Langley was our designated driver.

Langley looked like someone Vikings would fight over: hair like fresh ice, eyes like the light-blue of the Arctic ocean, skin like carved alabaster, and a mouth that always appeared as if it was on the edge of mischievous laughter. That impression was half true and half from the faint scar that ran across her right cheek. Langley was short and petite but gave the impression of being much bigger, one of those people who didn't just enter a room but filled it. Her favorite color was red, like her car and like the beret, sweater, skirt, and ankle boots she was wearing.

Leaning his elbows against the shiny red door of the BMW, Ollie spread his hands in mock consternation. "If only one of you harridans would go out with me, I wouldn't have to roam so far from home."

"I don't think any of us want what you have," Langley said.

"What's that?" Ollie asked. "Charm? Charisma?"

"Crabs?" Kate said, still sugar sweet.

"Always a delight to chat with you, Ollie," Langley said, revving the engine. "But for now, please move your Ralph Lauren–clad ass so Jane can get into the car."

"You're slipping, angel. It's John Varvatos."

Langley raised an eyebrow at him. "Freals, you're slipping if you think I care."

Ollie laughed, said, "Touché," and sauntered over to a dark-blue Mercedes with a driver waiting for him at the curb.

I got in and we touched pinkies, our friendship salute. Langley started to say, "Okay, lovelies, let's—" but interrupted herself to look at Kate. She sighed.

"You know what you need to do."

"No." Kate shook her head and made her eyes very wide. "That is why God created windshields."

"So you can crash your head through them?" Langley asked. "Put on your seat belt."

Kate sighed. "With the way you drive, Safety Officer Langley, it's hardly necessary."

"It's very simple," Langley said, holding up a finger. "The first rule of Langley Motors is: Don't talk back to Langley. The second rule of Langley Motors is: Don't talk back to Langley. The third rule—"

"Let me get a pen so I can take these down?" Five bangles tinkled on Kate's wrist as she pulled her seat belt across the faux-fur vest she was wearing over a cotton minidress. "It's sad that you have to lord this over me when I have no other options."

"You had the option to not run the second Mercedes your parents bought you this year into the front of Madame Yong's. There is such a thing as delivery, you know."

"That's brilliant," Kate said, clapping with mock enthusiasm. "I didn't know you could do impressions of my father. Do another one! Oh please?"

Langley shook her head. Her pale-blue eyes moved to me in the rearview. "Jane?"

"I'm locked in, ma'am," I assured her with a little salute, tugging on the seat belt strap that crisscrossed my ruffled T-shirt.

"Kiss ass," Kate said, rolling her eyes.

"No, just a law-abiding citizen," I countered.

Langley went on. "Here's the plan. We'll go to my house to get the costumes, then—"

My cell phone started to ring, interrupting her. I glanced at the caller ID, winced inwardly seeing the same number for the second time that day, and sent it to voice mail. Langley didn't like being interrupted and I didn't feel like talking to that particular caller anyway. "Sorry. Go on."

"After we get the costumes, we'll change at Kate's place on the beach and then walk over to the party so no one has to worry about driving. Joss is going to make everyone leave their keys at the door and I don't want anyone touching my baby."

A horn blared behind us. Turning around, I saw Nicky di Savoia leaning out the open window of her lemon-yellow Karmann Ghia. Nicky was David's ex-girlfriend and not a huge fan of mine. I waved.

She sneered. "Could you please discuss lip gloss or whatever hugely important issue you're debating elsewhere, vapid bitches?"

"Takes one to know one," Langley shouted pleasantly. Nicky kept honking, but Langley ignored her. She buttoned her red-leather driving gloves with care, signaled with her turn indicator, and slowly steered out of the driveway.

Nicky sped past us, flipping us off.

"Tsk-tsk, that's no way to drive," Langley commented. "DJ Kate, will you please do the honors?"

Kate flipped on the stereo and it started blaring Blondie. With "Heart of Glass" screaming from the speakers, I closed my eyes and pictured what we must look like. In my mind I framed the shot, the two of them with two different colors of blond hair up front, me with my dark hair fanned against the cream leather of the backseat of the red convertible, blue sky and green trees a blur in the background. It was a perfect image, the perfect snapshot of three popular girls embarking on a great weekend. I was happy, happier than I could ever remember feeling. I wished I could freeze the moment like that forever, *click*, to assure myself that it was real.

Because I still had trouble seeing myself in the snapshot. Kate Valenti and Langley Winterman were the top of the social pyramid. Even after two years I could hardly believe I was friends with them. Being popular wasn't something that came naturally for me. I'd worked at it. And paid for it.

Chapter 2

*I*t started the summer before freshman year. I still remember the day I told my best friend in Illinois, Bonnie, about my plan.

Bonnie and I had been best friends since my family moved in next door to hers when we were both seven and my pet turtle, Amerigo Vespucci, slipped through a hole in the fence and discovered her cat, Rolo. Like the man he was named for, Amerigo was a relentless explorer, always going off on his own and unafraid of anything despite being small enough to fit in the palm of my hand. He'd disappear for a day or two at a time and come back trailing leaves of unknown origin or strange splotches on his shell. I admired his courage and sense of adventure even as it mystified me.

Amerigo and Rolo became fast friends and so did Bonnie and I. Soon we were inseparable, planning elaborate funerals for the dead mice Rolo dragged in and making our own radio show and staying up late outside reading and giggling, then reading and gossiping, and later talking about boys.

We didn't have much luck with them. Which was why I decided, the summer before freshman year, to use my earnings from my summer business doing photo portraits of people's pets to go to Chicago and get a haircut and makeup and a new wardrobe.

Bonnie was saving all the money she made from her summer job as a junior lifeguard for the school spring trip to Spain. She thought I was crazy. "There's nothing wrong with you the way you are. Why would you want to be one of the Stall Sisters?"

Stall Sisters was Bonnie's name for the popular girls in our class because they seemed to spend most of their time in the restroom either fixing their makeup or crying. "Or both at the same time," she noted. "Which shows how stupid they are."

But I knew she was all talk. "It's a new year and a new school," I pointed out. "We can be anyone we want. Don't you want to be popular?"

"Why?"

Because popularity meant being accepted. Belonging. Never being alone. Because it was what everyone wanted.

"Not me," Bonnie said positively. "I'm not that crazy about the girls' bathroom."

"Do you want to die without being kissed?"

"You think popularity is going to get you kissed? Good luck with that, dream walker."

But it did. My makeover worked. People who had never spoken to me before started saying hi in the halls, and I managed to say hi back, and one day a group of popular sophomores came and sat at my table at lunch and I couldn't eat because I was so worried about spilling, but it was worth it. I got Bonnie and myself an invitation to a party being thrown by one of the most popular seniors. Bonnie hadn't wanted to go, but I convinced—okay, begged—her, and she finally gave in.

At the party Liam Marsh kissed me and like Sleeping Beauty, I was brought to life—social life. As his girlfriend, my popularity was guaranteed. So six months later when my mother announced we were moving to New Jersey so she could run a mayoral campaign and put herself "on the East Coast political map," I was devastated. Not just because of the popularity—by that point, Liam had become my whole world, the only solid thing I had. We said goodbye. I cried. He told me not to worry, we'd always be together.

The night before the first day of school in New Jersey, I got a text from Liam saying he wanted to be just friends. I took a bottle of vodka I found in the kitchen—Liam had introduced me to vodka the way he'd introduced me to all his friends—and a pair of nail scissors into the bathroom. When I woke up the next morning, I felt bad but not as bad as I looked. I'd hacked off my bangs and left myself with a strange fringe sticking out. So not how you want to look on your first day at a new school, but I was beyond caring. Or so I told myself.

Livingston High was smaller than my other school but more labyrinthine and scary. I endured lunch alone, studiously not looking at anyone, until the bell rang for fourth period. As I got up to go, my tights caught on the bottom of the cafeteria table and I got two huge runs in my right leg. Perfect.

Out in the hallway I watched as girls went by, arm in arm, or paused to touch pinkies with one another. Couples strolled along, guys staring straight ahead as their girlfriends nuzzled their necks. That had been me once. I realized I'd spent most of my freshman year with Liam's arm around my shoulders, his Irish Spring–scented neck near my cheek, and knowing I would never have that again made my stomach lurch. I felt too light, insubstantial, like I almost didn't exist. I was used to looking up at him, turning to him to decide what came next, what we wanted to do. *We.* I ached for *we*, hated *I. I* was lonely and untethered and abandoned and unloved. Unlovable.

I felt like I was going to be sick.

The bell rang for fourth period, but I couldn't face it. So I did the only thing I could think of: I went and sat in the girls' bathroom with my feet up on the toilet.

I'd been there about a minute when I realized that there was someone else doing the same thing next to me. Only it sounded like she was hyperventilating.

"Are you okay?" I asked.

There was a startled gasp. "I didn't realize anyone was in here."

"No one is."

"Um, you are? You're someone?"

"Not here." I'd meant to say it to myself, but it came out of my mouth instead. It was the kind of mistake, saying the wrong thing and seeming too insecure, that I dreaded.

There was shuffling next door and a tanned hand with two gold rings, attached to a fine-knit gray-cashmere-clad arm, appeared over the top of the stall. It was followed by a perfect oval-shaped head and a mane of wavy hair the color of fine brandy pinned back in that perfectly tousled way only people on television and the naturally gorgeous manage to achieve. The kind of girl who's never even realized she was popular because she always has been. I'd noticed her in English class earlier that day, surrounded by a group of other girls all clamoring for her attention. She was wearing a gray tunic with a leather-and-bone belt I'd seen in my mother's copy of September *Vogue*.

"I'm Kate?" she said, almost like it was a question. I'd come to learn she nearly always phrased things that way. She held out her hand. "Who are you?"

I stood up on the toilet and shook it. "I'm Jane. We have English together."

"Do we?" Her eyes went toward the ceiling like she was trying to summon a memory. "I don't remember seeing you."

"I just mov—" I stopped because the girl called Kate's lip started to tremble and she blinked like she was on the verge of tears. "Are you oka—"

Suddenly she started to cry. Without thinking, I reached my arms around to hug her.

She went stiff and sucked in her breath. I pulled back. "I'm sorry. I didn't—"

She swatted the tears on her face. "No, *I'm* sorry. That was inappropriate." She blinked. "I'm just going to get down"—gesturing with her fingers toward the floor—"and then go?"

"Right. Me too."

We both climbed off the toilets. I reached over and flushed even though I hadn't done anything and then I felt like a huge moron because what if she thought I'd done something? And I'd been like standing over it the whole time? Exactly the kind of thing a loser did.

I opened the door and went and stood at the sink next to her. At least I could look like I cared about hygiene. As I washed my hands, I thought maybe Bonnie had been right about popularity. Maybe it was all basically in the toilet, maybe—

"I'm guessing they're clean?" Kate said, nodding at my hands. She was about a foot taller than I was even though her brown knee-high boots were flat.

"Oh, right. I was just—"

And then she burst into tears again. Only this time she threw herself against me. My arms came up to hug her and she didn't pull away. She cried like that for a few minutes, then the heaving of her shoulders slowed down, stopped.

She stepped back. Suddenly the navy-blue puff-sleeved sweater dress with tights and ankle boots I'd thought was so cool when I put it on that morning now looked over-thought-out and dated. As I looked from my face—pale oval, blue eyes, pink lips, smudgy shadows under my eyes from the vodka, unfortunate hedge of dark short bangs—to hers—perfect despite the fact she'd just been sobbing—I felt a rising wave of panic and insecurity. Which wasn't helped by her saying, "Why didn't you leave?"

This time it definitely was a question, and not a friendly one. Her eyes were glittering and her jaw was set. "I mean, I didn't want anyone to see me like this?"

I was kind of surprised by her change in tone. "I told you, I'm not anyone," trying to make a joke.

In a flash her hardness transformed into confusion. She turned from looking at me in the mirror to looking me directly in the face, her brow furrowed. "Why are you being so nice to me?"

"Because you seem sad?"

She turned back to the mirror. "You mean weak." She grabbed a paper towel and started drying the tears off her cheeks. Only it was more like she was trying to rub them out.

"No, I mean sad."

She kept rubbing, her eyes avoiding mine. "Well anyway, thank you?"

"It was nothing. I'm sure you'd do the same thing for me."

She dropped the paper towel in the trash can and stared hard at her reflection. She might have perfectly symmetrical features and be model beautiful, but the expression on her face when she looked at herself was like she was looking at trash.

"In all honesty, probably not?" Now she smiled, but it was mirthless. When she spoke again, it was in a southern drawl, harsh and staccato: "I'm a spoiled bitch with a perfect life who's not even half grateful and never thinks of a thing but herself. At least that's how my daddy would put it."

It was my first encounter with Kate's amazing ability to imitate anyone's voice, and it was disconcerting. Between that and the anger beneath her words, I didn't know what to say. I can't even guess how long I would have stood there like a moron, nervously fingering my dark, short bangs, if the door to the bathroom hadn't slammed open then.

A blonde girl with the kind of confidence that came from always having been popular exploded through it into the room. Wearing shorts made out of some kind of brocade over lace tights, a sweater with ruffles down the front, and platform pumps with her mass of light-blonde hair tied into low pigtails with two satin bows, she looked more ready for a catwalk than a walk to class. She didn't even glance at me, just rushed to Kate, put a maternal hand on her cheek, and said, "Are you okay, Kit Kat?"

The Kate that turned to face her friend was nothing like the falling-apart girl I'd seen. She smiled like she was amused by the shorter girl's concern and said, "Yes, Mother Langley, I'm fine. I just had bad cramps."

The girl called Langley tilted back and put her hands on her hips. "Want fries with that?"

Kate's brow wrinkled. "Fries with what?"

"That whopper you just told."

Kate looked wide-eyed taken aback, but I couldn't help it, I started to laugh. Langley's eyes came to me then. "I like an appreciative audience. Who are you?"

"That's Jane," Kate told her. "She's new here? She gave me something to kill the pain." She winked at me.

Langley tilted her head to one side and studied me for a moment like I was a bio slide she had to correctly identify. Then she nodded, having located the right classification. "I'm not going to lie, you're cute, but the bangs are a bit extreme. Freals, did you do that yourself?"

I nodded. "My boyfriend from back home broke up with me." I couldn't believe I was admitting that. How pathetic did I look?

She came over and tried to push the bangs to one side. "Yeah, not going to work. Your tights, though, those are cool." She stepped back and assessed me again. "Do either of you have a pen?"

I fished one out of my bag and handed it to her. She immediately stuck it into her black lace tights and started to rip through them.

I was shocked. "What are you doing?"

"One for all—" Langley said.

"—And all for one," Kate finished, smiling not at me but at her friend. It was like a secret message passed between them.

A message I only understood a little later when, after having put a second run in her lace tights, Langley said, "Okay, I think we can debut this." Kate and Langley each took one of my arms and together we left the bathroom.

"Watch what happens," Langley said as we paraded down the hall. "We're about to make your year."

They introduced me to Elsa, the third member of what they called the Three Must-kateers because whatever they did, everyone else must follow. And it was true. By the end of the day, five other girls had runs in their tights. The next day most of the sophomores, three quarters of the juniors, and even a handful of seniors did too. And four girls had hacked their bangs off with nail scissors.

I'd arrived. Whatever the Mustkateers put their stamp of approval on—wearing sunglasses to class until the faculty banned it, wearing candy necklaces, wearing globs of red nail polish on the knees of your jeans because I was trying to paint Langley's nails at lunch and made a complete mess—everyone else approved of too. And that included me. I would never be lonely again.

Within weeks I was hanging out with Langley and Kate and Elsa all the time. And then came the morning when Elsa was found by the school custodian on the roof wearing nothing but a pair of anklets, after which she disappeared for a month to "relax" at a special hospital in Aspen. When she got back, I'd taken her place as one of the official Three Mustkateers. "Because there can only be three," Langley had explained.

"And we've chosen you," Kate finished for her, grinning.

"Besides," Langley added in an undertone, "with the number of voices Elsa has in her head, she doesn't need any more friends."

We touched pinkies and looking at our three arms, all with matching leather studded bracelets on them, I was too happy—and afraid of jinxing it—to ask how I got so lucky.

Once I'd been adopted by Kate and Langley, the move to Livingston had been great. At least until Joe Garcetti, proprietor of Garcetti Construction, showed up at one of the town hall meetings my mother was running, asked a question that stumped her candidate, thereby giving her the impression he was insightful, and took her out for dinner.

It wasn't that I didn't like him, although I didn't. It was that I didn't trust him. If there was shady business, he would be in it.

"What kind of construction-company owner gets calls at midnight?" I'd demanded of my mother.

She hadn't even paused in touching up her lipstick. "The kind with projects in Dubai."

Nothing I said stopped them from getting engaged or moving into the ten-thousand-square-foot brand-new house—with stone floors "flown in direct from Italy" and moldings as wide as my head—

that Joe called the "Chateau" (or, the way he pronounced it, the Chatoo). He'd rubbed his hands together as he showed us around the first time, and the image of my mother as some kind of goddess sacrifice got burned into my mind.

But it was her choice and she seemed hell-bent on going through with it.

In fact, during breakfast this morning, in the massive stone "Provençal-farmhouse-style" kitchen, my mother had said, "I thought this weekend you and Annie and I could go out for lunch after you get fitted for your bridesmaids' dresses."

"You're not serious, are you?"

She'd sighed and tried not to look upset, but I saw the anger in her eyes. "Why can't you find a way to like Joe? Annie adores him."

"Annie's only seven and her best friend is a Barbie she's decided is transsexual, so I'm not sure about her taste. And I don't care that you're getting married, I just think you might want to do it with dignity, not in a way where you make a fool of yourself. Do you have any idea how ridiculous you'll look having a formal wedding?"

"If you can't improve your attitude about this, I won't include you in the ceremony."

"Great. Don't include me. Don't include me in anything."

I'd stomped out of the kitchen and almost tripped over Annie, who was playing some kind of game tucked just behind the dining room door. She had her hands over her ears, humming. I stopped and said her name, but she just kept humming and rocking back and forth.

Damn. Seeing her there made my anger start to evaporate, and by the time I was heading back downstairs, I was ready to apologize. If my mother wanted to make a fool of herself by having some big formal wedding, she could do that and I could blame her for it for years to come in therapy. Joe might not be my ideal choice, but if he made my mother happy, then that should be enough.

I'd nearly reached the kitchen when I overheard my mother and Joe talking. Their voices carried easily across the stone kitchen.

He was saying, "I wish there was something I could do. I just hate to see you so miserable, Rosie."

"Let it be, Joe. It's a tough time for her. And grounding her will just keep her here with us, throwing a fit. I'm letting her go with her friends."

Kate's voice pulled me out of my thoughts and back into the reality of the butter-leather cocoon of Langley's backseat. Kate had wrapped her mane of silky honey-gold hair in one hand and swiveled so she could look at me. The sun caught at the curled tendrils playing around her face, making it look like she had a gold halo. As though she'd been reading my mind, she said, "Did you have any trouble with your mom about tonight?"

"No." I shook my head. "I didn't even have to give her any of the excuses we'd made up to stay out all night. She doesn't care enough about me to ground me, let alone care where I'm going."

I swallowed hard, swallowing back a lump that had unaccountably materialized in my throat. When we'd lived in Illinois, my mother had been a tyrant, wanting to know where I was all the time, with whom, until when. Before—

It didn't matter, I reminded myself. That was past history. Now she didn't want to know anything about my life. Anything about me. We lived in rough silences and occasional outbursts that did nothing but make the silence more appealing.

Langley shook her platinum head with wonder. "My grandparents demand such a precise record from me of everywhere I'm going that I'm thinking of hiring a private detective to follow me around and prepare a report. You're lucky."

"Totally," I agreed.

So why did I feel anything but?

My phone buzzed in my pocket, and with the touch of a chipped purple nail I quickly bounced the caller to voice mail once again.

But not fast enough. "Someone's popular today," Langley said, her light-blue eyes catching my gaze in the rearview. "Who is it?"

"Unknown number," I lied. I felt a warm blush creeping up my neck.

"I think Jane has a secret," Langley said in a singsong voice to Kate.

"No, really, it's probably just a telemarketer." I wasn't even sure why I was lying. I mean, Langley didn't like Scott because she thought his intentions toward me were "impure," but she wouldn't care if he called. I think the truth was, I felt a little guilty about the way I was avoiding him. But there had been something uncomfortable in our last few communications I couldn't define and didn't feel like dealing with.

I was spared having to think about it anymore because at that moment, Langley reached out to turn down the music and we pulled into the long driveway that led to the Winterman house.

Chapter 3

*I*f the monstrosity that Joe had built was a Chatoo, then the house Langley lived in with her grandparents was a palace, but a real one.

Mr. and Mrs. Lawrence Arthur Winterman were leading lights in New Jersey social and philanthropic circles and they somewhat terrified me, so I couldn't imagine what it must be like to live in the sprawling house with the gray-and-white-uniformed staff. But Langley had Maman and Popo, as she called her grandmother and grandfather, wrapped around her finger and they doted on her.

Mrs. Winterman was in the oak-paneled foyer when we came in, her lean straight pantsuit-clad back to the door, watching one of the uniformed housemaids adjusting a vase of flowers. Her pantsuits bore no resemblance to the blue polyester ones with the permacreases that my grandma and her friends wore down in Boca Raton.

"No, Ivanka, I said to the left." She gestured impatiently with a hand that held a massive emerald ring. "I can still see the camera. I want it hidden."

Langley announced, "I'm home, Maman," and moved to give her grandmother a cheek to kiss. "We're just going to my room to get my pajamas. We're having a girls' sleepover at Kate's house tonight. I put it on the calendar last week."

"That's right, dear, very good," Mrs. Winterman said. She rested the hand with the emerald on Langley's arm. "Before you go, will you check on your grandfather? And watch the new nurse especially? I think she's stealing his medication."

"Of course, Grandmother."

Recently Mrs. Winterman had developed a penchant for security, which, coupled with her overprotectiveness, was starting to make living in their house "more prison than palace," as Langley put it. "Where the guards wear Oscar de la Renta suits and specially blended Creed perfume," she had added.

"See?" Langley whispered now as we followed her red-suede ankle boots up the stairs to her room. "Crazy."

Langley's room was as neat and impersonal as a hotel and yet somehow suited her. The walls were cream, the furniture was either cream or blue, and the only personal items were riding trophies and ribbons and photos of her friends on the dresser. There was one of the three of us dressed up as sexy astronauts for Halloween, another of us dressed as sexy Girl Scouts to sell cookies, us dressed as sexy ninjas for—I didn't even remember now. Langley loved costumes and dressing up and since she did most of the planning, Kate and I nearly always acquiesced.

"Is this a new picture of Alex?" I asked, reaching for one of the frames to get a better look. Alex was the superhot Austrian prince or count or something she'd been dating since they hooked up at a riding event during the posh summer school she'd gone to in Scotland the previous summer. In this picture he was shirtless, wearing only a knitted ski cap and long johns and boots, apparently in the middle of a snowball fight. It looked a little cold for the absence of a shirt, but there was no denying he was superhot. We hadn't met him yet— he was flying in for her eighteenth birthday party next month—but Langley really seemed to like him.

"Don't touch it!" she screeched, poking her red beret out from around the corner of her closet. "It's—" She blushed.

I put it down and stepped away. "What?"

"I'm doing love magic with it," she said, emerging now with three bags and two shoe boxes. She stacked them carefully next to a chair. "It's embarrassing. And stupid." Her hand went to her forehead. "God, I can't believe I'm admitting this."

Kate snickered. "You're doing love magic? You? Miss Practical?"

Langley punched her lightly on the arm. "Stop it. Ivanka told me about it and I didn't want to hurt her feelings and—"

Kate nodded seriously. "Of course."

Langley addressed herself to me. "You just put a piece of his hair and some salt and you leave it there and it makes him think of you fondly. Not like you, Kate, with your voodoo."

Kate was lounging on the bed, one boot-clad leg tucked under her, the other resting on the floor. Her arms were wrapped around a stuffed dog. "It wasn't voodoo; it was Wicca, and it worked? I got the part of Stella in the play? Is your *love magic*"—she made quotes in the air with her fingers—"working?"

Langley glanced balefully in the direction of her phone. "Not today." Her mood shifted and she held out a pair of blue-and-silver silk-brocade platform sandals. "Jelly bean, these will look perfect with your costume. You should wear them tonight."

They were spectacular and so sexy, the kind of shoes that actually make you think you might hear a choir of angels singing. Which was why there was no chance I could wear them. I shook my head. "Those are your new Pradas. No way."

"Yes, way."

"They cost like a zillion dollars," I objected.

Still holding the shoes, Langley put her hands on her hips. "Freals, you have to wear them. I want you to. It's good luck to have a friend break your shoes in."

"Did Ivanka tell you that?" Kate asked, all innocence.

"Shut up." Langley returned to me, her blue eyes sparkling as she held the shoes out at arms' length. "The only thing I ask is, just don't wear them in the shower, no matter how much David begs. They're not waterproof."

I considered protesting again about borrowing the shoes—they really did cost more than a new telephoto lens—but I knew it was futile. I said, "Promise." In the end, everyone always did what Langley wanted.

Langley was in charge of our outfits for the night and she hadn't let us see them yet. She handed us each one of the bags with orders not to open it Or Else and we trooped back down the stairs.

From there we went to Kate's parents' beach house, where my surprise for David was taking place. Kate's father was the Reverend Joseph Carter "J. C." Valenti, preacher, bestselling motivational speaker, and patriarch of his own reality show *Living Valenti*. Reverend Valenti was on tour promoting the new season of the show as well as his Give It a Valenti Try! series of self-help CDs and day planners somewhere in Eastern Europe. Mrs. Valenti had taken Kate's two younger sisters to L.A. for a silent-meditation retreat and to meet with agents about a possible *Valenti Girlz!* spin-off show. Which meant we had the place to ourselves except for Zuna, the housekeeper. The idea was that David and I would have a picnic on the balcony outside, talk about the slight alteration to our summer plans I was going to propose and then…then there was Kate's parents' bedroom upstairs with the sixteen-head steam shower that, I'd been shocked to discover a few months earlier, was completely surrounded by mirrors.

Assuming everything went well.

When we got there, Langley unveiled our outfits. They were tube tops, puffy skirts, gloves that went to our elbows, and fairy wings. Mine was light blue to go with my dark hair, hers was lavender to contrast with her corn silk blonde hair, and Kate's was pale yellow to pick up the golden flecks at the center of her eyes. When I saw mine, I literally squealed with delight.

"You did good, kid," Kate told Langley in her mafioso voice. "Real good."

We changed in Kate's yellow-and-red-paisley bedroom at the beach house. Unlike her completely perfect exterior, Kate's bedroom always looked like it had just that moment been hit by a tornado. Every surface was covered with books or clothes or makeup or jewelry or dried flowers. "I don't understand how you ever find anything in here," Langley said, neatening the edges on piles of books.

Kate and I were at the mirror. I was sweeping on a final coat of mascara, and Kate was leaning forward to apply shimmer eye shadow.

"Can't find equals don't need," she said, moving to sort through a bowl full of necklaces.

Langley, already done with her makeup, went to peer into Kate's closet. Her expression was one of horror mixed with fascination. She stepped in and started poking at things. From inside her muffled voice said, "Hey, I thought you decided not to get this when we were at the mall last week."

Kate found the necklace she was looking for and reached around to clasp it. I would have offered to help, but I'd learned the first day we met that Kate didn't like to be touched unless she initiated it. "Get what?"

"This." Langley emerged from the closet wearing a purple fedora.

Kate's eyes got wide. "I—I changed my mind and I went back and got it?"

"You went to the mall without me?" Langley pouted, taking off the hat. "That's against the rules of friendship."

"It was just for a second?" Kate said quickly. She leaned forward to get a close-up of her mascara. "It's not a big deal."

"Kate—" I started to say.

She whirled on me, demanding, "What? Honestly, I liked the color, okay? Why are you giving me the third degree?"

Her eyes blazed at me. Her tone was so vehement I took a step back. "I was just going to tell you that your necklace isn't clasped right," I said.

She dropped her gaze and let out a chuckle. "Oh. Thanks."

Langley had moved to the top of Kate's dresser and was now flipping through a stack of photos she'd unearthed from inside a copy of *Our Bodies, Ourselves*. "Why don't you frame any of these? Like this one." She held out a photo of the three of us with David standing between Kate and me. We're all looking at the camera and laughing except Kate, who's gazing toward David with an unreadable expression.

"Why would I want to look at pictures of myself?" Kate asked, pawing through a tray overflowing with necklaces.

"It's not of you, it's of your friends," Langley explained.

"Um, I see you all the time?"

Langley threw up her hands, tossing the photo back onto the dresser. "That's not the point. But anyway, I like pictures. And I think we should get some film of the three of us. Because we are adorable. *Ooh*, let's do it in your parents' bathroom with the big mirror."

Kate looked at me for help. "Really? This is necessary?"

"Absolutely." I nodded solemnly.

Kate did her best stage pout. "Fine," she said, leading the way up the stairs to the master suite.

We took the camera up and filmed ourselves there, then set out for the party.

"Are you nervous?" Kate asked me.

"A little."

"She doesn't have to be. One look at her and David will melt," Langley said. "Just remember, not the shower—"

Kate said something under her breath.

"What?" Langley asked.

"Nothing," Kate said, adding too fast: "Just that it looks like rain, so the shower might not be the only place Jane could run into danger. Come on."

Kate's and Joss's houses were in a development on the part of the Jersey shore where all the streets were named after birds and all the houses were supersized. Joss's place was only three blocks away, but they were long and I had to concentrate to remember how to get back with David.

Of course, as it turned out, that didn't matter.

Chapter 4

*W*hen we got there, the party was a throbbing, gyrating mass of colorful bodies that parted like the ocean as we reached them with something like a collective exhaling of breath, as though everyone had been waiting for us. Kate, Langley, and I danced our way across the floor and they went with me in search of David.

As we approached, a gathering of sophomore girls flew out the door of the music room like newly hatched moths from a cabinet. Inside we found David, Ollie, and Dom sitting side by side on a leather couch. On the table in front of them were cups and the tall yellow bong David called Big Bird. David was wearing sunglasses, Dom was staring vacantly into space nodding his head up and down, and as I watched, Ollie reached up and stifled a yawn. They looked like the three monkeys, see no hear no speak no evil.

Dom gave an appreciative whistle when we came in and said, "Check out the fairy princesses."

Dom was like a golden retriever puppy, eager to please, sweet, and goofy. Or, as Langley put it, "More Play-Doh than Plato." He'd been in love with Kate for years, but it was hard to take Dom seriously, so he basically just danced attendance on her. "Don't you ladies look like a vision from a fairy tale."

David reached out and tugged on my skirt. "Sexxxy," he said, pulling me onto his lap. His eyes beneath the glasses were half open, his mouth had a lazy smile, and there was an eighth of an inch of stubble on his cheeks. "I like your surprise."

"This is just the beginning."

He raised his eyebrows and the smile got wider. "Do tell."

"Well—"

"No talking before knocking!" Dom called. "Let's get the ladies drinks so we can toast."

He led Kate and Langley out to the kitchen while I settled onto David's lap.

"I thought you weren't coming," I said to Ollie, who hadn't moved through the entire exchange. Ollie wore a dark-green military-cut jacket, jeans, and vintage brown Gucci loafers.

"My date got held up at a debutant-ball rehearsal."

David had been taking a bong hit while we talked and now, still holding it in, he nodded and said, "I was thinking about that earlier."

"About my date?" Ollie asked, frowning.

David exhaled. "No, man. Today in Mrs. Halverson's class, there was a spider." He kissed me on the lips. He tasted like gummi bears and pot.

"Dude," Ollie said. "If this is going to be one of your stony stories that doesn't go anywhere—"

"No, this is serious, Ollie. So I'm watching this spider building its web in the corner of the window. First it does the main parts, then the little connector rods. It's like so careful and precise, right? And then, just when it's done, Mrs. Halverson comes over and says, 'It's so stuffy in here I can hardly breathe. Let's have some air,' and opens the window. And boom, all the spider's work was gone." He paused. "Made me think, man, that was just like life."

I touched his cheek. "What do you mean, silly boy?"

"You work and work, and all it takes is one bitch to ruin everything."

Ollie stared ahead steadily and said, "I think it shows that sometimes for one person to keep breathing, something else has to stop." He turned and looked at me, right at me, jaw tight, his green eyes hard, glittering, and inquisitive. "Do you know what I mean?"

"Um, I guess?" As we were talking, David had moved his fingers from my neck and was now kneading my shoulders. I closed my eyes and leaned into him. "That feels fantastic."

His teeth nipped my ear. "It would feel better if we weren't wearing clothes. I like your surprise, but I'll like you even more out of it."

Ollie stood up, announced, "I'm going to get a drink," and took off.

I laughed at David and kissed him lightly on the nose. "This isn't the surprise. This is just *le amuse-bouche*."

"I like *le* sound of that." His eyes focused. "I thought of 139," he said. His fingers played along the edge of my tube top.

On our third anniversary David had given me a card with a list titled THINGS I LIKE MY GIRLFRIEND JANE EVEN BETTER THAN and he'd been adding to it ever since. The last one, BETTER THAN WEEKENDS WHEN DESPOT DAD IS OUT OF TOWN, had been number 138.

"What is 139?" I asked.

"I'll tell you when you give me my surprise," he said, and smiled mischievously. Even with his eyes at half-mast, he was so handsome I could barely believe he was mine.

"I can't wait."

"I don't want to wait. So when's it going down?"

"In just a few—" I broke off because I saw Kate waving at me frantically from across the room.

"I have to go."

"Seriously, fairy princess—"

"I'll be right back."

"—don't fly too far away."

I found Kate and Langley in an upstairs bathroom with flocked brocade wallpaper. Langley was crouched on the floor with her head over the toilet. "What's wrong? What happened? Was it something from lunch?"

"I didn't eat lunch." Her face still against the side of the toilet, Langley thrust her iPhone toward me. "Alex just e-mailed. He says he's not coming for my birthday party."

Langley had been planning her party for six months and the most important part of all was the presence of her boyfriend, Alex. "What? That's crazy. Why not?"

"I don't know. I tried calling him, but he won't answer."

"It *is* four in the morning there."

"That shouldn't matter. He must be with someone else." Her lip quivered and her eyes were pools of misery.

I pointed to the screen of her iPhone. "He signed it 'love, Alex.' Maybe something happened. He says he'll explain later."

Her hands were fists and her voice was rising with hysteria. "What can he say? There's no excuse for it. He's ruining everything. *Everything.*"

"Not everything, L.?" Kate's tone was quiet, soothing, her face filled with concern. A few wisps of dark-blonde hair fell forward as she leaned down to put her hand on Langley's shoulder. "Honestly, I'm sure there's a good reason and—"

"*Honestly,*" Langley repeated, mocking the word. She moved her shoulder from Kate's fingers. "Honestly, what do you know, Kate? Everyone loves you. Your parents, teachers, guys. Men follow you down the street just to tell you how beautiful you are. You have everything and you don't even care. But I have nothing. No one."

Kate recoiled like she'd been hit. She hugged her arms around herself.

"That's not true," she said quietly. She reached out and ran the fingers of her right hand along the edge of a large stone soap holder in the shape of a cupid. "I do care. And I don't have everything." Her voice got louder and more angry. Her hand closed on the soap dish. "You don't live my life. You don't know—" She broke off, shaking her head. "I'm going to go."

No! I wanted to shout. *This can't happen. No fighting.* I got that knot of panic in my stomach I always got when they fought, even just pretend. The feeling I got at the thought of anything ruining our friendship, of being alone again. I had to make this better. I stood in front of the door, took a deep breath, put my hands on my hips, and said, "Kiss and make up, you two."

There was a long pause. They both looked at me.

Then Langley said, "Kiss and make up. I bet the boys outside would pay to see that."

We all laughed and the tension was broken.

Langley stood and wrapped her arms around us both. "I'm sorry. I was just so disappointed in Alex. I should know better than to trust any boys. I love you two. You are the best friends I could ever have or ever want in the world."

We each kissed our pinkies and brought them together in salute. "All for one," Langley began, "and one for all," Kate and I finished off.

Langley frowned, took my face in her hand, and turned it toward the light. "Speaking of which, someone has been wearing off her lip gloss. You need another coat before you go tell your boy the news. Pout for me."

I pouted and she glossed me.

I remember that moment, the three of us in the mirror, Langley with her light-blonde hair, Kate with her honey brown, and me with raven black, three fairy princesses indeed. This was my life, I thought. Like a Clairol commercial. And it was perfect.

Five-and-a-half hours later, I'd been left for dead in a rosebush.

Friday

Chapter 5

I stood at the tip of the dock, shaking my head. "Come on, Jane," the pretty brunette camp counselor said. She was floating just off its edge, beckoning to me. "Come on, the water's great. Just jump."

I heard the buzzing of cicadas in the bushes around the lake and felt the sticky midwestern air and the splintery boards beneath my bare feet.

The water was brown and thick with weeds. I knew this because my best friend, Bonnie, told me about them. "They grip your ankles like slimy tentacles and won't let go," she said, wiggling her fingers menacingly in my face.

"Jane Freeman, you have to jump." A new voice spoke behind me. I turned and saw one of the boys' counselors, Cass. I'd had a crush on Cass since the first day of camp, when he took a bee stinger out of my foot. "I know you're not chicken," he said.

I was. I absolutely, positively was chicken. But with him smiling down at me, brown curly hair and blue eyes with thick dark lashes, I didn't want to admit it. "Go on," he said, broadening the smile.

To please him, to save face, I jumped. At first it was great. Bonnie had just been pulling my leg. I laughed, at my fear, at my stupidity, at the exhilaration of being in the cool water.

And then I felt it. First one and then another oleaginous tendril slipping along my skin. What began as a fawning caress was soon a series of slimy ribbons looping around my ankles. I felt the long weeds wrapping themselves around my calves and thighs, like sea witches grasping my feet with greedy fingers, trying to drag me into their underground lair. The more I struggled, the tighter they gripped me.

Stop moving, a voice in my head said. You'll be fine.

But I didn't, I couldn't. I fought and fought, getting weaker, until I had no choice. I couldn't go on. My body, nearly airless, went limp. I stopped moving.

And then, like magic I was free. The weeds unwrapped. I slipped away.

My lungs ached for air, my chest felt like it was going to cave in. I kicked with all my force, arms pushing forward, parting the greenish-brown water around me. There, above me, I saw it, a spot of shimmering sunlight. With my last remaining strength I broke through the surface of the water, gasping for breath, triumphant at having pulled myself back to life.

I opened my eyes, blinking the water out of them. And found myself staring into a gaze filled with malice.

"You stupid bitch. I hate you," a voice I knew but didn't know said. "Goodbye, Jane."

I was hit with a wave of devastating pain and I felt a hand pushing me back under, pushing me into the brown water, back into the darkness, to the weeds. The tentacles reached for me again, imprisoning me. My arms and legs were trapped. Water was pouring into my open mouth and my throat stung and I couldn't breathe and there was

a long wailing sound and someone said, "Get her back under!" and—
Blackness.

Scratching.

A woman's voice. "Mr. Carl St. James. White lilies in a green vase."

More scratching.

"Nicola di Savoia. Balloon bouquet in shades of pink with a Mylar alligator balloon."

"Pontrain Motors family. Bucket of four-flavored popcorn."

A man's voice. "That's the one I like. Pass that over, will you, Rosie?"

I hate it when Joe calls my mother that. That's the first thing I thought when I regained consciousness the second time. Before even realizing that I could hear, that I was awake, that this time it was for real.

My eyes flew open and I saw him there, my soon-to-be stepfather, gorging his face with four flavors of popcorn.

My mother was sitting in a blue upholstered chair next to him, her legs together, ankles crossed, in the posture she described as Casual but Respectful when she made me and my sister, Annie, master it. She was wearing jeans with a perfectly ironed crease down the center of each leg, a white silk blouse with a bow at the throat, and an American-flag stick pin. She was rail thin and looked misleadingly delicate. Her hair was a perfect gold bob with bangs that ran straight across her forehead.

Beneath them the red-framed glasses she used when she was working were pushed forward on her nose. The scratching I heard was the sound of her burgundy-enamel Mountblanc roller ball making notes on the leather-bound pad in her lap.

I watched her for a moment, seeing her the way I always did

recently, as a stranger. Like someone I was seeing on television, not someone I lived with.

I followed her gaze to my younger sister, Annie, who was standing near a shelf half filled with bouquets. For reasons that undoubtedly made sense to her, Annie was wearing the special red-velvet dress she'd gotten at Christmas, now a few sizes too small. It would have been obscenely short, but any hint of impropriety was erased by the black-and-white-striped tights and yellow rubber boots with duck faces on the toes she'd paired it with. At seven, Annie looked like a mini-version of my mother complete with an air of maturity far beyond her years, red-framed glasses, and golden bob—although my mother's was dyed—but Annie was very much her own person.

My mother reached a hand toward her now. Annie lifted one of the bouquets and held out the card nestled beneath it.

"Arthur and Susan Kazarhi," my mother said aloud as she wrote on the pad. "Pink-and-white orchid in green-patina planter."

Joe lounged on my mother's left, ankle on his knee, arm across the back of my mother's chair, taking up as much room as possible. I'd heard people say he was handsome, but to me he looked like a gorilla. He had hairy hands and the perpetual shadow of a beard. He was wearing a blue-and-white-checked button-down shirt with gold cuff links and khakis. The shirts were specially made for him, as he'd tell you if you were unfortunate enough to talk to him for more than five minutes. Expensive, but can you beat the feel? Here, touch the fabric. What a guy, that Joe.

Joe must have felt my glare because he was the first one to notice me. His face split into a grin. "Well, isn't that a sight for sore eyes. Look, Rosie, Sleeping Beauty has awakened."

My mother looked up instantly. Too fast, in fact, not giving herself time to compose her face, and what I saw, in that moment, was fear. And age—it was like she'd aged ten years since I saw her last.

Then the fear vanished and she was smiling, perfect lipstick, just the right degree of concern in the eyes. "Jane, darling!" She set aside the notebook and came toward me. "We were just making a list of people for you to write thank-you notes for and—"

Thank-you notes? For what?

My mother trailed off, the brightness fading. "Janey, oh, my precious girl." She was at the side of my bed now, clutching my hand. Which was when I realized I couldn't feel anything. "Jane, do you know where you are?"

Or speak.

Horror, terror washed over me.

My chest tightened and I felt tears pricking my eyes and a scream started in my stomach and tried to work its way out, but it couldn't. It was trapped, a prisoner in my own body. *What is going on?* I wanted to scream. *Someone tell me what is happening!*

Nothing came out.

Tears blurred my vision and I felt like I was suffocating. My brain sped, *Where am I how did I get here what is this let me out where am I?* but no one heard, no one answered. Everyone was talking at once, saying things I couldn't understand, coming in and out of focus. "Don't leave me, Mommy make it better, Mommy—!" I knew she stood next to me crying, I knew somehow that there were tears falling on my arms, and I couldn't feel them.

I couldn't feel them.

I was completely isolated. Completely alone.

The fear that coursed through me then was white hot and chilling at once. I was being buried alive, I was stuck, trapped, alone, forever.

My heart began to race. *I have to get out of here I have to be able to move this can't be happening to me this can't be happening!* The heart-rate monitor started to beep more quickly as my pulse picked up. The me inside me tried to claw its way out, fighting, twisting, pushing. Dying. *I have to get out of here, I have to escape.* My vision blurred, went black. *I'm in danger. Let me out let me out.* The heart-rate monitor beeped faster.

I felt my throat closing up. *I'm going to die, I can't breathe, oh God, please please let me out, let me—*

The heart-rate monitor began to shriek and my mother's face, chalk white, was replaced by a face I didn't know, the face of a woman in pink scrubs with big yellow suns grinning on them.

"Shhh, baby," she said, smiling down at me as much as the suns on her shirt. "I know this is all a shock, but it's okay. It's all going to be okay. But you've got to calm yourself down."

She held my eyes with hers and there was something about that, about her steady gaze and soothing voice, that seemed to reach deep inside me. "Relax, sweetheart," she said, and as though she'd hypnotized me, the monster fighting inside of me stilled. "Let's try to do this on your own without more medicine. Breathe with me, baby. One in, nice and slow, now let it out. Another breath in, that's good, you're doing great, and out."

After four breaths, my throat opened up. After six, the heart-rate monitor started to beep more slowly.

"There's a good girl," she said to me. "And waking up just in time for lunch, too. It's chicken stew. Hope you don't regret it." She laughed, a ringing peal that blanked out the humming and beeping of the machines around my bed and made the room feel human for an instant. I think I fell in love with her then. "My name is Loretta and I'll be your guide through the world of critical care for the next few hours."

"Is she okay?" my mother demanded. "What happened?"

"She's better than okay, aren't you, sweetheart?" Loretta said. "Did you see how she focused on me and responded to my words? Shows there's little if any cognitive impairment."

Little if any cognitive impairment. What were they talking about? *What did that mean?*

Loretta turned to me. "Keep breathing, baby. It's natural to be a bit disoriented when you wake up, what with the drugs and all you've been through. But you'll feel better in no time, you'll see. There's a clock straight in front of you on the wall. Can you see it?" I moved my eyes to it. It said one fifteen. "You just blink once for yes or okay and twice for no or bad." Like it was normal not to be able to speak.

I blinked once, and there was a collective exhaling of breath. It wasn't until later that I learned they weren't even sure if I would be able to do that. Based on where I was hit on the head, I could have been fine or—as Dr. Connolly put it when he appeared a minute later—"One millimeter more to the left and bang, you'd have been no better than a rutabaga."

Dr. Connolly looked like he might have played football in high school and still talked about it. He was tall with fading red hair and cheeks halfway to florid, like someone's jovial but slightly inappropriate dad. "I'd say it's a classic case of hit-and-run," he said. "Like what happened between wife number three and me. She hit me for divorce, I started running!" He winked at Joe.

Astonishingly, Joe didn't wink back.

According to Dr. Connolly, despite the broken rib, 103 thorn piercings, a concussion, a broken leg, and (hopefully temporary) paralysis, I was lucky. "You should have been dead," he told me.

He went on, enumerating all the things that could have been

wrong with me but weren't and hypothesizing that my paralysis was in part due to swelling on my spinal cord and partially psychological. The swelling of my limbs was a result of the drugs and would go down soon. "Long as you're a strong brave girl and your luck keeps up," he said, "you've got a good shot of coming out of this good as new. We should look for some improvement over the next few days. Feeling in the limbs is good. If you can feel your toes, well, then"—he laughed—"you're doing better than me."

Hit-and-run? Should get better? Swollen limbs? It was too much to take in, too much to try to process, so I found myself staring down at the body that was mine but not mine. I had the sensation I sometimes got of seeing everything through someone else's eyes, like watching the neighbors' TV from across their yard. There was the white hospital gown with blue stars on it. My arms, covered in gashes, were at my side. My left wrist had clear tape holding down three IVs that went to a machine out of my range of vision. My right hand had a monitor of some kind taped to it, attached to a dozen rainbow-colored thin wires. Beneath the hospital gown I could see that I was wearing what looked like a diaper.

A diaper. Oh my God. What if this was my future? It seemed silly, but that was the thing that got me crying again.

My tear-blurred eyes moved to my mother. Through Dr. Connolly's speech, especially as he got to the part about how I should ultimately be okay, the nerve at the edge of her left eye began to twitch. That meant she was struggling to keep the anger that was always fluttering just below her perfectly manicured surface away. As any one of the testimonial letters hanging on the wall of her office could tell you, she was an amazing and accomplished woman and had earned the reputation that she could get anyone "short of Hitler" elected. Her candidates described her as a "rock," "unflappable," and "the most reliable thing this side of the John Deere tractors my constituents are proud to manufacture right here in our town."

She showed Dr. Connolly and Loretta to the door and turned to face me. None of those letter writers would have recognized her then. Her picture-perfect smile was gone and her eyes blazed. "My God, Janie, what were you thinking? How dare you? How dare you do this to yourself? To me?"

How dare I do it to her? To *her*? I felt even more like I was watching this from a great distance, like this was a play about someone else.

She rifled through her purse and pulled out her silver monogrammed compact mirror. "Look," she ordered, holding it right up in front of my face. "Look what you did."

I looked and another scream rose in my throat. The distance vanished. This was me. And I was horrifying.

Half my face was swollen like a balloon. There was a bandage wrapped around my head, my hair was matted in knots, one of my eyes was half closed with a massive yellowish-purple bruise around it, and my lower lip was torn and twice its normal size. The left side of my face was covered in stripes of brown where thorns had ripped across my cheek. There was a bruise on my shoulder going up to my neck.

Hot tears welled up again and I closed my eyes. I felt nauseous. The girl in the mirror was awful, disfigured. Disgusting. She couldn't be me. She *couldn't*.

"Do you see?" my mother was in my face demanding. "Open your eyes and look, Jane!"

I did, but I stared at her, not myself. Why was she doing this to me? Let her look if that's what she wanted.

"I think you look like a warrior after battle," Annie said into the silent standoff between my mother and me. "I think it makes you look tough."

My mother whirled on her, taking the mirror. "It does no such thing. She looks horrible, like—"

And like one of the summer storms we used to get in Illinois, she exploded suddenly from rumbling thunder into a torrential shower of tears.

She buried her face in Joe's shoulder and sobbed. "Quiet now, Rosie," he said, patting her hair. "Jane is in enough pain."

At last, something that Joe and I could agree on. With his arm around her, he guided my mother into the bathroom next to my bed and shut the door.

Hot tears ran down my cheeks. You might think that if you were paralyzed, at least you couldn't feel pain. But it isn't like that. You can't move, but you can hurt. You can hurt more than you can imagine.

Chapter 6

*A*nnie did what she always did when she was nervous—she started talking. "Kate and Langley were here earlier. The doctor said you'd be allowed to have visitors because it will help you recover."

Her words were like knife points pricking me. What could Kate and Langley have thought when they saw me? What would David think? I was horrible. A freak. I wanted my face back.

"They were really nice. Kate made fairy wings for Marvin out of toilet paper." Marvin was the Barbie doll that Annie had decided was actually a man trapped in a woman's body. "And Langley showed me how to put on eye shadow, but Mom made me take it off. They woke you up before and took the breathing tube out, but you got scared, so they had to put you back under anesthesia. An induced coma, they called it. The doctor said your face was puffy from the sleeping medicine, but now that you are awake, it will go back to normal."

I was only half listening, still thinking about how I looked. I found myself getting angrier and angrier with my mother for not letting me get my eyelashes dyed the week before, when Langley and Kate did it, because then at least my eyes wouldn't look like little pig eyes the way they did when I didn't wear mascara. Angrier and angrier at her for not caring where I went, for not paying attention. She had time to pay attention to Joe, but for me she was too busy, I was too much work, too much—

"I wore my best dress because I wanted to look nice when you opened your eyes." She tugged at a thread on the corner of one of my blankets. "They said you might never, but I knew you would. I knew you wouldn't leave us."

The sweet craziness of her wearing her special dress jolted me from my selfishness. *Oh, little sister,* I wanted to say. *I'm sorry you have to go through this.*

She went on, pulling at the thread more deliberately. I couldn't see her eyes, only her long dark eyelashes, made longer by the magnification of her glasses. "Mom was just scared, that's why she acted all angry," she said. From the time she could talk, which had happened when she was only fifteen months old, Annie had been our mother's number-one fan. Even though she was only seven now, in some ways she was the most mature member of our family. "She didn't mean to yell. She was so scared you were going to die and then when you lived, she just had too many feelings, and they kind of all came out at the same time. Because she loves you so much. You know how she does that."

There was no reason for me to argue with Annie. Let her keep an ideal image of our mother as long as she could. I blinked once.

"And—" She paused, then rushed on. "I brought you something."

She went to the corner of the room and started digging around in the backpack she carried with her everywhere. Inside she had two books (in case she finished one), a fruit roll up, twenty dollars (five of them in quarters), a Swiss army knife, and an extra set of shoelaces. I'd never bothered to ask how she settled on those items.

When she came back to the bed, she was holding a toy stuffed dog with a worn patch on his head and his right foot. It was technically mine, but I hadn't seen it or thought about it in years, not since we left Chicago at least.

As though she could read my mind, Annie said, "I kept it. I sleep with it sometimes. I hope that's okay."

I meant to blink once, but instead I blinked a lot of times because my eyes pricked with tears.

Memories—memories I kept locked very far away—came flooding back now and I couldn't stop them. Sitting with my father on the old rocking chair in his study, having him read me poetry. I must have been really young because I remember I could get my whole body into his lap. That's how I picture us, both with our shaggy dark hair and pale skin. "Bastard children of the lusty Spanish sailors routed in the battle of the Spanish Armada and the kind Irish lasses who took them in" was how he described his ancestry, always with a twinkle in his blue, blue eyes. As much as Annie resembled our mother, I resembled our father, or at least I inherited his coloring and his wide-spaced eyes and strong chin and slightly too-big mouth. I don't think I ever had the twinkle, though.

I loved his study, the brightly colored rag rug on the scarred golden-planked floor, the way the white molding around the window was so thick with repainting that it had lost all detail, the bookshelves that covered every wall surface, the sheer yellow curtains that turned the light a buttery color where it slanted across the unruly piles of paper on his desk and landed in a pool right in front of us. It wasn't grand—not like Joe's house, where the moldings were pristine and the windows were tinted and the rugs were so deep they came up to your ankles and the books all had matching red-leather spines that have never been cracked—but it felt like home.

I could sit there for hours listening to him read aloud to me, but what I loved most was when he read poetry, and in particular when he read the Robert Frost poem "Road Not Taken."

My father went from himself to a shadow in only three months. At first when the doctor said he was sick—"Some kind of muscle-wasting disease. We don't know what it is"—it was hard to believe. He still looked like Dad, and sounded like him. But soon he began to change. It was like watching someone fade out of a photograph, each day becoming paler, smaller, washed out, more ephemeral, until only their outline and one trait—a nose, the way the shoulders slope—remained. And one day you looked at the photo and even that frail residue had vanished.

The last time my father left the house, he was gone for hours. We were frantic—he barely had the strength to get himself into and out of the shower at that point, so the idea that he was somewhere, driving, made my mother crazy. But when we rushed into the garage after hearing the door open, he was getting out of the car, beaming. He was clearly weak, but he seemed better, more alive, than he'd been in weeks.

"Where the hell have you been?" my mother demanded. Even then she had to yell at him.

When he told her he'd been to the mall, she stared at him, aghast. "How could you have been so stupid? You'll tire yourself out and—"

"What? Get sick and die? Oh, Rosalind, my darling, that's going to happen anyway."

He'd gone to a toy store to buy one of those stuffed animals with a voice chip in it that you give to people saying "Happy birthday" or "Merry Christmas." This one was a dog with floppy ears, and he'd rigged it to record the whole of him reading "Road Not Taken."

"All you have to do, anytime you miss me," he said, holding the dog out to me with a shaking hand, "is push his left foot and you'll hear my voice." He tried to push it, but by then his fingers were too weak, so I did it and we listened, together, to him reciting my favorite poem.

It was our last shared moment. After that he went to the hospital. "I'll come back good as new," he said. "I won't ever leave you, Janie girl, that I promise."

He never came back. He broke his promise. He disappeared forever. He left me alone and I didn't want to be alone. I changed—everything changed after that. He'd been wrong, I saw. The road less traveled led to heartache and loneliness.

I'd shoved the dog in the back of my closet after he died and forgotten about it, or tried to, but apparently Annie hadn't. She was holding it toward me now. "I know maybe it's not your favorite poem anymore but, well, I figured maybe it could still keep you company."

No, I wanted to say. *Get it away from me. I can't stand it. He lied. He knew he wasn't coming back. He abandoned us and then Bonnie—*

"Do you want to hear it?"

I couldn't blink twice fast enough. *NO!*

Annie nodded but slipped it in the bed next to me. If I could have, I would have pushed it away, but I couldn't and now I was trapped. I tried to turn my face away from it but managed only to avert my eyes.

"Please, Jane," Annie said, standing at the side of the bed, her voice so soft and small sounding. "You have to get all better. You have to come home."

She smelled like Bonne Bell lip gloss and raspberry fruit leather. Behind her red-framed glasses her eyes were huge. She looked wise beyond her years and like a very scared little girl all at the same time.

Fear and love and hope stared out at me. I had trouble swallowing. "Promise?" she squeaked.

I blinked once. Yes.

The bathroom door opened and my mother and Joe emerged. Her eyes were pink, but she'd washed her face and, of course, reapplied her lipstick.

"I'm so sorry, sweetheart," she said, coming to take my hand for the second time. How ironic that this was more than she'd touched me in months and I couldn't even feel it. Her voice trembled. "I don't know what came over me. I—we—have been so terrified. So afraid you wouldn't wake up or when you did—" She broke off. "I couldn't imagine losing you. And when the doctor said you would be okay, when you woke up, I guess I just—" She swallowed, dried her eyes on her sleeve. Her sleeve! "The pressure just exploded. I didn't mean what I said. I know this was just an accident, that you didn't—didn't *want* this to happen. But the way things have been between us…And you sneaking off to a party…I—I didn't behave well. I'm so very sorry. You understand, don't you?"

She began to sob again and Joe ducked into the bathroom, reappearing with a Kleenex. She took it with the hand she'd been using to hold mine and put the other one on his arm.

I blinked once. A nice thing about not being able to talk, I was learning, was that it spared you having to say anything you didn't mean.

I was spared even more by Loretta knocking and coming back in. She smiled at everyone, oblivious to the tension that hung like humidity in the air, and said, "It's nearly visiting hours and I think someone here could use a sponge bath. If the rest of you will excuse us?"

Everyone filed out obediently, even Joe. Loretta, I decided, was a woman to learn from.

She wasn't big, but she was strong and managed to get me out of bed and into a wheelchair. I couldn't feel the floor, the chair, her hands. But it wasn't like floating. It was terrifying, like being completely out of control. I started to breathe fast again and she stopped what she was doing.

"Look at me, sweetheart," she ordered.

I did.

"You're going to be fine. This is all temporary. You've got to calm yourself down."

Temporary, I told myself. *Calm down.* I nodded.

"You'll see. Before you know it, you'll be singing and dancing."

My breathing started to return to normal.

"Good girl," she said, and moved around to the side of the chair. She unhooked monitors from my fingers. "Won't need most of this much longer," she said cheerily. The IVs stayed with me, now hanging from a hook on my right. More tubes were gathered on the left. I was like a traveling medical exhibit.

This is all temporary, I repeated to myself.

She pushed me into the bathroom and said, "Feast your eyes on this five-star accommodation."

It wasn't bad, actually. The entire room was covered in white tile. On one side were a toilet and a sink with a mirror above it. On the other, separated only by a curtain but on the same level so that you could easily move between them in a wheelchair, was a big showerhead.

Loretta talked as she carefully undressed me. "It's nice to finally meet the famous Jane. You know your mother hasn't left your bedside since you were brought in. Sat there talking to you the whole time. Talking *about* you, too. I hear you're quite a girl. Good student, great sister. Popular." She tugged the hospital gown off my arm. "Your mother kept telling everyone, wanted everyone to know how important it was that you could see, get all better. 'She just has to be able to hold a camera,' she said. 'You should see her pictures. She's a brilliant photographer.'"

I wondered how many blinks it took to say "Stop lying."

Loretta moved me onto a bench on the shower side of the room. She turned on the hot water, then looked around.

"Someone took my bucket!" she said in mock horror. "You sit tight where you are and I'll be right back."

I sat there, listening to the sound of the shower and feeling the steam begin to rise against my cheek. It smelled like Coco Chanel in here, my mother's perfume, and looking beyond the half-open curtain I saw that she'd left her makeup bag on the sink. Of course, Rosalind Freeman would never for even a moment look anything less than perfect even when her daughter was nearly dead.

I took a deep breath, closed my eyes as the small room filled with steam. The warm, moist air felt wonderful, almost like normal. Maybe I was going to be okay. Maybe—

I must have dozed off. A noise roused me and I peered past the curtain to see if it was Loretta coming back, but no one was there, just the toilet and the mirror.

The mirror on which was written in all-capital letters, faint but unmistakable:

YOU SHOULD HAVE DIED, BITCH.

That's when my voice came back in a long, gurgling scream.

Chapter 7

*L*oretta flung the door open. "What is it, sweetheart? What is this fuss about?"

I gaped at the mirror. "Mirror," I said. "Look."

"Your voice is back, honey!" Loretta said as she turned to look at the mirror and my eyes followed hers.

Nothing was there. Opening the door had stirred up the steam and made the letters disappear. Condensation dripped down the surface, but the writing had vanished. Loretta reached out to wipe the fog away.

"No, wait. Don't you see it? Someone wrote a message on the mirror. They wrote that I should have died."

I thought I could make out a faint trace of the letters, but it could also just have been water droplets. Loretta peered at the mirror, shook her head, and wiped it with a cloth.

"You're on some pretty heavy narcotics and one of the side effects can be—"

"Not a side effect. It was there. Words." I was crying now in frustration. "A threat."

"But sweetheart, no one came in or out of here while I was gone."

I stared at her. "Must have."

"I was just outside the door. Your room is empty."

I focused on the steamed-up mirror. Was I going crazy? Had I hallucinated the words?

The only other option was—

"Loretta," I said, trying to sound casual.

"Yes, kitten?" She was filling the plastic tub she'd gone to get with water, but she looked at me over her shoulder. Her expression was open and honest and kind and I knew, with every bone in my body, that she wouldn't have done anything to mess with me.

"Nothing. I just—you're sure no one could have snuck in while you stepped out? I can't believe I just imagined it."

"Don't feel bad, kitten," she said. "Nearly everyone sees something odd when they're on as much medicine as you are." She dipped a cloth into the basin of hot water. "Was one patient in here, swore he saw a rainbow donkey piñata hanging just above his bed like one he had at a birthday party as a child."

She shifted my weight. "And a little girl was convinced that fuzzy mice were running around her bed. Her mother said she'd been asking for a pet mouse for ages. Best I can imagine is that the hallucinations come from something buried in your mind, maybe a wish."

"I don't wish I was dead."

"No, I suppose you don't. But it did get you talking again. Maybe you were just looking for the right trigger to get your words back."

Maybe she was right. After all, not being able to talk had turned out to be temporary like she said.

By the time she was done bathing me, I'd stopped shaking and nearly accepted the fact that I must have hallucinated the message. I mean, if no one had come in or out of my room, let alone the bath-room, wish or no wish, it had to have been in my head.

Which meant no one wanted me dead. No one hated me. I'd made it all up.

"Your mother will be happy that you can speak again, no matter what caused it."

My mother. She'd be thrilled with a new sign of my return to "normal," but I was pretty sure she wouldn't like the hallucina-tion part.

"Is there any way we could keep this from her? I mean since it was just something I made up and not a real threat? I don't want to make a big deal of it." I cleared my throat. It felt raw—I guessed from the breathing tube that had been down it.

"How about I'll tell Dr. Connolly what happened and let him decide about telling your parents, how's that?"

"Thank you."

"Now let's get you dressed," she said, deftly sliding my arms into a new hospital gown, this one white and green. She pushed me in front of the mirror as she combed my hair out.

"What do you think?"

My first thought was, *At least I still have my hair.* David loved my hair. Maybe it was that, or maybe because the swelling had started to go down in my face or because I was prepared from the time before, but this time looking at my reflection, I was more fascinated than horrified. The white grid of the tiles framed my face—black eye, hash marks on the cheek, fat lip—as though it was on a drawing board like an avatar being created. Not the avatar I would have cre-ated for myself, though. This one would definitely have been some kind of underworld villain.

But I could recognize my eyes, my hair, my lips, my smile. I could imagine them coming back how they had been. I could be pretty again. Me again.

"Well?"

"The green dots on the hospital gown really bring out the yellow around my black eye," I said.

"There's that twinkle in those beautiful eyes your mother told me about. She said you had a great sense of humor."

"Is there any chance at all you could put some of my mother's mascara on me? On my good eye. I don't want anyone to see me like this."

"I promise you, everyone is just going to be glad you're alive. No matter how you look, you'll be beautiful to them."

"You don't know my friends."

"Teenagers." She shook her head, but she rifled through my mother's makeup bag and found the mascara. "Look down, I don't want to poke you and cause any more damage." When she was done, she said, "Okay, kitten, are you ready to meet your public?"

"I don't have a choice, do I?"

"No."

I took a deep breath.

Loretta wheeled me out of the bathroom and tucked me back into my bed, covering the diaper with a blanket, before opening the door to the outside corridor. She went out and Annie came in. By herself, I was relieved to see.

She started talking immediately. "We went to the cafeteria. They make good hot chocolate there, but Joe says to stay away from the cinnamon rolls. There's a police officer outside waiting to talk to you. Your hair looks pretty." She stopped abruptly, then swiveled her head from side to side as though desperate for something else to say. "Look." She pointed at the windowsill, where a large bouquet of roses had appeared with some kind of object tucked next to it. "You got another bouquet, and it came with a teddy bear. Cute." She picked the bear up and held it toward me. It was wearing a muscle shirt that said GET WELL BEARY SOON!

I grimaced. "That's not cute, that's awful. You better tell Mom who it's from so she can add it to the list."

"The card says 'from your secret admi—'" She dropped the card and looked at me. "You can talk!"

She swung toward the door, clutching the doorjamb and leaning out into the hallway to yell, "Mom, Mom, Jane can talk!"

There was a chorus of "*shhhs*" from the nurses' station, followed by the sound of high heels running up the corridor fast.

"Hi, Mom," I said when she rushed into the room.

There were tears in her eyes. "Oh, thank God," she said, taking up her place at the side of my bed again. "I was—we all were—thank God you can talk. How did it happen? When? Oh, thank God, thank God."

"All of a sudden in the bathroom I just had my voice back." It wasn't a complete lie. My mother looked at my hand. "Just my voice. I still can't move the rest of my body."

"That's enough for now," Joe said heartily. "We'll just be patient and you'll be good as new in no time."

I couldn't move, but I could still feel anger rising inside of me. "How do you know? Did you get a medical degree while I was in the shower?"

"Jane!" my mother said warningly. "There is no cause for rudeness."

A quiet tapping on the door spared me the rest of whatever she would have said and woman with dark hair in a navy-blue police uniform stepped into the room. "I'm sorry to bother you so soon into your recovery," she said, "but I have a few questions that could help us find who did this to you." She gave the impression of being competent and tidy, from the neat bun of her hair to the clear polish on her short fingernails.

My mother assumed her best authoritative manner. "Officer—"

"Rowley, ma'am."

"Officer Rowley, my daughter only just came out of a coma." I had this feeling like she said the word as though she was savoring it. I could already hear her spinning it for cocktail parties, using the anecdote to highlight how brave and capable she was. "This is hardly the time for her to be grilled."

"I know, ma'am, but your daughter is the only one who can help us figure out what happened to her. It's imperative that we get as much information as we can, as quickly as we can, and Dr. Connolly says if she can speak, your daughter is up to answering questions." She turned to me. "Do you remember why you were walking alone on the street so late at night?"

Walking? Alone? I didn't remember anything. My mind was completely blank. "No."

"Was there a particular reason you went to Dove Street?"

Dove Street? I'd never heard of it. "No. Where is that? Is that near here?"

My mother's lips got tight and she swallowed. "Dr. Connolly says that this forgetfulness is normal but that she'll probably recover her memory soon. He's one of the best in the country."

That did it. "Stop saying I'm normal, that I'm going to be fine," I said, raising my voice. It shook. "You don't know that. You just want to make yourself feel better. I'm paralyzed, Mother. *Paralyzed.* For once look at me. See *me* for what I really am."

My mother's lip trembled. "Jane. Don't say that. This isn't you, this is just temporary."

"You don't know that. You *don't* know what's going to happen. No one knows. I could be like this forever." I tasted tears on my tongue.

"Jane, please. Not now."

"Why does the time matter? Why not at"—my eyes went to the clock—"three ten? Will it be better at four fifteen? Five twenty-seven? Anyone can see that I'm a mess. That we all are."

Now tears quivered in my mother's eyes. "Why are you doing this?"

"Why are you?" I demanded back.

It sounded like the beginning of a hundred fights we'd had over the last two years. "I'm just trying to do my best for us, Jane. For all of us. Why are you so angry at me?" she'd say, and I'd shoot back, "Why are you so angry at *me*?"

And we'd look at each other the way you do when you see someone on the street you think you recognize, but not quite. Someone you wish with all your heart were there but who is actually just a stranger. And you feel a kind of deep longing that hurts like a huge gash and your inability to fix it leaves you frustrated and angry and bone-deep lonely.

Now my mother shifted her eyes to the policewoman and when she spoke, her voice was even, but I could see her knuckles were white and clenched. "I apologize for interrupting," she said to the officer. "We're all under a lot of stress. Please go on."

The policewoman gave her a benign smile and returned her focus to me. "The night of the party. You stepped outside. Maybe you were just getting some fresh air? Or meeting someone?"

Meeting someone? Had I been? I have a sudden flash of memory, of being on a street talking on the phone. "Where's my cell phone?"

"No cell phone was found with you. Could you have left it at the party?"

"I just—I have this idea that I was talking to someone on it. When I was walking around."

"It hasn't been recovered, and there was no sign of one around the scene of the accident. Do you remember anything else? Anything about the car that hit you?"

"No."

"Wouldn't there be marks on the car?" Joe said with an air of importance, like he just discovered nuclear fusion. "Shouldn't you be looking into that?"

"There is very often damage to the car in question, and certainly that's something we'll look at when we have a suspect." The policewoman returned her focus to me. "Do you know of anyone who might want to harm you?"

Before I could answer, my mother said, "No one would want to hurt Jane; she is very popular."

"I have to ask, ma'am." The policewoman focused on my mother now. "What about you? Do you or your husband—"

"I don't have the honor of that title *yet*," Joe said, with a proprietary grin. I wished I could slug him.

"Fiancé, then. Do either of you have enemies?"

My mother rolled her eyes. "I am a political consultant, of course I have enemies, but none that would cause physical injury, especially to a child."

"Are you sure?"

"Quite sure."

"It would be bad for business," I said.

My mother's mouth tightened with the effort to resist reprimanding me.

I was interested to hear what Joe had to say about having enemies, but he just said, "That's irrelevant." Cop-out. Then he went on the offensive. "Is this just a fishing expedition or do you have any leads, officer?"

"We are exploring a variety of possibilities."

"Meaning?" Joe challenged.

The policewoman didn't seem to like him any more than I did. "Meaning we are doing our job."

Joe stood up. "Can I talk to you outside, officer?"

"Yes, when I'm done here, I'd be happy—"

"You're done here," Joe told the woman, tilting his head toward the door.

Their eyes locked. "I would like to have a word with Jane alone."

"She's a minor," my mother said. "I have a legal right to be present."

"Jane isn't a suspect, she's a victim, and I have some questions that she might be more comfortable answering without anyone else present."

"I demand—"

"It's okay, Mom," I said. "I'll talk to Officer Rowley alone."

My mother got the thin-lipped look again, but she went, taking Joe and Annie with her.

Officer Rowley pulled a chair up next to the bed and sat down. Close up, I could see that her nails weren't just short, she'd bitten them. Maybe she wasn't so perfect after all. "Now, Jane, when I asked if you had any enemies, I felt like you had something to say before your mother stepped in. What was on your mind?"

What had been on my mind was a feeling of someone watching me, someone who hated me. It was like a feathery flick of a memory from the party, more of a sensation than a fact. How would I explain it? "I thought someone was staring at me"? That, coupled with hallucinating a threatening message on the mirror, wouldn't make me seem insane at all.

No, I was going to stick with things that were concrete and I actually remembered. "I don't know," I said finally. "Maybe it was something that happened at the party."

There was a knock on the door and Loretta came in, three quarters concealed by a huge bouquet of flowers. "I'm going to have to take up weight lifting if you're sticking around," she said. "These are the biggest ones—" She stopped, seeing Officer Rowley for the first time. "I beg your pardon, am I interrupting?"

"Yes, I'm afraid so."

She set the flowers on the windowsill next to the others. "Apologies. I'll get right out of your way." She stopped at my bed to say, "They're from Oliver Montero, in case you were wondering. Your mother already wrote it down."

"Thanks, Loretta."

"You okay in here alone?" she asked.

"Yes."

When the door closed, Officer Rowley resumed. "You said you think maybe something happened at the party. Could it have been something bad enough to make you want to commit suicide?"

I'd been looking at Ollie's flowers, but my eyes zoomed back to the policewoman. "What? I didn't want to commit suicide. Why would you ask that?" Just because I hallucinated the writing on the mirror did not mean I wanted to die. A chill was starting to creep through my body, as though tendrils were wrapping around my limbs, pulling me down into a deep dark place.

"Based on your injuries and the angle of impact needed to make them, this wasn't a normal hit-and-run. It looks like you were kneeling in the middle of the street, waiting for the car to hit you." She leaned back in her chair, her ankles crossed, pad on her knee like she was relaxed, but I could tell she was watching me closely.

"Kneeling? In the street?"

"Yes. Do you have any idea why you would have been doing that?"

I was stunned. "No. I have—no."

"There are generally only two explanations for that kind of behavior. Either the person is trying to kill themselves—"

"I told you I wasn't trying to kill myself."

"—or the person's on drugs." She let that sink in for a moment, then leaned forward, inviting confidences. "Did you take anything?"

"No."

She studied me as though assessing whether I was telling the truth or not and gave a small nod. "Did you eat or drink anything at the party that could have been drugged?"

I had to think about that longer.

I'm in the music room with David and Ollie. I'm sitting on David's lap. I'm—

I'm holding a drink.

But where did it come from? I've got nothing. No memory.

"I don't know. Maybe. I don't remember."

This time she looked at me like she wasn't sure she believed me. She closed her notebook and stood up, sliding a business card on the table next to my bed. "Here's how to reach me if you recall anything else."

You should have died, bitch.

The full impact of what she was getting at suddenly hit me. "Do you really think that someone might have drugged me on purpose? To—to hurt me? That this wasn't an accident but someone out to get me?"

"I don't think anything yet. We're investigating. Your being drugged could be unrelated to what happened," she said. She was watching me closely. Something distrustful, maybe mocking, in her expression reminded me of my friend Bonnie from Illinois.

"But if that's true, then it was someone at the party," I said. "One of my friends. Why would one of my friends want to hurt me?"

"Only you can answer that question, Jane." Her gaze moved toward the new bouquet. "Lilies, tulips, hydrangeas. Lovely and expensive. You have a generous boyfriend."

"They're not from my boyfriend, they're from his best friend," I corrected.

"Ah." She tapped her card with a ragged fingernail and went to the door. "Call me if anything occurs to you."

Chapter 8

*H*er words, that mocking glance seemed to linger in the air like the heavy perfume of Ollie's flowers even after the door clicked closed. Friends didn't try to hurt you, I wanted to shout after her. Friends protected you from being hurt. If you had friends, you were never alone. And I had friends. Dozens of them. I tried to look at all the flowers on the windowsill, but my eyes drifted beyond them to the sliver of sky above. It was bright blue with a lone cloud floating through it. Perfect weather for a ditch day.

Langley and Kate and I had planned to spend it at the Livingston Country Club working on our base tans. I closed my eyes now and the whirring of the machines around me became the humming of cicadas in the flowering bushes that surrounded the pool. It was punctuated by the soft thwack of tennis balls and the tinkling of glasses as the staff conveyed carts filled with tableware from the dining room to the pool pavilion to set up for the annual Memorial Day dinner dance that night.

I should have been there, stretched out on a lounge, critiquing everyone's new bikinis, drinking iced tea, and picking on a Cobb salad. I should have been there with them and not here, alone, surrounded by machines, unable to move, my body bruised, my face not my face.

Why would one of my friends want to hurt me?

Only you know the answer to that.

I didn't have any answers. Just unanswered questions and huge blank spaces in my mind, blank spaces so big I felt like I could drown in them. I was alone, and lost, and free falling. Once, developing negatives during photography camp the past summer, I'd had the feeling that my world was slipping away from me, like I didn't know which way was up. I felt that way now so strongly I could almost smell the pine trees. I closed my eyes and the memory came flooding back.

The photography camp had been a special intensive program for high school yearbook and newspaper photographers from around New Jersey. It took place out in the woods, under an enamel-blue sky with evergreens marshaled like sentinels around a series of real log cabins. But despite the rich natural palette, I'd signed up for an old-school black-and-white photography elective where we were working on real film, doing everything from taking the pictures to printing the negatives and the photos. When you develop the actual pictures, you can use red lights in the darkroom so even though it's dark, you can still see. But when you're developing the negatives you make the pictures from, it has to be pitch black.

I'd never experienced anything like that complete darkness and it threw me. I kept blinking, expecting my eyes to adjust, to be able to pick out the outlines of things, maybe a seam of light from the door.

Nothing. Just pure, all-engulfing dark.

When that realization settled in, I started to freak out. I felt like the ground was sliding out from under me, like gravity ceased to exist. I knew the table with all my supplies on it was in front of me, but my fingers wouldn't work, I couldn't find them. A trickle of sweat ran down my back and my hands and knees began to tremble and it was like someone was clenching my chest. I couldn't breathe, I had to get out, only there was no out, I couldn't find the door, the floor was sloping, where was the exit, I was trapped, I was going to die here, I'd never get out, I was—

I was gasping for air when he spoke from behind me. "Close your eyes," he said, next to my ear.

It should have been terrifying to have a strange guy so close to me in the dark, but it wasn't. It was reassuring. Grounding. I closed my eyes.

"Now take a nice big breath."

I took a breath. And then another.

"You're okay," he went on. "You're fine. It seems different, but it's the same as when the lights are on. Everything is still there."

Like magic, it was true. I was fine. My hands stopped shaking. I found all my equipment just how I'd laid it out, and I managed to thread the film into the negative-developing tank and seal it up. I wasn't even the last one done.

It seems different, but everything is still there. It had been true then, and it would be true now, I told myself.

When the lights had gone on in the darkroom, I'd looked around to see who had helped me and was astonished when the guy who always sat in the back by himself during critique wearing a fedora and making notes came over and introduced himself.

"I'm Scott."

"I'm grateful. Jane." I held out my hand.

"Nice to meet you, Grateful Jane."

"No, it's just Jane." He raised an eyebrow and I realized he'd been making a joke. "Right, you knew that. Anyway, I am. Grateful, I mean."

"No need, Just Jane."

"How did you know what to do?"

"I'm a student of the way that perception impacts reality," he said, sounding a little pompous. Then he grinned. "Plus I've been there. First time I did my own negatives, I totally freaked."

He and I sat together at dinner at one of the scarred wooden tables with generations of initials carved into its top, and over institutional pizza and fizz-less soda I learned that he wasn't shy, just thoughtful, that he lived in the town next to Livingston—"the sketchy town where you and your friends go to buy beer." He was both the photo editor of his school paper and the head yearbook photographer and dreamed one day of having a gallery of his own. In the meantime, he planned to go to law school because you have to pay the bills somehow and fund it half with scholarships and half by doing commercial photography work. Over the next three weeks and innumerable cups of watery coffee, "Just Jane" was shortened to J. J. and we became good friends. He was more intense and focused than anyone I knew but also more passionate, ramming full speed ahead into anything that interested him.

I caught up with him one afternoon after a particularly harsh critique of his work. He veered off the path and into the forest, head down, fast. Pine needles crunched under my feet as I ran to keep up.

"Are you okay?" I asked when I caught him.

He turned to me, beaming. The sunlight filtered through the bluish-green trees, picking up the gold flecks in his eyes. He looked alight. "Hey, J. J.! Wasn't that great?"

"The critique? But they—" I tried to figure out how to say it nicely.

"—they hung me out to dry," he finished, grabbing me by the arms and spinning me around. "I know. Did you notice how not a single person could criticize the composition or the angle or the technique? It was all about how the photos made them uncomfortable."

I nodded.

"It shows I got to them. My photos had an effect. That's better than simple like or hate." He exploded in a rich, rolling laugh and curled his hand into a fist of triumph. "They're going to keep thinking about it. Perception can make reality. Change one and you change the other. That's art."

Perception can make reality. The darkroom felt different with the lights off, but everything was actually the same. Everything was still there, right where I'd left it.

It would be like that now—everything where it should be. But not being able to remember was making the world feel so weird, so alien. My life was still my life. My friends were still the same people they'd been before.

Which meant so was I.

Why would one of my friends want to hurt me?

Only you know the answer to that.

I didn't. I didn't because it wasn't possible. No one wanted to hurt me. My life was nearly perfect. I got along with almost everyone. People signed my yearbook with things like "You're the best!" and "Love you!" and "Let's get together this summer!" Friends didn't harm friends—having friends meant never being alone and unprotected. Never being abandoned.

I opened my eyes and discovered Kate and Langley standing near the foot of my bed. My best friends. They were smiling at me, and Langley waved. I looked from one to the other of them and a voice in my mind screamed, *Bitches!*

Chapter 9

*T*he word had swooped into my brain like an alien invasion and left me feeling just as rattled and confused as if I'd woken up on a spaceship. Something tugged at the edge of my consciousness like an image seen only out of the corner of your eye, but I had no idea what it was, no idea where that word, and the fury that accompanied it, came from. I loved Kate and Langley. They were everything to me.

In the next instant the anger was gone. But the residue of strangeness lingered like the bad aftertaste of food court Chinese food even as I realized how crazy I was being. If this was the kind of thing I could think about my two best friends, then hallucinating writing on a mirror was nothing. Kate and Langley *always* looked perfect. It was who they were. And who I was. It was part of what I liked about them and myself.

Langley was wearing a puff-sleeved T-shirt with cherries embroidered on it, a denim flared miniskirt, white lace kneesocks, and the Marc Jacobs Mary Janes we'd flipped a coin for when we saw them on sale two weeks earlier. Her lip gloss was fresh, her platinum hair just the perfect amount messy. She looked like Goldilocks on a slightly punk bender.

Even dressed casually in a green-gray long-sleeved T-shirt dress that matched her eyes and brown motorcycle boots, Kate managed to exude grace. Her wavy hair was held off her face with sunglasses and each time she moved, the armful of gold bangles she was wearing gave a pleasant tinkling sound.

Langley, naturally, made the first move, rushing toward me and saying, "Oh my God, jelly bean, I am so happy to see you awake!" She threw her arms around me as well as she could and hugged me.

Kate, moving more slowly, came around the other side and laid her fingertips on my hand. "You have to stop worrying us this way," she said, bending to give me a kiss on the cheek. There was something strained about her voice, her manner, like she was playing at being carefree. Up close, I noticed she had a cut on her lip. She smiled and said, "Honestly, I feel it aging me prematurely. My mother will never forgive you if I have to start Botox at eighteen."

"We can't have that," I agreed. "What happened to your—"

"Everyone is talking about you!" Langley interrupted. There was nothing strained or weird about her. She'd seated herself on the windowsill and now she picked up the teddy bear wearing the muscle shirt that had arrived earlier. She stretched the T-shirt to read it and made a face. "*Beary* soon? Who gave you this?"

"A secret admirer," I said. "It came with the roses."

"Isn't that in slightly poor taste?" Kate asked.

"The bear?" I asked. "Or sending roses? Actually, yes to both."

"I think it's sweet," Langley said. She pushed aside the vase of flowers from Ollie to seat the bear in the center of the windowsill. "There, now you can see it from anywhere in the room."

"Lucky," Kate said.

"Yes, I feel like one of fortune's most favored right now."

Kate laughed, her genuine ringing peal, and for a moment all the tension was gone. "At least you look nice with your hair slicked back? Very French and jejune."

"Would you like fries with that whopper?" I asked.

Langley smiled. "That's my line. But I'll let you have it since you're hobbled." She hopped off the windowsill and pulled a DVD out of her bag. "Enough chitchat, we have something to show you."

Placing my mother's laptop on the table next to my bed, she slid the disc in and pressed play. The opening chords of David's band's best song, "Highway Man," started. It was the background music behind a video of all my friends telling me to get well, get better, hurry back. The Bryson twins mooned the camera and T. C., Marla, and Poppy, our freshman little sisters, read a poem and Vivian and Boz beat-boxed while Winston did the robot and pretty much everyone in our class and the class below appeared doing something. They'd even managed to get Ollie, who wouldn't let me take a picture of him "because you never knew what someone would do with it," to appear standing in front of his Range Rover in Kate's driveway saying, "Fix yourself up and get back here." It looked like instead of spending the day at the country club, Langley and Kate had covered every inch of Livingston to interview all our friends, and as I watched it, I was touched. That they had done it, and that everyone had agreed to participate. *See*, I wanted to tell that weird voice from earlier. *You're wrong*.

Everyone looked happy and perfect, like they were in a music video or a hip catalog. One of the double-page spreads where it's like you just caught a bunch of absurdly attractive guys wearing nothing but strategically ripped jeans and leather necklaces and girls in cargo shorts and ruffled shirts and rain boots with tiaras perched insouciantly atop accidentally loose braids running through a stream in the middle of nowhere on the way to some fantastic bohemian picnic where they would drink sodas in old-fashioned bottles and be clever and witty and have the most marvelous time.

That reminded me of Scott again, of the series of photos he did that he called Still Lifes with Aspirations. "People playing parts without even being aware of them," he'd explained when I asked him about the theme. "You know those pictures that come in the frames you buy at the store? They show the perfect vacation, perfect wife, perfect child. It's like lining those up on the dresser and pretending they were really yours."

"But you shoot candids. Of real people."

"Who are really posing. Playing at being real, living the way they think they should, hoping that if they make it look right on the outside, it will be right on the inside."

"Isn't that a little cynical?" I asked him. "Couldn't people just be happy?"

Scott's eyes twinkled. Unlike a lot of people, he enjoyed it when you questioned what he said. "How do you know they're happy? I think every smile hides a secret. You can learn the most about people when they don't know you're watching them." Then he went through and pointed out details in the photos that showed the space between appearance and reality, some troubling thing you didn't see at first that suggested the perfection could unravel at any moment. "These images are like Christmas ornaments, shiny and pretty and reflecting back what people want to see. But they're hollow—they're all surface." His eyes went dark and intense and sometimes when he got that way, he could be a little unsettling.

"I like surface," I said to him, because it was true, and because I wanted to defuse his seriousness. "I want to believe in the possibility of perfection."

"Maybe that's why you pretend everyone is dead in your photos," he said, a statement, not a question. "Because only the dead can be perfect."

"That's not true!" I'd told him then.

"No tensions simmering under the surface, J. J.? No hidden fault lines waiting to shake things up?"

No, I'd said, and I'd believed it. I still believed it. I wished he was here now to see my perfect friends and the perfect video. It *was* possible. My life was really like this. The DVD was the proof.

None of these people would drug me. None of them wanted to hurt me. They were *friends*.

The final minute of the DVD cut to the night of the party, when Kate and Langley and I were getting ready in Kate's parents' massive pink-marble bathroom. We were in our matching fairy costumes— Langley in lavender, Kate in yellow, me in blue—as Langley filmed us in the gold-framed mirror. I watched these three girls with their tight, effortless friendship—I pick a thread off Kate, I can't find my lip gloss so Langley lends me hers—and it made me smile. I was so lucky.

The three of us did our pinkie salute and made kissy faces at the camera in the mirror at one another, at some invisible audience. Then the scene moved to the party and the camera work got wobbly because we were dancing. Langley spun around, panning across the sea of bodies, and when she got back to Kate and me, Nicky di Savoia was there, hugging me. Nicky said something, gave me a kiss on the lips, and handed me a red plastic cup.

My mind veered back to the party.

We step into the room and Nicky, like a force of nature, comes barreling toward us across the dance floor. It's almost like she has been waiting to see us. She's wearing a yellow minidress with tiny silver beads in a pattern on the front, a lynx stole wrapped around her neck, and gray motorcycle boots. She ignores Kate and Langley and grabs me by the upper arms. She's holding a red plastic cup in one hand.

With her other she taps me on the nose. "I owe you an apology. I was wrong about you. Okay?" She hugs me tightly enough for me to realize that the stole is real fur, then kisses me right on the lips. "I know we haven't been that close recently and I'm sorry. Let's be super-nice friends again."

"Sure, okay."

"Good." Her fingers caress my face. "Your skin is so soft, like a baby. I love it. Let's make a toast to you and me." She holds the cup up, says, "To Nicky and Baby Jane," and tips it in my direction. "You first."

I take a whiff—it smells strong—and go to hand the red plastic cup back to her, but she's dancing with her fingers all over Todd Quigley's face. She says, "Baby, you hold on to that for me, will you? I'm busy," and goes back to mauling him.

"I wish she'd take E all the time," Kate says. "She seems so much more at peace."

"If that's what you want to call that." Langley nods toward where Nicky and Todd are now making out. "I call it something you desperately want to forget in the morning. Come on."

We walk across the floor to the music room, and a group of sophomore girls fly out like newly hatched moths from a cabinet.

I keep Nicky's cup.

I kept Nicky's cup.

Did that mean Nicky drugged me? And then tried to run me over?

"Nicky?" I said aloud without meaning to.

"I know. She was so wired last night." The video had ended and

Langley popped the DVD out of my mother's computer and put it on the windowsill next to my other presents. "The way she went off on Ollie was surreal."

"What do you mean? Why was she yelling at him?" I asked.

"Not just yelling," Langley said, her eyes wide for emphasis. "She kept saying, 'How do you like Kicky Nicky?' and giving it to him in the shins."

Kate leaned in confidingly to say with a wicked smile, "Which was admittedly kinda fun to watch?"

"For a preacher's daughter you're a bit on the evil side. You know that, right?" Langley asked.

"Part of my charm." Kate batted her eyelashes.

"Why do you think Nicky was freaking out?" I asked.

"It's Nicky." Langley shrugged like that was answer enough. "We tried to find her today, but there were a few people who didn't get back to us to be on the first part of the video."

"Probably still sleeping the party off," Kate said. "I bet a lot of people are?"

Did she and Langley exchange a look?

Langley said, a little too eagerly, "The doctor said we should talk to you to help you remember what happened Thursday night."

"Although frankly, if I were you, I might not," Kate said.

"What do you mean?" I asked them.

"Well, since the night included Crippen break dancing—"

"Literally," Kate put in, "as in 'break the coffee table and an urn.'"

"—and a lot of sophomores in unfortunate knockoff dresses, you're better off not remembering. The whole thing was more faux than fun."

"My memories are so sketchy. I remember walking in and then looking for the boys."

"We found them in that media room watching some special about the mating practices of bonobos and getting high," Langley reminded me. "You crawled into David's lap, but since Kate and I aren't huge *Chimps Gone Wild* fans, we went in search of drinks and Dom came with us."

"I remember that. And I remember sitting and talking to David and Ollie." I riffled through my mind. Something about spiders? "Wait. I remember being in some nutty bathroom with you guys because—" I recalled Alex's bad behavior then. "Oh, sweetie, I'm sorry. Alex is a jerk," I said to Langley.

"It's okay. It turns out that his father is being honored by the Austrian government that weekend and that's why he can't come, so it's not that he didn't want to see me."

"So are you back together?" It was a bit hard to keep up with things between Langley and Alex, especially since none of us had ever met him and their entire relationship existed over phone and IM. But Langley had said that he might be The One, meaning The One she liked enough to get over her dismay about anything messy and actually have sex with, which meant she genuinely adored him.

"I don't know. He's on probation for making me wonder." I laughed, which made the cuts on my face sting, but I didn't mind. It was good to feel something, even pain. Langley went on. "That's not what's important. What else do you remember?"

"After the bathroom it's just a big blank space."

"You don't remember anything?" Kate asked. "Like where you went?" She was leaning forward, a crease between her eyebrows. Her gaze, her tone seemed more intense than necessary.

"No. The doctor says that could be from trauma or from the hit I took to the head." I didn't mention what Officer Rowley said about being drugged. "Did either of you see me at all after I left the bathroom?"

"No." Langley shook her head. "Kate and I were together all the time, but you disappeared."

Kate nodded. "We assumed you were with David, but then we saw him and he was—"

"—looking for you too," Langley finished. "That's when we got worried and went driving around, but you'd just vanished."

Why did I feel like they were talking too fast? Covering something up? Langley was smiling too much and Kate's eyes kept wandering from me to Langley to the door. Was there some drama behind the scenes that everyone was covering up, had something—

"Excuse me." Langley's voice interrupted my thoughts. "But what is *she* doing here?"

Chapter 10

*A*t first I thought Langley meant my mother, but then I realized she was looking at the dark-haired girl standing slightly behind my mom in the doorway. She had one of the blue-satin padded hangers my mother favored with a suit jacket on it dangling from her index finger while she feverishly typed notes into a BlackBerry with her other hand.

"She's Jane's mother's intern," Kate whispered.

My mother had an intern? I had no idea. "Who is she?" I asked.

"Her name is Sloan Whitley," was all Langley said, but her tone suggested that Sloan Whitley might be synonymous with Satan's Girlfriend. It caught me off guard, especially because Sloan looked slightly familiar to me, like I'd seen her somewhere recently, and the impression in my mind was that she was nice.

"Was she at the party?" I asked.

Kate answered. "Yeah, I think I saw her there. Right, Langley?"

Langley shrugged. There was definitely something odd going on. Sloan trailed my mother and Joe into the room, still typing.

"…and Hetty Blanstrop at the *Post*," my mother finished her sentence. "Ask to speak to Hetty directly. Do you have all that?"

"Yes, Mrs. Freeman," Sloan said.

"Sloan, do you know all the girls? My daughter Jane in the bed, obviously, and her best friends, Kate and Langley. Sloan is a sophomore at your school. She wants to work in politics one day." Bright smile.

Everyone murmured hello. Sloan blushed. She glanced at me fast, nodded quickly at Kate and gave Langley an unsure smile, then set the hanger on a chair and stepped outside to make her phone calls.

My mother hugged Kate and Langley and gave them each an air kiss on the cheek. "Girls, I'm so glad you're here. We're about to have a press conference announcing a reward for information about what happened to Jane." She lobed a telegenically perfect sympathetic glance in my direction.

"A reward?"

"The police said it would help, so Joe has agreed to give a ten-thousand-dollar reward for information leading to the apprehension of whoever did this to you," my mother said, smiling at him.

"Thank you, Joe," I said, meaning it but hating having to. "That is very generous."

"Anything I can do to help," he explained, suddenly bashful. "Wanted to do more, but that Officer Rowley said it wasn't necessary."

My mother patted his face and beamed on him the way I remember her smiling at my father at the breakfast table on the nights after they'd had me babysit so they could go out to dinner together. Their fingers would brush as she poured him more coffee and they would both jump back a little in this shy way and even though I felt a little left out, I knew this was love, and I wanted it for them forever.

Now she was doing it to someone else. "You are a wonderful man," she told Joe. My stomach tightened.

She turned back to my friends. "Would you two be willing to answer phones for an hour later?"

"Of course," Kate said. The tension in her had become even more intense once my mother arrived and I had the sense that she couldn't wait to leave.

"I'm sure we could round up a lot of volunteers," Langley confirmed, pulling out her BlackBerry. "How many people do you need?"

"Um—" For a split second, my mom looked lost. Then she snapped back into focus. "Coordinate with Sloan, if you don't mind. Sloan? Sloan?" My mother went over to the door, muttering, "Where is that girl?"

"I think she stepped outside to make—" Kate started, but my mother had her head out of the doorway.

"Sloan," she called. "Sloan? I need—oh there you are." Sloan seemed to take my mother's demands with complete calm. It was only my friends and I who upset her. "Sloan, I want to go over the script. Joe, please take Annie and wait for us on the front steps of the hospital. Kate and Langley, thank you for all your help. True friends. Jane is lucky to have you."

Langley winked and as she bent to give me a kiss on the forehead, I caught a whiff of her Jo Malone grapefruit cologne. It was so familiar, so soothing, like the promise of normalcy. Kate gave me an air kiss on the cheek and whispered, "Get better, sailor girl."

That gave me a lump in my throat. "Thanks," I said to both of them, meaning it in big ways and small.

"Don't be absurd," Langley said. "What else were we going to do? Sit around at home and wish you were with us?"

The lump in my throat got bigger.

They gave me a pinkie salute, even though I couldn't feel it, and moved to the door. Langley turned to wave one last time, but Kate crossed the threshold fast, like suddenly she couldn't leave quickly enough.

And then I was alone. Well, with Judge Zonin, "The last word in justice," on the television who filled the slot right before the five o'clock news. With his thick wavy hair precisely graying at the temples, a spray-on tan, and very white teeth Judge Zonin looked to me more like he should be selling toothpaste or the good life than dispensing justice.

Two guys standing behind podiums faced Judge Zonin, both with their heads shaved. One of them wore a suit and tie; the other was more casual in a long-sleeved sweater that clung to his pecs.

"And then he calls my girl," Pecs was saying, pointing to the guy in the suit. "Using my cell phone he calls my girl and starts stepping out with her."

That was when it hit me: David hadn't been on the video. It was weird that I hadn't even realized he'd been absent. Now that I did, though, it bothered me.

"Is this true?" Judge Zonin asked, his eyebrows rising so high they were almost lost in his fancy hair.

"Is simple math, man." The guy in the suit turned over a palm. "He got her on Friends and Family, right? I use his phone to talk to her; it's free for everyone."

Was that why Langley and Kate were so strange? They didn't want me to notice that David wasn't in it?

"You were supposed to be my friend, yo," Pecs said, gripping the podium like he wanted to punch someone. "Friends don't play that way. Steal my steady, steal my phone. But both? No."

Probably sleeping it off. That's what Kate and Langley had said about Nicky, and it was probably true of David also. He was just sleeping it off. Or practicing. A lot of times he got so absorbed in practicing he didn't answer his phone. Or the door. Like that time two weeks earlier. And when he had finally come to the door, he'd been annoyed that I had interrupted him.

The guy in the suit spread his hands. "Just sound business, man, and the free market at work."

Pecs hit the podium now. "Free market this—one day you're gonna to pay for what you've done. One day soon. And I ain't talking about reimbursement for the phone."

"You're scaring me there, sir," Judge Zonin said.

He was scaring me too. And then I realized, it wasn't him. His words were an almost perfect echo of what Nicky had said to me during our last real conversation.

Chapter 11

*N*icky and I had been assigned as biology lab partners at the beginning of the year, and the second week of classes she'd invited me to her house to work on an extra-credit project. I was surprised because I was enough of a geek to do that, but I didn't think she was. Nicky di Savoia was cool in a way that went beyond popularity. Her dad was a famous music producer and her mother was a former supermodel and the whole di Savoia family was always showing up in the copies of *Gotham* and *Vanity Fair* my mother had lying around the kitchen.

The di Savoia house was invisible from the street, hidden behind thick hedges and a tall wall. Inside was a stone castle—complete with a moat.

"You have your own drawbridge?" I asked incredulously.

"Yeah. We need it, there's an alligator in the water."

"No way."

"It's a miniature one. Okay, it's an invisible one. But just pretending it's there has had a great effect on the twins' obedience."

The twins were Nicky's five-year-old brothers, Marc Antonio and Gian Luca. Like Nicky, they'd been adopted from an orphanage for refugee children, only Nicky came from Brazil and her brothers were from Vietnam. They ran up to greet her as soon as we stepped from the garage into the massive Tudor-style kitchen, and if I'd been surprised by Nicky wanting to do extra credit, I was even more surprised seeing her with her brothers.

"What was your favorite thing at school today?" she asked Marc Antonio first.

"I caught a ladybug."

"Tell what you did with it," Gian Luca said, smug.

"I ate it. Tastes just like chicken."

"Marc Antonio is the chef in the family," Nicky explained. "He'll eat anything once."

She was amazing with them, asking them questions about their friends and teachers and getting them a snack and cleaning off their faces and examining with great solemnity a scraped knee and an invisible splinter. Watching them together made me make a resolution to pay more attention to Annie. Or really any attention.

Mr. and Mrs. di Savoia came into the kitchen "to see what all the laughing is about," and I couldn't help it, I stared at them. Not because they were both exotically gorgeous—he was Native American and Italian and she was Somali American—or because her dad had tattoos over every visible inch of skin.

I stared at them because they were barefoot and holding hands.

I couldn't remember the last time I'd seen my mother barefoot except getting out of the shower, and even then she usually stepped right into slippers. And parents holding hands? Never.

They got into an intense discussion with the twins about what to cook for dinner that night while Nicky and I went up to her room.

That was a surprise too because it was filled not with music posters like I would have expected but with American Girl dolls. "I can't help it, I love them," she said.

I went to touch one and saw her flinch a little.

"Sorry. It's just I don't usually, you know, handle them without gloves." She looked sheepish. "Oh my God, I'm acting like such a geek I'm embarrassed for myself."

"Not at all," I said. "My mother still has the clothes her Barbies wore in special dress bags she made for them."

"Wow. I'm going to remember that next time David makes fun of me for being so anal. He makes me close the dolls' eyes if we're making out up here."

David was her boyfriend then and they were the coolest couple at Livingston High, so the thought of them making out surrounded by dolls—even dolls with their eyes closed—was really funny. "How long have you been going out?"

"David and I? Seven months, five days and"—she checked her clock—"sixteen hours. We met in line for a midnight showing of *Casablanca*."

"That's so cute," I said. "He must be the best boyfriend ever."

She rubbed her wrist. "He is. For sure."

I had dinner with the di Savoia family and afterward we played a game of miniature golf on the indoor course they'd just installed in the basement, complete with a steam-spitting volcano. "I'd rather have my boys hitting each other with sticks here than attacking other people's kids in public" was how Mr. di Savoia explained it, but based on the way Mrs. di Savoia snickered when he said that, it was clear it was as much for him as for them. Each hole had a dance you had to do before you could shoot, and some of them had secret handshakes, and I could hardly remember a time I'd had more fun. As I left, Mrs.

di Savoia took my hand and gave me a kiss on each cheek and said in her slightly accented English, "I hope you will visit again. It is rare for Nicola to bring a girlfriend over. Come back soon."

Nicky blushed. "Mom."

"I'd love that," I said, and totally meant it.

Langley and Kate found me at my locker the next morning at school.

"Where were you yesterday, jelly bean?" Langley asked, peeling the silver foil from an ice-cream sandwich. One of Langley's many enviable qualities was that no matter what she ate, she never put on any weight. "We kept calling and calling you."

"I was at Nicky di Savoia's working on bio. Did you know there's a mini-golf course in the basement of their house? With a volcano?"

"Seriously?" Kate asked, sipping her latte. "Don't let my father hear that, he'll put one in except instead of a volcano, it will be a statue of him." She got pensive for a moment. "Of course, that could be fun to shoot balls at."

"And you could dress it up." I shouldered my bag and the three of us started to walk toward AP European History.

Langley nibbled the edge of her ice-cream sandwich. She always ate it the same way, nibble, lick, nibble, lick, from the outside in. "It sounds like you had fun."

"I did."

"I wouldn't hang out with her too much, though."

I stopped walking. "Why not?"

Langley stopped too. "Haven't you heard the rumors? Licky Nicky? Likes to suck dicky?"

"I've never heard anything like that," Kate said.

"Me either," I agreed. "What are you talking about? She dates David Tisch."

Langley shrugged and started walking again. "I guess he hasn't heard them either."

Maybe because I was listening for them, I started hearing the Licky Nicky rumors after that. At first it was just a trickle, but soon everyone was talking about it. One guy said she'd blown him in front of one of her dad's gold records, another told about a hot night on top of the miniature-golf-course volcano, the kind of details that gave the rumors authenticity. I was in the hallway once when a senior boy came by and said to her, "Hey, Nicky, hungry? How many licks would it take you to get to the center of this?" and grabbed his crotch. She started getting more withdrawn, so I didn't see her as much, and when our bio rotation ended, I didn't see her at all. I heard she and David broke up, but I didn't know the details.

The last time we talked was in early December. There was a weekend of Indian summer, so I took Annie to the park and Nicky was there with the twins. It was a little more than a month after I'd started dating David and I thought it might be awkward, but she came over in response to my nervous wave and said, "So, I hear, you and David."

"Yeah."

She gave me a weird look. "Enjoy that."

"Um, thanks?" She was turning to go when I stopped her. "Want to get a coffee or something later?"

"Why? So you and your friends can destroy my reputation some more? There are easier ways to steal someone's boyfriend."

"What are you talking about?"

"I know where those Licky Nicky rumors came from. I didn't want to believe it at first, but how could I not? When the 'details' started filtering out. My dad just finished his miniature golf course and you're one of the only people to go down there."

"You think I started those rumors?"

She didn't say anything, just stared at me blandly.

"Why would I?"

She gave me a hard look. "Don't act naive. *'He sounds like the perfect boyfriend,'*" she mimicked my voice. "And now you have him. Although I should thank you. I was looking for a way to break up with him and that made it easy."

"Nicky, you have to believe me, I didn't start any rumors."

"I don't *have* to do anything. And what I really don't have to do is stand here and talk to you."

She started walking away, then turned and looked back at me. "The sad part is, I really liked you. I thought you were cool. Now I just feel sorry for you. Don't you ever get tired of being the pawn between those two? Their little doll, doing whatever they say?"

"That's not how I am."

She shook her head. "Right. One day you'll wake up and realize how expensive this is."

"What do you mean?"

"You'll learn the true price you've paid for your boyfriend and your popularity."

Someone else had said something similar to me once. But they were both wrong.

"Jealous much?" I shouted at her but also not at her, at a memory, at someone far beyond hearing. She was. She was jealous about David, about my friends.

She laughed, gave me the finger over her shoulder, and kept walking.

That was the last time Nicky and I talked.

And then at the party she'd hugged me and kissed me and said she wanted to be my friend. And she gave me a drink.

All of which was weird. But for some reason I still couldn't imagine Nicky drugging me.

Unless she and David—

No.

But David hadn't been on the DVD, I reminded myself. And neither had Nicky.

It didn't make sense. Although after hallucinating the writing on the mirror, and my weird reaction to seeing Kate and Langley, I didn't feel like I was exactly the best judge of what made sense and what didn't.

The flowers, the bouquets and cards, those were real. Weren't they?

I wanted to cry out in frustration. And then I wanted to do it even more when the phone started to ring.

I willed my arm to work, but I couldn't lift it. "Help!" I shouted. "Someone—"

Loretta came in, lips pursed, shaking her head. "No one should be putting calls through to you." She picked up the phone. "Room 403, who is speaking, please?" She started to frown, her eyes got wide with surprise, and finally she smiled. "Why, thank you, your voice isn't too hard on the ears either. Let me see if Miss Freeman is available."

Loretta held the phone to her chest. "A David Tisch would like to speak to you."

Something about the way my eyes lit up told Loretta all she needed to know. She held the phone to my ear. "David!" I said, louder probably than I needed to.

"Hey, babe. How—how are you doing?"

The familiar bass of his voice sent a wave of pure joy through me. And something else unexpected that felt like—relief? I didn't know what I had been afraid of, but hearing his voice made it vanish.

"I'm good now. Are you coming to see me?" I didn't want to seem too desperate, even though now that I had him on the phone, I felt like I needed him. Needed to see him.

It sounded like he exhaled. Like he felt relief too. "I can't to-night, but I'll be there first thing in the morning. I just wanted you to know I was thinking about you. And babe?"

"Yes?"

"Better than cupcakes. That's 139."

I couldn't stop smiling, even though it hurt. "No way."

"Yes way."

I felt so happy. Normal. This was normal.

In the background I heard voices and I heard a siren. Or maybe it was on my end.

"Where are you? It sounds like you're in a parking lot."

"Something like that. Listen, I gotta run, but I'll see you soon."

"Promise?"

"Super-promise. Love you, babe. You take care. Stay soft."

"Love you too."

I heard him say, "Hey, wait up—" and then the phone clicked off. Who was he meeting? What lucky person got to see him now?

It didn't matter. I'd see him tomorrow.

He sounds like the perfect boyfriend, I heard myself say to Nicky.

He was.

I grinned at Loretta.

"My goodness, couple more doses of him and you'll be doing jump-ing jacks out of here," she said. "I guess you hardly like him at all."

"Hardly."

"You got off the phone just in time, your mother's about to be a star." Loretta turned up the sound as the five-o'clock-news jingle started to play.

My case made the first slot. An ambulance with a siren blaring went by and then the shot moved to my mother. I'd expected a podium—she liked podiums for her candidates—but instead she was standing on the front steps of the hospital with Annie and Joe beside her on her left, like a perfect family. On her right, in the place she always made me stand ("to balance the image"), was little Sloan. But that didn't bother me. Nothing could bother me.

I thought about Scott's Still Lifes with Aspirations and how every one has a telltale detail as I watched. I took in Annie's non-matching socks, the whiteness of my mother's knuckles, the way Sloan kept looking over her shoulder and—hold up, did she have a hickey? Nice one. That was one of the first habits I'd had to train David out of when we started dating, because you never knew when my mother would need a family photo op. Too bad for you, Sloan, I thought, you can't quite replace me yet.

After them there was a report about a fireman who rescued a child from a cougar that got loose from someone's private wild-animal collection, an interview with wild-animal trainers about how you shouldn't have a private wild-animal collection, and a piece about a convenience store heist where they made off with a case of Butterfingers, $143.72, and several issues of *Playboy* using iPods disguised as tasers.

They teased the Memorial Day weekend hot dog taste-test challenge before cutting to commercials.

Orange juice. Michigan. Two-for-one drinks at Friday's. In my mind I saw David and me enjoying it all, arm in arm, always with a sunset behind us.

I spent the rest of the night watching television and thinking about all the things David and I would do when I was better.

The last ad I saw before turning off the television was for something called Scar-B-Gone. "Get rid of unsightly scars in just ten days with our miracle cure or your money back," and my mood skyrocketed. David loved me. My scars could become invisible. Everything would go back to the way it had been.

I had yet to learn that there are scars no miracle cure can heal. Scars buried so deep you can't see them or reach them or stop them from aching. Scars that can kill you.

Saturday

Chapter 12

*T*he planks of the dock were warm beneath my feet. It was hot and I could hear bees buzzing in the shrubs behind me. In front of me the brown water of the lake was smooth and inviting.

"Just do it, Jane," the pretty camp counselor said. Her head bobbed off the side of the dock, water drops glimmering on her eyelashes, blonde hair splayed out around her. Her eyebrows needed to be plucked.

As I watched, her head tilted back and her body floated up, arms out. Her hair surrounded her like a mantle and a serene smile played on her lips. Her eyes were open, pupils fully dilated. A trickle of blood came from her mouth.

I have to save her, I thought.

I dove into the brown water. The weeds tugged on me, pulling me down. Relax, they said. Let go. Don't fight it.

I fought until I couldn't anymore and then I gave up. The weeds released me and I swam hard, pumping my muscles up toward the surface. I was almost there but not close enough; I wasn't going to make it, my lungs were burning, out of air. I was dying, drowning.

A hand reached down through the water. It was a hand with a ring and I recognized it. I grabbed the hand and it pulled me up, pulled me out, dragged me to the surface. I splashed into the air like a flying fish, gasping for breath.

I opened my mouth to thank my savior and saw them.

The eyes. Eyes twisted and filled with hate. Mocking me. Laughing at me, taunting me. Eyes that wanted me dead, eyes that envied me, right above me. I opened my mouth to scream and a voice said—

"Hey, lover lips."

My mind cleared. I was staring up at David.

Like always, he was wearing sunglasses, and their lenses were showing me two distorted images of myself. He bent to kiss me on the forehead and I felt the brush of the guitar pick he wore on a chain around his neck against my skin and smelled Prada for men. He only wore that for special occasions.

My heart soared.

He had a T-shirt that said COME BACK TO LEBANON! which was one of his favorites and jeans and a day's growth of stubble and he looked amazing. I felt suddenly nervous. How did I look? He was so handsome and I was so—

"How's my brave girl?" he asked, taking my hand. The way he called me brave, the way he smiled at me, made me want to cry. "You look like a princess who's seen a few things."

"I feel like one."

"I'm so proud of you, babe," he said, and even though I didn't know why—what had I done?—it made me happy.

"Thank you."

"I'm working on a song about you," he told me. "Already have most of the chorus worked out."

He was writing a song for me. That was—I felt tears pricking in my eyes.

"Aw, don't cry, babe. You know I love you."

"I love you too."

He looked at me over the tops of his glasses and winked. Then he straightened up and pointed a thumb behind him. "Look who else came along to give his most sincere regards."

I don't know why, but somehow seeing Ollie there was a shock. The flowers had been odd, but now it was like some part of my mind was tensed. The atmosphere in the room seemed to shift as he stepped closer to the bed.

"Thank you for the flowers," I said. "They're beautiful."

"Oh yeah, sure. Always send flowers to ladies in distress." His tone was casual, normal, but he rattled his car keys against his right leg nervously. "How are you feeling? I mean, your spirits good?"

It was an odd question, but the answer was easy. "Great now," I said, smiling at David.

Ollie nodded to himself. "Yeah, you look okay. How's the head?"

"Still a bit slow. A lot I don't remember."

"I expect." He looked at me for a moment with one of his unnervingly intense gazes and repeated, "I expect. Probably better that way. No reason to ask a lot of pointless questions." Then turned to David. "I'll wait for you outside, man. Don't be too long, it's ten of eleven now and I want to get to the Apple store before it gets busy."

"Be out in a few, buddy."

God, he was so weird. As soon as he left, the strange feeling in the air disappeared.

David sat down on the chair next to my bed. He pushed the hair off my forehead with his left hand. "How come you can even look great when you're all busted up, lover lips?"

I laughed hard. It hurt my face and a little in my chest, but it was still the most wonderful sensation. I felt like I hadn't truly laughed in ages. "Don't be ridiculous."

He slid his glasses off his nose. I could see his eyes were a little glassy, but he wasn't too stoned. "Would I lie to you?" He gave me that crooked smile, the one that I had fallen in love with the very first day we hung out, when I didn't even imagine he could be interested in me.

It had been a Saturday at the beginning of the previous October and Langley, Kate, and I were manning a booth at the Livingston Days Faire, raising money for the no-kill animal shelter in town where Langley volunteered. We were selling cookies, so Langley had decided we should dress as sexy Girl Scouts, and since things had been on the rocks between her and Alex then, Kate and I had acquiesced to make her happy.

We'd only just finished setting up our booth when David and Ollie came by. Kate waved them over and began recruiting them to be our plants at the fair. "All you have to do is go around saying in loud voices how great our cookies are," she explained. "Then we'll do the rest."

Kate and David had been next-door neighbors since they were little, so she knew him pretty well, but I'd never talked to either him or Ollie before. They were super-popular seniors and I'd always been a little intimidated by them, but they stuck around all afternoon, pretending to be our bouncers and funneling people to the booth. "Step right up and get a load of these lip-smacking good morsels," Ollie would say, and David would put in, "And the cookies are good too!"

They were funny and clever and really easy to hang out with. David spent most of the afternoon talking with Kate and Langley while Ollie talked to me. Even then he had a way of looking at me that made me feel like he was looking through me, but it didn't quite have the edge of not liking what he was seeing. That came later.

The day of the fair, he was nice and surprised me by knowing a lot about photography and art and galleries in New York. And after we'd sold all our cookies, he invited us back to his place for a barbecue. The idea was thrilling—a barbecue with two popular senior guys—but Saturday was family dinner night at my house and I knew there was no way my mother would let me out of it.

It was mortifying to have to tell Ollie and David that I had to spend Saturday night with my mother, sister, and Joe watching *Muppets Take Manhattan*, but instead of making fun of me, David offered me a ride home. He and I had hardly talked at all during the day, so at first it was a little weird—

Me: This is a nice car.

Him: It's new.

Me: What kind is it?

Him: Audi.

Me: Did you pick the color green?

Him: Naw, my mom did.

—but then he looked at me out of the corner of his eye and asked if I'd ever been a real Girl Scout.

"I was, back in Illinois before we moved here," I admitted.

That was the first time I saw the crooked smile. "Thought so. You've got this innocent thing about you that's like sexy and sweet all at once. I couldn't stop watching you today."

I stared at him, dumbstruck. He took his hand from the steering wheel and put it on my knee. "Maybe we could go out sometime?"

That's when I blurted, "But I thought you liked Langley."

He looked at me quizzically. "What do you mean?"

"I mean you talked to her all day and didn't even look at me once."

"See?" he said, pushing my hair behind my ear in a gesture that would become familiar. "There's the sweet-innocent thing. That's how you play the game, lady girl. You never talk to the girl you're interested in, you talk to her friends. Play a little hard to get, peak their interest." By then we were at my house. He pulled over and turned off the ignition. "I mean, I don't go around asking girls out if they're not going to say yes; I'm a sensitive guy." He made an earnest poetic face and I laughed. "There you go, making fun of me."

"I'm not making fun, I'm—"

He kissed me softly on the lips and when he pulled away, he had this surprised expression on his face.

"Wow," he said. Our foreheads were close together, his fingers on my chin. He paused like he was waiting to see my reaction.

"Wow," I echoed. It seemed like the right thing to say. This was it, I guessed. The way kissing was supposed to be. It had been nice. Warm and pleasant.

He tilted his head back, resting his cheek against the headrest, and ran his fingers through the tips of my hair. He looked at me for a long time, like he wanted to know me, like he thought I was special. His fingers moved from my hair, down my arm, finally twining through mine. His gaze was warm, admiring, and I felt like he was seeing the me I wished everyone would see.

"Would you—" His eyes moved away from mine, then back, and he stammered, "I—I mean, would you go out with me?"

There was something so moving about how vulnerable he seemed, how nervous. How much he really seemed to care what I thought.

"I'd like that."

He exhaled hard. "Phew. I was worried there for a second."

"That I'd say no?" I was incredulous. Had anyone ever said no to this guy before?

"That maybe you didn't feel what I felt when we kissed." He was stroking my palm. "But you did, didn't you?" He didn't wait for me to answer. "Good. I'll pick you up at eight next Saturday night."

"Actually Saturday night is the one night I can't—"

"You'll work it out," he said, smiling. He was looking at me in this completely different way now, more confident, his eyes half open. He brought my hand to his lips and kissed the back of it, like a prince in a fairy tale. "I hate being disappointed and I know you won't disappoint me."

I wouldn't, I decided. No way.

I met Langley and Kate at Livingston Bagel the next day for brunch. I waited until we'd gotten through the previous day's gossip about Elsa dying the hair of all her stepmother's collectible dolls rainbow and the two freshman girls who had been caught with ecstasy to tell them my news. "David? Asked you out?" Langley was so incredulous she dropped her fork and pushed aside her chopped salad.

"I know, I couldn't believe it either."

"You're not going to go, are you?" Kate said. She began closely studying the ends of her hair.

"Um, yes. I mean, I thought so. Why?"

She looked at me. "He and Nicky just broke up. Aren't you worried you're just a rebound fling?"

This wasn't what I was expecting. I'd been expecting them to be happy for me, not—cautious. Kate had finished her study of her hair and was staring past me with her eyes unfocused, the way she got when she was working on getting into character.

"What's wrong? I thought you would be excited."

"I am," Kate said, her eyes sliding back to me. "Of course I am. I just want to make sure you don't get hurt. David is—he's not exactly a monk."

Langley had returned to her salad. "I was just surprised. Personally, I think it's great," she said, nibbling around the edges of the mouthful on her fork. "And so what if it is only a rebound, you guys will have a few fun weeks together and then you'll both date other people."

"Sure," I said.

Instead David and I were now nearing our eight-month anniversary. I still smiled every time I saw his name on my caller ID or caught a glimpse of his car. I couldn't believe he'd picked me. And if anything, he seemed to like me and want to spend time with me more with every passing week.

"I feel like I can trust you," he said on our fourth date. "Like I can tell you anything," and I felt so important, so loved.

He *did* confide everything to me, too—about the time when he was seven when he'd overwatered his father's bonsai collection and his father had beaten him so hard his mother had to take him to the hospital. "Told the nurses I had an accident," he said, matter-of-fact, no blame. "What could she do? If she'd said anything else, the man would have beaten her too." About the time when he was twelve that his father made him go for four days without food or water because he'd forgotten to check the water filter in a prize-fish tank. It was no wonder David had inherited a little temper.

But there was also this soft, sweet, boyish side to him that I adored. The side that could sit and tell stories to Annie for hours, that loved old romantic movies or anything with the Muppets, that made tiny mewing noises when I rubbed his feet. He would bring me little presents for no reason, a necklace with a heart on it, an action figure of Wonder Woman because I reminded him of her. Things that meant something to him, that he hoped would mean something to me.

And there was the time, after we'd been going out for a month, when I woke up to the sound of knocking on my bedroom window. I opened it and he was there, shivering, even though it wasn't that cold.

"Can I come in?" he asked, his voice unsteady.

"What's wrong?" I asked, helping him over the threshold.

His eyes were clear and looked so bereft, so sad. I'd never seen anything like it.

"Can we, can you just love me for a minute?" he asked, and fell into my arms.

He started sobbing and, still holding him, I lowered us both onto my bed. For a long time we just lay like that, him in my arms, me comforting him like a child. He gripped me hard, so hard it hurt and left bruises the next day, but I didn't care. That was him, how passionate he was. When his sobs had subsided, he looked at me and smiled more sweetly than I'd ever seen before.

"I love you, Jane," he said. "More than I've ever loved anyone."

I lost my virginity to him that night, a token of love, of the trust he could have in me. He was wonderful and sweet and loved me. The only time we fought was if I had to break a date with him, but in a way, that just made me like him more because it showed how much he cared.

"So you're really feeling better?" David said now, next to my hospital bed. He was fingering a beat against his leg, the way he did when he was anxious.

I nodded.

"Well enough to tell me what that surprise of yours was that I didn't get to experience? It's only fair, I already coughed up 139."

I felt my chest tighten. I knew it would all be okay once I told him, but right now I didn't want to do anything to ruin how good it was having him there. Besides, I might never get better and then it wouldn't matter anyway. "Nope. I'm still saving it."

"That is just mean." He pouted with his gorgeous mouth.

"I know you can be patient." I noticed he had a scratch on his face. "What happened to you, babe?"

His fingers went to it. "Nothing."

"Tell me."

He shrugged and pushed the sunglasses up his nose and stared into the middle distance. "Guess I was a little more out of it than I thought Thursday and I nicked the Despot's car when I pulled in. We had a little tussle."

"David," I said, genuinely concerned.

"Babe, you got bigger things to worry about. So tell me, what do you do for kicks in this here town?"

"Well, cowboy, it's a real hoot. Sometimes my mother comes to bother me, sometimes I get to bathe." I was tempted to tell him about the writing on the mirror, but I didn't want him to think I was being weird. "There's a police officer who visits. But I don't think she likes me much because I can't remember anything."

"What *do* you remember?" he asked. His fingers went a little faster.

"I remember coming in and sitting on your lap—"

"I remember that too," he said. Smiled. "You looked amazing in those little fairy wings. And that, what do you call that top you were wearing?"

"A tube top."

"Yeah. Nice." I felt his gaze move away from me, like he was picturing that. Picturing how I had looked.

Suddenly I was acutely aware of how different I looked now. Now I had bruises on my face, I couldn't move. Everything was—wrong. Different. "Was that the last time you saw me at the party?"

That seemed to jar him back to the present. Behind his sunglasses his eyes crinkled and his mouth got firm the way it did when he got angry. "What are you getting at?"

His reaction surprised me. It was the way he acted when some-one disagreed with him or questioned what he said. "I'm not getting at anything. I'm just trying to piece together what happened. The doctor says some of my paralysis might be mental, so the more I can recall, the faster I'll be able to move."

"Sounds like BS to me. Why *wouldn't* you want to move?"

I bit my lip. "I don't know. Maybe you could help me by helping me remember."

His jaw loosened slightly. "Seriously? You don't remember any-thing? You're not jerking me around?"

"No." I was relieved to see him relax slightly.

"Well, then I think the last time I saw you was when you aban-doned me for the girls." He pulled the hand he'd had wrapped around mine away. "Like you always do."

My relief evaporated and I went totally cold inside.

Chapter 13

"**I don't always abandon** you for my girls," I insisted.

"Really? What about two weeks ago?"

What was going on? I had the sensation my world was slipping out from under me again. "We've been over that. You said you understood. You said you'd give me another chance."

"Yeah," he said, clenching and unclenching his hands, his body rigid. "Well, maybe I was wrong."

Two weeks earlier David had the afternoon off from his job at the music store and we'd planned to hang out. During lunch Langley had been called to the principal's office because her grandfather had been having trouble breathing. By last period she'd texted us to say that he was okay, but it seemed like she wasn't. This was Langley, who prided herself on being independent and not needing anyone, but she sounded so shattered it was clear that she needed a dose of the three Ss—shopping, Slurpees, and sisterhood. It's what friends do.

I left David a message that I'd be late and then headed to the mall with the girls. I didn't hear back from him, but while we were out, I made Kate and Langley stop to get his favorite cupcakes. In the past when we'd fought, I'd brought cupcakes for him as a peace gesture and it usually ended in me licking the frosting off of him.

When they dropped me at his house on the way home from the mall, no one answered the doorbell. His green Audi was in the driveway, and stepping back, I saw the curtain in his window move, so I knew he was home. I rang again. After a minute the intercom went.

"What?" he demanded. Not friendly. It was a good thing I'd splurged for the half-dozen cupcake pack.

"Um, it's me, babe. I came by to say I'm sorry about today. And I brought you something."

"I'm busy practicing," he said, although I thought I heard music in the background.

My heart hammered. I hated his moods, his insecurities. I wanted him to understand how much I loved him. Why was it so hard sometimes? "It's cupcakes." My voice sounded meek.

"This just…isn't going to work, Jane. It's not that easy." Yes, definitely music in the background. In fact, he was listening to the Doors, "Light My Fire," the song we always made out to.

"What are you talking about?"

"You and I. Not like this."

Was he breaking up with me over the intercom? I started to shake. "Can we at least talk? Face-to-face?"

"I don't know." A pause. "Fine, wait there."

He came down a few minutes later wearing only jeans with his lightning-bolt-patterned boxers poking out the top. They were my favorites because he looked so insanely good in them.

He crossed his arms over his lanky chest, perfectly framing the small patch of freckles right above his toned abs. "So. Talk."

I had to drag my eyes from his body. "I'm sorry. I didn't realize this would be such a big deal."

"Not a big deal? We had a plan, babe, and you bagged it at the last minute."

"But we were just going to hang out in your room."

"Just? Because hanging out with me isn't enough for you? It *used* to be. Look, babe, if you're not committed to this relationship, if your friends are so much more important—"

"It's not like that. Langley needed me."

"You know, you're using Langley an awful lot this way. Like I'm thinking maybe you're just not that into this anymore."

"This?"

He shifted his weight and shrugged his freckle-sprinkled shoulders. "Us." His face was hollow, a mask. A stranger.

I felt desperate and my voice came out high and tight. "No, David, it's not that. I am. I'm just trying to be a good friend. Besides, how many times have you canceled for band practice?"

He stepped back and put his hands up like I'd punched him. "Whoa. Did I just hear that right? Are you comparing *shopping at the mall* with my *band*?"

My heart sank into my stomach. What was I saying? "No, of course not. I—I'm just sorry. I didn't want to hurt you and I didn't think you would care that much and I'm really sorry."

His gaze was focused on something over my head, like he couldn't even bear to look at me.

I was crying and when I went to dry my eyes, I realized I was still holding the cupcakes. "Here. I got you these."

He didn't move.

"I'm sorry," I said, my voice barely a whisper. "Please don't leave me."

"Leave you?" He frowned.

I was so upset I didn't even know what I was saying. "I mean forgive me. Please forgive me."

Without looking at me he said, "I need some time," took the cupcakes, and closed the door.

I'd walked home in the middle of the street, not even caring what happened to me. I was numb, frozen from the inside out. When I got home, Annie was doing something weird in the downstairs powder room. She saw me and came running out and stopped and stared. "You look sad," she said.

"I'm fine," I muttered.

She evaluated me through her thick glasses. "I'm playing Bride of Slime. Want to play with me? You can even be the bride."

That was an honor, but not one I could accept right then. "No thanks. I've got to do my homework."

She hugged me. "I'll be in my office"—she pointed to the powder room—"if you change your mind."

I watched her go back to playing and for a moment wondered how she could be so oblivious to how other people acted, what they thought, what was normal, and yet be so confident that she was adored.

Later that night David dropped by my house. I was listening to music, so I didn't hear the doorbell or even his knock on the door of my room. I didn't realize he was there until he had his hands on my shoulders, looking over the top of my head at what I was writing on the computer screen.

"'Photography as Social Commentary,'" he read aloud. "What's that for?"

"AP European History," I told him, closing the document before he could read more. I turned to face him. "Did you come here to help me with my homework?"

He smiled and sat down on my bed, pulling my rolling desk chair toward him so I was between his knees facing him.

"I spent all afternoon thinking," he said.

"I spent all afternoon crying."

"Oh, babe." He ran his left thumb over my cheek, across my neck, down my arm, following with his gaze. He started to massage my hand. I knew it turned him on to touch me like that and I felt my body respond.

He breathed out and raised his blue eyes back to mine. "We're so good together, aren't we?"

He kissed the palm of my hand softly. I swallowed and nodded.

He kissed the inside of my wrist. "We shouldn't fight, should we?"

I shook my head.

He dropped my hand and leaned toward my mouth. I was desperate to feel his lips on mine. "You know what you did today, canceling like that, was wrong, don't you?"

I nodded.

"Say it," he said, his mouth inches from mine, smiling, teasing.

"Yes."

"Otherwise you wouldn't have brought me cupcakes."

"That's right."

"But you won't do it again, will you?"

"No." My tongue darted out to try to reach his lips. He laughed and pulled me from the chair onto his lap. "Do you want to kiss me?"

"Yes," I breathed. His mouth came down over mine, hard and fierce and possessive as his hands moved over my back. I loved it when he held me like that, like I was his, like he would never let me go. I could imagine how we looked, me on his lap with my hands on either side of his face, his lips biting mine. Tendrils of desire curled through me.

Maybe it was the stress of almost losing him that did it, but I felt bold, wanton.

I pushed him so he was lying on my bed and was thrilled by the expression of surprise mingled with pleasure on his face.

I'd read in one of Kate's mother's *Elle* magazines that you can train your man to do things he doesn't want to do if you combine telling him about them with pleasurable sensations. I straddled him. "We're too good together to fight, right?"

"Right," he answered, gazing up at me, his eyes dancing with amusement.

"But you understand that I have responsibilities to my friends." I tugged suggestively at the bottom of my T-shirt like I was going to start a striptease. I knew he loved seeing me in my bra, so I stopped just above my belly button. "Right?"

He gulped. "Right."

I pulled my T-shirt over my head. "Especially Langley, who has no other family and needs her friends. You know that it's not a question of me picking her over you." I'd never been so forward before, but judging from the way his breathing got short, he liked it. His reaction spurred me on. I moved the fingers of one of my hands slowly up the thigh of his jeans and leaned my mouth to his ear to whisper, "It's a question of being a good friend." My fingers reached his belt. "Right?"

He moaned. "Jesus."

My hand hovered over his guitar-shaped belt buckle. "Say it."

"Yes. Right."

I shimmied him out of his jeans. There was a streak of frosting on his upper thigh, just under his boxers. It must have fallen there when he was eating the cupcakes, I thought, glad to have the chance to lick some frosting off him after all.

Later we lay with our legs tangled together, in our underwear, looking up at the ceiling. I could picture us, me in my boy-cut white-and-black-polka-dot panties and white kneesocks, him in his lightning-bolt boxers, my head on his shoulder, the fingers of my hand tracing the strong drummer muscles of his forearm.

"That was amazing," I said.

"Mmm-hmm," he agreed sleepily.

"You know I love you, David," I said.

"Yeah, I know, lover lips."

I went on one elbow. "I do."

He tucked my long dark hair behind my ear. "Yeah. It's just that I don't want to be made a fool of, you know. I trusted you with everything. You're not playing me, are you? Doing other guys behind my back?"

That's what all his possessiveness was about. My heart nearly broke for him as I understood it wasn't anything I did, it was because of what had happened with Nicky. That's why he was so sensitive. "Of course not," I said. "I'd never hurt you."

That night he had rubbed his nose against mine and said, "Maybe you can have another chance."

Now, in my hospital room, sitting stiffly beside me, he said, "Maybe I was wrong. Maybe I shouldn't have done that."

I felt panic rising in my throat. "Why did you say that? Why shouldn't you have given me another chance?"

"You want to know what happened the night of the party so badly? Fine, here's what happened: I was sitting there waiting for you and your 'surprise' like some kind of well-trained puppy, while you were supposed to be off saving the world or your friends or whatever. I trusted you. I believed you. I believed in us. And then Elsa came to have a little talk with me."

Chapter 14

Elsa. **Elsa Blanchard.** When I'd first come to Livingston, I thought of her as Elsa the Rich Girl because she drove a Porsche, had at least two diamond tennis bracelets, and always wore Chanel from the limited edition sunglasses perched on her head to the custom-made ring on her pinkie toe. Even the ankle socks she'd been wearing the time the school custodian found her passed out on the roof of the gym before her "extended relaxation vacation" had been Chanel.

My mind went back to the party.

I get up from David's lap and turn around to give a cute wave, but instead of David, I get a glimpse of Elsa strutting toward him.

She's wearing a satin tuxedo-shorts jumpsuit from the Chanel resort collection, complete with a top hat. She has a pearl necklace with a huge jeweled Chanel symbol slung around her neck, a big red ring on her left hand, and platform sandals with bows up the back. She looks really cool, and if it were anyone else, I would be jealous, but Elsa only dates college guys, so it's actually a relief. I know David is in good, or at least safe hands.

I turn back and—

"I bet you can guess what she said." David's jaw was set, his posture as straight as the IV pole next to my bed. Machines clicked and whirred, making white noise to fill the silent void between us.

He was right, I could guess what she'd said. Although it was hard to believe she'd do it. It never occurred to me that Elsa had the power to tell David something that would destroy all my plans. Destroy us.

That same day two weeks earlier when David and I had been fighting, Mr. Jergens the art teacher had called me and Elsa into his room.

"I have good news and I have bad news," he'd said. "Which do you want first?"

Elsa and I had been distant acquaintances since I'd gotten to Livingston, but she was the editor of the school paper and we'd become friends at photography camp the previous summer. Before that, I'd always gotten this vibe from her that she didn't like me and I assumed it was because she'd been the third Mustketeer with Langley and Kate until I came, and I sort of took her place.

She laughed when I got up the courage to ask her about that one night last summer when she and Scott and I were talking around a crackling campfire.

"I was only friends with them because my stepmother insisted," she said. Elsa's stepmother, Mary-Ellen, was twenty-seven years younger than her father, a collector of dolls, and a notorious social climber. Elsa put on a staccato voice to mimic her saying, "Knowing the Right People now will ensure you move in the Right Circles later, sweetie pie." Elsa shook her head. "She'd usually get to that line around the third glass of Chablis—pronounced 'cha-bliss' by her, by the way," Elsa explained, taking a swig of vitaminwater. "But really she wanted to use me to open social doors that were otherwise shut and triple bolted from her. She didn't quite understand how having been a beauty queen in Idaho wasn't enough to get her into the fold of Livingston's upper crust. So I tried, for her, because she's actually very sweet, but I couldn't do it. You have no idea how glad I was when you showed up and I could make a safe exit."

I was shocked but tried to keep my voice neutral. "What do you mean?"

"It takes a neurotic to know a neurotic. Like Langley. The sad orphan. She needs acolytes, people to think she's important."

"What's wrong with wanting to be important to people?" I asked, a little harshly.

"There's nothing wrong with wanting to be important. What's wrong is using other people to make yourself feel important."

"That's not what Langley does." The conversation was making me uncomfortable in a way that went beyond having to defend my friends.

Elsa thought about it. "Maybe it's not to you. But that's how it felt to me. And Kate. Always happy, that's how she wants everyone to see her, but actually she's deeply miserable. She's always acting, always fooling everyone. It's a power trip. Like the way she needs everyone to think she's carefree. Really she's just careless—or at least she could care less about anyone but herself."

"That's not true," I burst out. "She's totally not self-centered. And she's one of the most generous people I know."

In the flickering light of the fire I saw Elsa give a rueful grin. "Given who you hang out with, that's likely."

"Ouch," Scott said.

Elsa put up her hands in mock surrender. "Just kidding? Anyway, when you came along, it was more like you were their newest victim than my replacement."

"No one could replace you," I said, to try to change the topic.

"Here, here," Scott agreed, his face all lean planes and glowing skin in the light of the fire.

Elsa gave me a pretend tip of the hat. "I'm glad you're happy. Personally those two scare me. Once I looked in Langley's eyes, and I swear there was no emotion there. Nothing. Then you look in Kate's eyes, and they're even scarier because it's like looking into a swirling pit of darkness. Both of them are seriously messed up. I thought you must be vapid to want to spend time with them and not worth my interest." She smiled at me. "Turns out I was wrong. Although your taste in friends is still a bit suspect."

"She picked us," Scott said from his place on the other side of the campfire, where he was smoking a hand-rolled cigarette. "We bring the noise and the funk."

Elsa shook her head at the cigarette when he offered it. "Sure. But we'll see what happens when we get back to school."

I didn't pursue my defense of Kate and Langley because I didn't see the point. She wasn't right. She couldn't be. Kate and Langley wouldn't be so popular if what she said was true. If that's what Elsa had to tell herself to feel better about not being friends with them, that was her issue.

Plus I liked hanging out with her and I didn't want to pick a fight. She and Scott and I spent a lot of evenings together talking about the ways we'd each capture a shot or who our favorite photographers were. We hadn't hung out since school started again, but I didn't think we were enemies. Not even the day Dr. Jergens called us both into the art room to tell us about the internship.

He was beaming. "The good news is, I just got a call from the Getty Images people about their summer internship and they loved both your work."

I was speechless. Getty Images was known for having the highest-caliber photographers in the field, the most Pulitzer Prize winners, the best. Getty photographers hogged the front pages of all the major newspapers in the world, had the covers of *Time* and *Newsweek*. They were the top.

"What's the bad news?" Elsa asked.

"The bad news is, there's only one position available. I tried to convince them, they even lobbied internally, but only one of you can go. You'll each have to write an essay about your philosophy of photography to break the tie. And I'm afraid you only have a week."

The essay I'd been working on the night David came over, about photography and social justice, was what broke the tie in my favor. I'd won the internship.

When Mr. Jergens gave us that news, Elsa had smiled and said, "Congrats. I'll buy you a vitaminwater to celebrate."

"Awesome."

"Remember, Elsa," Mr. Jergens reminded, "you're still their next choice, so if for any reason Jane can't take it, it will be yours."

"Make that a poison vitaminwater," she'd joked.

I was excited, but it was a huge commitment, nearly the entire summer. It would mean commuting by train into New York City, so I'd have a lot less time to spend with my friends and David. And in particular it would mean canceling the ten-day camping trip he and I had been planning to take.

I should have told him when I first found out I was a finalist, but it was the day we had our fight, and besides, I didn't know if I'd get it. And then I was going to tell him the day I found out I won—I even canceled on Langley at the last minute to do it—but his band had a gig and we didn't get to talk. It wasn't that I was putting it off, I was just waiting for a good time.

David liked it when things went the way he planned so I knew he'd be upset about canceling the camping trip. But he loved me, so he'd also have to be happy for me. This was an amazing opportunity. "Like getting your band signed to a first-look deal at a label," I'd rehearsed saying in my head.

That was just part of the speech I'd planned for the night of the party. The picnic Kate and Langley had helped me organize had all David's favorite foods, ending in cupcakes. I was going to soften him up with buffalo chicken wings in the first course, move to Kobe beef sliders after, and as they were settling in, I'd tell him about the internship. We'd have chocolate cupcakes and champagne to celebrate, and then it would be into the sixteen-headed steam shower for a different kind of dessert. It was the perfect way to show him that we could have fun even if we weren't camping.

The not-perfect way was Elsa going up and congratulating him on me getting an internship that would take me away most of the summer. Which was apparently what had happened.

He looked at me now with such hurt and betrayal and said, "I just didn't want to be made a fool of again, all right? Having everyone know my business except me."

"I'm so sorry. I didn't think it was that big a deal—"

"Not a big deal? That you have, like, plans behind my back?"

He was so stubborn, so afraid of being hurt. I was desperate to get through to him. "Please, sweetheart, I'm sorry. It wasn't my idea. And I know I should have told you about it as soon as I knew—"

"Yes."

"But I wanted to make sure to tell you the right way. So you wouldn't freak out."

"Mission not accomplished," he said.

Tears burned in my eyes. I needed him, needed him to love me now more than ever. Now that I was ugly and broken. I couldn't face being alone. "I made a mistake. I admit it. Nothing happened, I didn't commit to anything. Everything can go back to just how it was, all our plans, everything. You gave me another chance before. Could you do it again?"

He was watching me closely.

"Please. I love you so much. And I'll owe you one. Next time it's your turn to mess up."

Like he couldn't stop himself, that crooked smile came out of nowhere. "Hmm. Intriguing."

"Say yes."

He hesitated, scratching his chin like he was trying to make a decision. "Very well. But you have to get it right."

"What do you mean?" I said, exhaling with relief.

"Last time when we had that fight? I didn't just say I'd give you another chance. What I said was—"

And suddenly I was back there two weeks earlier. Back in my room, back on my bed.

David said, "I guess I could give you another chance."

Our lips met in a long, deep, slow, sinuous kiss. I pulled away slightly to tease, "Only one chance?"

He brought my fingers to his lips and started kissing them. "Maybe one chance an hour."

He spoke the words now, in my hospital room, and it was like we'd been transported back to that moment together. He stood and reached out for my fingers, but my hand was stuck in a tangle of cords. "Um, this is a bit awkward."

"Maybe we can save that part for later. Since I can't even feel my fingers."

"Oh yeah." He bent over. "But you can feel your mouth, right?"

"Yes."

The kiss hurt a little on my bruised lip, but I didn't want him to stop. It made me feel normal again, hopeful. I could have continued it all day if Ollie hadn't come in then and said, "David, man, we have to go." He jingled his car keys in his hand.

"Chill, buddy," David said, barely lifting his lips from mine. "Can't you see I'm busy giving my lady-girl mouth-to-mouth? Your phone can wait."

"Seriously, man. It's the fuzz."

David stood up like he'd been tased, but it was too late.

"Hello, Mr. Montero," Officer Rowley said. "And Mr. Tisch. How nice to see you both. Do you have anything to add to your statements yet?"

"No, ma'am," Ollie said, looking—and sounding—like Livingston's number-one upstanding citizen. His voice was relaxed, but the knuckles of his right hand were tight where his fingers wrapped around his car keys.

"Very well, then we won't detain you."

"We can go?" David asked.

"I've just come to talk to Jane. Unless you want to stay and answer questions."

"No, that's cool." He shot me a peace sign from down near his belt and a small intimate smile. It was filled with promise and love. "Be seeing you, babe. Stay soft."

Chapter 15

Officer Rowley closed the door behind them and pulled a chair up next to my bed. "I see you've received several new bouquets and cards."

"Yes."

"But the largest ones are still from Oliver Montero."

"I guess. I haven't really been ranking them."

She smiled the fakest smile I've ever seen. "Of course. A girl with your degree of popularity would never think that way."

I didn't even understand what that meant. "Have you been questioning my friends?" I asked.

"We're trying to get to the truth." Moving with precision and no haste, she opened her notebook and uncapped her pen. She looked at me for a moment.

"What can you tell me about Nicola di Savoia?"

"Nicky? She's a girl at my school."

"How would you describe your relationship with her?"

"Okay. Why?"

"Based on your tox screens, you were both dosed with a drug called Paratol. She exhibited the same memory loss you've been showing and reports some of the same symptoms, but more mildly."

"What's Paratol?"

"It's a prescription sleeping medication. For some people it has hallucinogenic side effects, so it is highly regulated and not easily available."

"We shared a drink at the party. She gave it to me."

"Why didn't you mention this before?"

"I only remembered it last night—her handing me this red plastic cup and telling me to drink almost as soon as we got to the party."

"She gave it to you? You're certain of that?"

I nodded. She made a note on her pad. "Did anyone else touch the cup?"

I hated the way she was looking at me, like I was a criminal. The way she was talking about my friends. "No." I paused. "I didn't do anything wrong."

Her eyes left her pad to focus on me. They were cool, completely without emotion. "No one is saying you did." Back to the pad. "Did you share anything else?"

I ran through the memory in my mind. Nicky coming up right when we got there and wanting to make peace. Giving me a kiss and the cup and telling me to drink. Refusing to take the cup back when I tried to give it to her. "I can't think of anything else we shared."

"Besides a boyfriend, of course."

That caught me off guard. I felt flustered, pinned, and I could sense heat rising in my cheeks. "I guess. I mean, sure. But Nicky and David broke up a few weeks before I started dating him. I didn't steal him from her." I was aware of talking too much, sounding defensive. I took a breath. "What I mean is, we didn't *share* him. And she broke up with him. So it's not like she wanted him anymore."

"You'd be amazed how seeing your ex with another woman can reawaken powerful feelings," Officer Rowley said, straightening the pad she had resting on her knee. She seemed almost human for a moment, vulnerable. Then her eyes moved from the pad back to me and she was all business again. "Did you see her again at another time during the party?"

"I don't think so."

But even as I said it, I felt like something was wrong. There was something tickling the back of my mind, telling me this didn't make sense. "Wait. Since there's no reason Nicky would drug herself, someone must have drugged both Nicky and me, right?"

"That's one way to look at it."

"What's another?"

"Your mother has a prescription for Paratol."

I didn't know my mother had trouble sleeping. All those nights when I'd come in late and she'd never even mentioned it, I assumed she just didn't care. Had she been drugged? She'd never had problems sleeping before—that I knew of.

"Miss Freeman?" Officer Rowley's voice recalled me to the hospital room.

"I'm sorry, what were you saying?" I was struck by the fact that maybe there were as many things about my mother I didn't know as there were things about me she was in the dark about.

"Nicky says that she drank from the cup *before* giving it to you and felt fine, but when she drank from it after *you'd* held it, she started to feel weird."

I shook off the thoughts about my mother. "Wait, are you suggesting I drugged her?"

"If, as you say, no one else touched the cup and if Nicky drank from it before you with no ill effects, that's certainly how it looks."

I felt like I was on the deck of a ship that was being tossed in the waves with no firm footing, no way to know which way was up, what was true, what was false. "No way. Nicky made a mistake. She didn't drink from the cup after I did. She gave it to me and went off to dance."

"She says she did. And right now, Miss Freeman, since she hasn't withheld information from me, I'm inclined to believe her."

The sense of reality heaving below me intensified. I felt my stomach lurch and my body went hot and cold at once. "What information have I withheld?"

"Like that you had a big fight with your two best friends at the party that night."

"What?" I was bewildered. "I fought with Langley and Kate? Did they tell you that?"

"No, but several people witnessed you yelling at them and walking away from a room you'd been in with them saying"—she flipped through her notebook—"that's it, it's over, I'm ending this."

I had a flash memory then of Langley in front of the door of a room. It's dark; the door is beige with gilding around the moldings of the panels. Her hand is on the knob; it's gold. Or was it Kate? It was all hazy, a blur. But I didn't remember fighting with either of them.

This was horrible. I was losing my mind. I couldn't remember, but I knew, *knew*, I wouldn't have drugged Nicky. Would I? I felt battered, exhausted, like I could no longer separate truth from illusion. I had to get a grip. Find the facts.

"What else did people tell you?" I asked, forcing myself to refocus on the harsh fluorescent lighting of the hospital room. But the nausea in the pit of my stomach, the growing sense of dread, of being about to drown in my own self-doubt, didn't leave me.

"That you weren't alone when you left the party, although no one seems to have observed who you were with. Do you remember that?"

"No."

"You're certain?"

I was crying now. "I don't know what you want from me. I've told you everything I can."

"You didn't tell me about the cup with the drugged drink in it until now."

"I only remembered it a little while ago." Please, I wanted to beg. Please believe me.

"Right." She nodded once, desultorily.

"I had no reason to drug Nicky." A thought dawned on me like sunlight slicing through storm clouds. "If you believe her, that I put something in the cup, that means I drugged myself. Why would I do that?"

She gazed at me as though I'd just walked into a trap. "Why would you kneel in front of a speeding car?"

"What if I didn't see the car? What if I didn't know it was there?"

"An invisible car?" Given her tone, I was surprised she didn't snort.

The storm clouds closed up over me again and I felt like I was being sucked into darkness. Everything Officer Rowley said made me more confused, more unsure of what really happened. My memory felt like the gap-toothed smile of a creepy crone from a fairy tale, where the spaces between her teeth give you glimpses of a scary dark place that wants to eat you up alive.

Officer Rowley kept talking, but I wasn't really paying attention. Because I knew what was bothering me now. I was back at the party, thinking about the plastic cup.

I get up from David's lap to find Kate and Langley. I kiss him and pick up the red plastic cup and carry it across the room toward the stairs.

I turn to give him a cute wave, and I see Elsa talking to him. He's in good hands, I tell myself.

I turn back and crash into something—the balustrade of the staircase?—dropping my purse. It's open, so everything scatters all over the floor and I put the drink down to pick it all up.

I put the drink down and left it there.

Which meant I didn't drink any. So it didn't matter what was in it.

But this discovery did nothing to help my case at all. Because it didn't answer the question of how the drug *did* get into my system. And it only made it look more likely that I knew there was something wrong with the cup and purposely avoided it.

It only made me look more guilty.

"That's all for right now, Miss Freeman," Officer Rowley wrapped up. "Do you have anything to add?"

I was trapped. The truth wasn't what was going to help me.

"No."

Chapter 16

"*A* dollar seventy-nine for your thoughts," Langley's voice said from the door of my room. I must have been really distracted because I hadn't heard her approach. I looked at the clock and saw that it was a little past noon. "Not that they're not worth more, it's just that's all the cash I have on me."

As she walked into my room, she slid her phone into the outside pocket of her Miu Miu purse, which was weird, because she always kept her phone inside. She'd only put on mascara and lip gloss, and she was wearing a T-shirt and cardi with baggy jeans, leopard flats, and a newsboy cap over her hair but no other accessories, which made her much less put together than usual, like maybe she rushed here.

"Are you okay?" I asked.

She looked aghast. "Am I okay? You're the one we're supposed to be worrying about. That is so you, jelly bean. I'm fine, don't think about me."

"You're lying. What's going on?"

Her face fell apart in an instant. "It's Popo. He's—there's been a bit of a setback."

"Oh, Langley, I'm so sorry."

She wiped her eyes, pulled a hair off her sweater. Swallowed. He and her grandmother had raised Langley together since she came to live with them, but Popo and Langley had a special bond.

He was the one who started her car every morning in the winter to make sure the heater would be putting out warm air by the time she got in. He was the one who attended all her dressage competitions, always with some little piece of jewelry or object that she'd been secretly coveting as a present. He was the one who snuck her wads of hundred-dollar bills "in case she needed a soda" at the mall. He wrote the letters to her when she was away for the summer school session at Gordonstoun in Scotland, and he was the one who sat by her bedside reading *Little Women* when she had a cold, even now.

Or he had until recently. Although the name Lawrence Archibald Winterman, former president of New Jersey Gas and Electric and chair of a dozen boards, still commanded towering admiration, the man himself was in decline. Six months ago, he'd fallen down the back stairs of the house and broken his hip and it wasn't healing as well as it should. Since then, despite the care of a full-time nurse, he'd had infection after infection, each one taking a toll on the whole family.

"What is it this time?"

"He's having chest pains. The doctor is running some tests, but we won't get the results until Tuesday. I think it's because of my grandmother."

Langley's grandmother was convinced that the nurses they had to care for Popo were stealing from her, so she was constantly trying to sneak up on them and installing surveillance devices to catch them in the act. All her precautions had really achieved was to create an atmosphere of tension and a rotating string of nurses who quit because they found the conditions intolerable.

"She's just looking for something to control," Langley explained with a resigned smile. "She's like my mother that way. When disruptive things happened in one part of her life, things she couldn't stop like the air-conditioning in the trailer breaking, she'd become extra rigid in another part and put us on some crazy diet or become obsessed with my posture."

It was hard to imagine Langley as anything other than a pampered East Coast girl living in a palace, but she'd actually spent the first eleven years of her life living in a trailer outside of Tucson, Arizona.

Once, when I asked Langley what it was like, she'd said, "The trailer was so snug with the two of us in it, it was like living inside a doll's house."

"Maman practically bought out the entire stuffed-animal selection at FAO Schwartz when we found out Langley was coming to us," her grandfather told me one day when the three of us were having tea in his study. "And that first night Langley took them all, the giant deer, the giraffe, the lion, and used them to drape a sheet and make a tent so she could feel cozy because her new room was too big. That's my girl." He'd squeezed her hand and looked at her with such pride that I was jealous. "That's my resourceful, smart girl."

I hadn't learned why Langley went to live with her grandparents until the class ski trip to Killington my first year in Livingston. Everyone else was excited to go in the Jacuzzi after skiing, but Langley and I had both said we'd rather stay on the mountain longer. In my case, anyway, it was a lie—it was a dreary, freezing day—and I'd changed into jeans and a big nubby fisherman's sweater and gone and hidden myself in the snack bar. It was a cavernous octagonal space with a wooden-beam ceiling and huge windows looking out at the mountains. Because everyone else was on the slopes, the wood-plank tables arrayed around the octagon were nearly all empty.

Until five minutes after I sat down, when Langley slid in next to me. She was wearing jeans, camel-colored Louis Vuitton snow boots, and a light-blue parka with white fur trim around the hood that perfectly framed her face.

"Okay, jelly bean. What's your excuse? Why aren't you going to the Jacuzzi party?"

I felt my breath catch. Her directness caught me off guard. "It's a long story."

She looked at her watch. "I'm guessing that we have a couple hours before everyone gets bored and wrinkled and forgets we weren't there so we won't have to answer any questions about why. If it's longer than that, I might need popcorn."

"Why don't you want to go in?" I asked as she slid out of the parka and pulled the sleeves of her white thermal shirt up over her knuckles.

"You tell me yours, I'll tell you mine."

She and Kate and I had been nearly inseparable for two-and-a-half months, but this was the first time I had really been alone with Langley. I don't know if it was that I wanted her to like me or if it was just that I really needed to tell someone. Without thinking, I blurted, "Last November, back in Chicago, my best friend, Bonnie, died in a Jacuzzi." The words sounded strange—like a character in a movie was saying them, not me.

Langley's light-blue eyes got huge. "My God. I'm so sorry. What happened?"

"I don't know, really." I watched the steam come off my hot chocolate, letting it pull me into the memory. I was afraid, but also slightly exhilarated. I'd never discussed this with anyone before. "It was at a party," I said finally.

When I'd told Bonnie about the party, her reaction had been, "No and also Way."

"You can try all your mind tricks on me, Jedi," she'd said, "and I shall not waver. Why would you want to go to that? I don't even know any of those people and neither do you. Plus your mother is never going to let you go to a party thrown by a junior."

Bonnie had a brother who was a few years older than her, which meant her parents had gotten being protective out of their system, but my mother hadn't and was worse ever since my dad had died earlier that year.

"I'll sneak out," I'd said. "And not knowing them is why we *should* go. To meet new people. Do you want to die without being kissed?" I pulled out my best Jedi mind trick. "I heard Mark Ellis was going."

It had been a little crooked to name her senior crush, but it had worked.

"Fine. I'll go as your chaperone," she'd agreed at last. "But for the record, this is a seriously bad idea. I'm packing my paperback *Harry Potter* in my bag so at least I have something to do while you're making a fool of yourself."

Langley's voice came to me then, across the scarred wooden table of the ski-lodge snack bar, saying, "Did she hit her head? How did she die?"

"I—I don't really know. I was off with someone else. By the time I saw her, she was just lying there in the Jacuzzi, with her head lolling back and her dark hair floating all around her, gazing up at the sky like she was looking for the Big Dipper. She looked beautiful, peaceful. Like Ophelia from Hamlet, you know?" Langley nodded. "Her face was such a perfect pale oval in the moonlight and her eyes glittered. At first I couldn't believe she was dead. And then—" I stopped. Hot tears came running unexpectedly down my cheeks and fell into my hot chocolate.

Langley put an arm on my back. "Then what happened?"

I met her eyes. "Then all I could think was, God, she needed her eyebrows plucked." I started to sob then for real, huge shaking sobs that racked my entire body. "Can you believe that? She was dead and that was all I could think of. Her eyebrows." I pressed the palms of my hands to my eyes, jamming the tears back in. I didn't deserve to cry about this, didn't deserve any sympathy.

"That happens a lot," Langley said, rubbing my back. Her voice was soothing, kind. Maternal. "That you fixate on one weird detail. It's normal."

I kept my head in my hands. "They said she OD'd. That she committed suicide."

"Did she?"

"That's what they said."

There was a beat of silence. Langley broke it saying in the kindest, sweetest voice, "That must have been awful for you, jelly bean. Just awful."

I lowered my head to the table, cradling it in my arms. "I made her go to the party," I said, just loud enough to be heard. It was another confession I'd never made to anyone. "She didn't want to go and I made her go. If I hadn't convinced her to go, it wouldn't have happened. If only I had—"

"No," Langley said. "Stop that right now. Your making her go did not make her take her life."

"You don't know."

Langley put her hands on my shoulders and pulled me back up, but I didn't dare to meet her eyes. "People don't kill themselves because they're not having fun at a party. If they do something like that, it has much deeper and older roots." She reached a finger under my chin and lifted my face. "Look at me, Jane Freeman."

I did. There were tears in her eyes too. Their expression said that she understood, understood what I'd said, and maybe even what I didn't. She gave me a small, sad smile completely unlike the one she usually had. It was tender, loving.

"You were not responsible for what happened to your friend. You did not make her overdose."

I hadn't realized what a burden carrying all those secrets had been. Sharing them now, sharing them with Langley, felt like someone had lifted a lead blanket off of me. I was filled with a sense of gratitude that was almost euphoric. "Thank you," I said. "You— you're amazing."

She shook her head and this time she gave me her characteristic Langley grin. "Don't thank me, thank Dr. Phil. I learned everything I know about psychology from him."

I laughed, my face still wet and stinging with tears.

"It must have been hard losing your best friend like that," she said.

"It was." *But not just in the way you know*, I thought. Because there was still one secret I was keeping. I stared down at the table, tracing the place where someone had carved B. G. + A. F. 4-EVER into its surface with my pinkie as I wondered if I should tell her the rest. Make a clean break of it. Finally, at last, tell someone the whole truth.

I looked up at her, her face expectant, her blue eyes sparkling like the icicles that hung outside the window, and I just couldn't. I was too afraid of what would happen if I did. Too afraid that she'd see me for the coward, the loser I was and decide I was unworthy of her friendship.

Instead I said, "What about you? What's your Jacuzzi trauma?"

Whatever I was expecting wasn't what happened.

Langley pulled up her thermal shirt and I saw a long puckered scar that disappeared into the waistband of her jeans and crossed her pale white torso. "It goes all the way down my thigh."

"How did you get it?"

She looked away. She was quiet for a long, long time and I thought she might have changed her mind. Then abruptly she said, "My mom grew up in Livingston, in the same house my grandparents live in now, you know." I had no idea where this was going. Was this about their pool?

She went on. "When my mom was eighteen, she got pregnant. Her parents, well, Maman, really, gave her an ultimatum. Either tell who the father of the baby was or move out. My mother and Maman are a lot alike, both stubborn, and neither of them would budge. So when she was six months pregnant, my mother moved to Lynx Arches, Arizona."

"Sounds exotic."

"The natural part of it is really beautiful. Big blue sky, red mountains. Most people live in trailers, so architecturally it leaves something to be desired."

"Why did your mother choose Arizona?"

"I think because it was as different as possible from Livingston. Plus she didn't want her parents to be able to find her, so she used a fake name, which means she didn't have a diploma to show, so the jobs she could get weren't great. Waitressing. Secretarial work. Small-appliance repair shop. " She stared out the panoramic window at the mountain, glowing pinky orange in the sunset. "For a while she was the assistant to a locksmith and she'd bring locks home at night and practice opening them. The best was when she worked at the bakery." Her gaze moved to me and she smiled ruefully. "That's how I learned to frost cakes. You didn't know I could do that, did you? I'm actually an ace froster."

"I'll keep that in mind for my next birthday."

"You should. My mother believed you had to make your own luck, and in order to do that, you had to have skills. She taught me to sew and shoot and fix almost anything. And then the spring when I was eleven, she was teaching me to swim."

She poked at one of the mini-marshmallows in her hot chocolate until it dissolved. "Every Tuesday and Thursday after school we'd meet at the trailer and go to the community pool. It was our ritual, to make up for the fact she had to go to work before I got up because bakeries open so early. I always pedaled my bike home extra fast those days because I loved swimming lessons with her."

She was sitting more still than I'd ever seen her, but with the setting sun lighting up her corn silk hair she seemed to shimmer. "One Tuesday, I got a flat tire so I had to walk my bike halfway and I was a little later than usual. I was just locking it up in the back when I smelled something weird. I looked up and I saw smoke coming from under the front door.

"The trailer was on fire." Her fingers worked their way around the rim of her paper cup, unrolling it. "I used my sweater to pull open the door and flames exploded in my face. I called to my mom, but she didn't answer. So I ran through the flames into the house. That's how I got the scars."

She kept her gaze very level. "I was too late. The—the fire had already spread and my mother was—they said she died of smoke inhalation, so the burns on her body, she never felt—never had a chance—never—"

She breathed in sharply and tightened her jaw. Her eyes were fixed on the wood-beam ceiling of the ski lodge, her hands clenched into fists, knuckles white with the effort not to cry.

I wrapped my arms around her, conscious both of her strength and of my weakness. She'd been honest, naked with me, telling me everything. I hadn't been able to do the same. I'd left out one part of my story. The hardest part. I opened my mouth to tell it, but it caught in my throat.

When her breathing returned to normal, she pulled away and faced me. "I'm sorry."

"For what? I'm—I feel really honored you told me."

She nodded and cupped her hands around the mangled cup of hot chocolate, studying it as if it held the answers to all life's mysteries. "I miss her," she said. "I don't like to show it around Popo and Maman, but I miss her every day. I wonder what my life would have been like if that didn't happen. If I'd come home sooner. If I'd been able to save her."

"Langley, you were a hero that day. You were so brave. Your mother would have been proud of you. And she'd be proud of what you've become."

She shook her head, still staring into her hot chocolate. "Do you really think so?"

"Who wouldn't be proud of you? You're the light of your grandparents' life. You're smart, beautiful, fun, adored, and popular."

"I am pretty great, aren't I?" she said with a tenuous smile, She looked brave and vulnerable all at once. I marveled at her.

"Yes."

She winked. "Takes one to know one."

Tell her, a voice in my head said. *Tell her the rest.* Before I could, Langley was finishing her story.

"Anyway," Langley had concluded that day in Killington, "my mother never finished teaching me how to swim. So I still don't know.

And the scars always remind me. You won't tell anyone, though, will you? About what happened or about my scars? My grandparents don't like people to know."

As I'd been listening, I'd been thinking that Langley reminded me of someone and I realized who it was. She reminded me of my intrepid turtle, Amerigo. They were both brave; they'd both been through a lot and used it to make them stronger. They were both survivors. I couldn't even imagine having half their courage and strength.

Including the strength to show vulnerability. "Your secret is safe with me," I assured her.

She smiled. "I know. I know I can count on you."

With her hair pulled carelessly back and under the industrial light of my hospital room, the scar across Langley's cheek was more visible. "You should be with Popo," I said. "Not here with me."

"Don't be ridiculous. You need me. Besides, I can tell that something is bothering you."

"It's nothing."

"Good, then it won't take you long to tell me what it is." She went to the windowsill and picked up the bear in the T-shirt. "Tell the get-well bear your problems, jelly bean. He's a beary good listener."

"Stop," I cried, laughing. "I give in."

She came back and settled herself into a chair next to my bed. "Is it about David? I ran into him and Ollie in the parking lot. Or, I should say, Ollie almost ran me over. He's a menace in that huge Land Rover. No wonder he has a driver most of the time. David's been so worried about you; he's been calling me for updates. I'm so glad you got back together."

"Got back together?"

She blinked. "I mean got together. Your mother was very cagey yesterday about not letting him come by."

Of course. I should have known my mother was interfering.

"So, what's wrong?"

"I know this is going to sound weird, but did we have a fight? At the party?"

"You and David?" she asked. All of a sudden her tone was wary.

"No, you and I?"

She looked surprised.

"It's just, some people told the police officer that we did and I have this memory of you standing in front of a door and me not wanting to go past you. Or something. It's weird."

Her face cleared, but she started twisting the friendship ring on her right hand. "Oh. Well, yeah, kind of. I was trying to keep you from leaving the bathroom. You—I don't know what happened, but you were really upset at David and you were sobbing and you kept saying, 'I can't take it anymore. It's over. I'm done, it's done. I just want to end it.' And I just thought—I thought it would be better if you didn't do it like that. That night."

"That must be what people heard. Why they thought you and Kate and I had a fight. Do you know what happened?"

"No, I found you crying like that."

"And I said I wanted to break up with David?"

"You said you wanted to end it...that you wanted it to be over." She shrugged. "Maybe you meant something else." Her voice was soft, softer than normal, and I had to strain to hear.

"Like what?"

I felt like I was seeing it in a film that kept slipping. Some frames were in focus, but others I couldn't pull up. Langley in front of a door, looking upset, and me saying those words I could sort of imagine. But why? What could I have seen that would have made me want to end things with David? And if something *had* happened, wouldn't he have mentioned it? Wouldn't I have been able to tell when he came by?

You're just being paranoid, I told myself firmly. Like the writing on the mirror, this was probably just something my brain was making up with the help of heavy medication.

"Thank you for keeping me from making a fool of myself," I said. "David may have his flaws, but I still love him."

"Of course you do. That party was just strange. Did you hear that Elsa totaled her Porsche? She drove into a post."

"What?"

"Yeah, and not just that. Apparently she was hallucinating or something and became so belligerent with the paramedics that they had to restrain her."

"Was she drunk?"

"It's *Elsa*," Langley said. "The girl so clean she even brings her own bottled water to parties."

That was true. Elsa didn't drink or do drugs. She was strange enough without that. "Was it a neurotic episode?"

"Who knows. But it's weird, right?"

It felt great to talk about something other than myself, to get into the rhythm of gossiping with Langley again, even if I was worried about Elsa. She went on, "Ollie said he heard that she had a nervous breakdown and got sent to the Bahamas to live with her real mother, but I heard they put her in a mental hospital for observation."

"Was she okay? I mean, physically?"

"Yeah, I guess she was fine, just a few bruises. So who else has come to visit you today? Has Kate been here?"

The rapid change of topic unsettled me for a moment. "No. Um, not yet."

"I'm sure she'll be here soon. She's so upset. She really loves you." There was something about the way she looked at me then that made me uncomfortable. Did she know?

No, no one knew. Not even Langley. Especially not Langley.

"I should probably get going." She smiled down at me. "You poor baby. Are you in a lot of pain?"

"A little." I looked toward the IV rack she was standing next to. It had three bags on it and four digital monitors. "I think they're keeping me pretty doped up. The hardest thing right now is not re-membering. Oh, and not being able to move." I'd wanted my voice to sound joking, but it came out more like a weak croak.

"You're going to get all better. I promise." She leaned down to give me a kiss on the nose and her arm must have rested on the cord to my IV because all of a sudden a wave of pain crashed over me.

The heart-rate monitor started to squeal and Loretta rushed in and Langley retreated to a corner and I was hyperventilating.

My God, the pain.

Black and white spots flashed in front of my eyes and there was a roaring in my ears and my body was convulsed in a spasm of agony as though my skeleton was trying to crawl out. I heard screams, my screams, and I felt a prick on my arm.

Then I was swimming, swimming through the brown water, and someone was yelling, *Get out of the way, you jealous bitch*, and I swam to the top and broke through the surface and—

Suddenly everything was fine. My body relaxed. My eyes cleared. My ears stopped ringing.

Everything went back to normal. Even better than normal.

Loretta leaned over me. "We had to knock you out there for a moment. How are you feeling?"

"Great," I said, and meant it.

But that wasn't true of Langley. The color had drained from her face and she was trembling, slumped in a chair in the corner as though trying to make herself as small as possible. "My God, I'm so sorry," she said. "I didn't mean to hurt you. I didn't mean to hurt her."

Loretta gave her a nice smile. "Don't worry. Just an accident with the IV line. No permanent damage done."

Langley's head was buried in her hands. "I feel awful."

I beamed at her. I didn't know what Loretta had given me, but I felt great. "I'm fine. Nothing wrong. And now I know how much I need that IV."

Langley looked at me from between her fingers. "Yeah, I guess you do."

Never one to miss a party, my mother rushed in just then, in a cloud of Coco Chanel and questions. "What was that? What happened?" Joe followed her.

"Just a little mishap, nothing to worry about," Loretta assured them.

"Are you certain?" my mother demanded. "Jane looks pale as a ghost."

"Not a ghost yet, Mother," I told her.

"That's not funny," she snapped.

I looked behind her. "Where's Annie?"

"She's at the Monteros' for the day playing with Dora." Dora was Ollie's younger sister. Turning, my mother saw Langley for the first time. "Langley, darling, so good to see you here. How are your grandparents?"

Since Langley's grandparents were two of the most socially prominent people in the area, it was important to ask this, even with a daughter paralyzed in the hospital. One couldn't let a little thing like near death interfere with one's manners.

"They're doing as well as can be expected, and they both send Jane their best wishes."

"Please thank them for us. It really means the world to us."

"Have there been any new developments?" Langley asked.

"The police have credible evidence that it was the robbers who held up the convenience store. They hit Jane when they were speeding away."

"What does 'credible evidence' mean?" I asked.

"A vehicle matching the description of the robbers' was sighted in the vicinity of the ten fifty-seven. That's a hit-and-run in the ten code the police use," my mother explained like she'd just graduated from the police academy. "And the striations on the skid marks are a possible match to the getaway vehicle."

"Ten four, Officer Rosalind," I said.

Her lips got thin, but she ignored my snarky tone and addressed Langley instead. "We're holding a news conference about it in a few minutes to try to get information about the robbers' whereabouts, if you'd like to stay."

"So that means they'll catch whoever did this," Langley said. "That's great news."

My mother nodded. "What it means is that Jane is a casualty of the rising crime rate in this area. A symbol of what is at stake for us all."

If I could have clapped, I would have. "That line's a winner," I told my mother. "I hope you're planning to use it on TV."

"This constant negativity and sarcasm is so—" She stopped talking, and if I hadn't known her better, I might have thought she was about to cry.

But I did know her better. "You can't imagine how hard it is for me to maintain," I said. Which was true. I wasn't like this with anyone but my mother. For the first time, as I stared at the wrinkle across her forehead, I wondered why.

She sighed and reached tentatively for my hand. "Don't you see, darling, it means this can all be over soon."

Oh yes, that was why. I didn't know what she meant by "all" or "be over," but I did know that one of us was still completely paralyzed. And would be no matter how many convenience store robbers she caught. It was more evidence of how she refused to see me as I really was. Refused to see the person in front of her, now or ever.

Langley stood up from the chair she'd been sitting on, sparing me from having to think up an appropriate retort. "I wish I could stay for the press conference, but I have to be getting home. My grandfather."

"Of course, dear. Thank you for coming and cheering up our poor girl."

"My pleasure."

"You see, Mother. Everyone thinks I'm a pleasure to be with but you."

Langley kissed me on the forehead, giving me a whiff of grapefruit. "Goodbye, jelly bean. I'll try to come by again later."

"Take care of Popo. That's more important." I meant it. She was so sweet to spend time with me when her own life was so rocky. That was what Langley was like—always ready to be strong for you, no matter how much she needed her strength herself.

My mother followed her out the door, but Joe lingered behind, hovering near the foot of my bed. He coughed once, cleared his throat. "Jane, I don't understand why you're so angry at your mother, but I want to be sure you know that she is really upset about this."

"She doesn't seem to be. She seems to be having the time of her life." My voice sounded petty and small, but I didn't care.

"That's your mom. She's a trooper."

"How would you know? You've only been in her life a year. How can you tell what she's like?"

Joe huddled with his hands in his pockets, seeming sort of sheepish. "I love her and I admire her, so I've made a special study of her. I just—I just want you to know that everything she's doing, she's doing because she cares."

"All my mother cares about is how things look for her press conferences."

He sucked in breath through his mouth as though I'd slapped him. "That's not fair. And I'm pretty sure you know it."

"Fine. Thank you for delivering that message."

He looked like he was going to say something else, then shrugged to himself and left. I kept my eyes on my flowers and balloons and the get-well bear on the windowsill. Those were from people who actually cared. People who *liked* me for who I was, not some imaginary perfect daughter I *should* have been.

The phone next to my bed started to ring. Maybe it was David again. Just the thought gave me tingles all over, and without thinking about it, I reached out and picked it up.

"Hello?"

"How are you today, Jane?" a voice that wasn't David asked. I didn't recognize it, but I didn't care because as it spoke, I realized I'd just regained use of my left arm. I tried the right one. Yes, that one too. I could move. *I could move!*

"I'm great, how are you?" I answered.

"I'm well. Looking forward to our eventual meeting."

That was starting to sound weird. "Wait, who is this?"

"Don't you know?"

"No."

"I'm the person who tried to kill you. Or, I should say, who is *going* to kill you."

My entire body went cold. "This isn't funny."

"I assure you, I'm dead serious."

I swallowed. "What are you talking about?" Now my arms were working, but my brain felt more numb than ever.

"We both know what happened to you was no accident."

I started to shake.

"Don't we?" the voice needled.

"Who *is* this?!" My hands clasped around the receiver were freezing. "Tell me who you are."

"That's for me to know and you to find out. See you soon."

The line went dead. A guy I'd never seen before came into my room holding a cell phone in his hand and a large box cradled under his arm. He looked from it to me and said, "Hello, Jane."

Chapter 17

"**Get out! Get out!** Help!" I shouted. "*Loretta!*"

The guy dropped the cell phone.

Loretta rushed in. "Yes, sweetheart, what is it?"

I pointed at the guy. My arm was trembling. "He—he's going to kill me."

"Who, Pete?" She looked at the guy, who was now stooping to retrieve his cell phone. "I doubt it."

"Someone—someone just called to say they're going to kill me. And then he walked in."

Loretta came closer to me and pulled out a flashlight. She shined it in my eyes. "Look up for me, sweetheart. Good. Now left." She clicked the light off.

"I'm not hallucinating. I didn't make it up. Someone called me."

With her finger on my wrist she said, "Tell me what happened, sweetheart."

"The phone rang and I picked it up."

"You picked it up? You moved your hand?" She was gazing at me with surprise.

"Yes. I can move both my arms now."

"The Lord works in strange ways. The phone rang and you picked it up and what happened?"

"The voice on the phone said what happened to me was no accident. That they would finish what they started. And that they'd see me soon."

"I see. And then what?"

"Then he"—pointing to the guy, who was now slouching along the wall, looking amused—"came in. This isn't funny, by the way."

"I'm not laughing at you. I'm laughing at that bear." He pointed at the windowsill. "It's—kind of hideous."

Loretta had gone out for a moment, but she came back in now. "That's Pete," she said. "He's volunteering here. Like a candy striper."

"I'm not sure *volunteering* is the right word." He pushed off the wall and came toward the bed holding out the box. "I was supposed to deliver this."

It was wrapped in paper that said WACK ATTACK all over it, clearly from the Just 4 Teens! section of the Hallmark store.

"I don't want a stupid box. Are you two listening? Someone called and threatened to kill me." I enunciated each word. "We need to tell the police. I didn't hallucinate it this time, Loretta. Someone called me."

Loretta said, "I already have security on the way up along with—"

There was a noise in the corridor and my mother and Officer Rowley came in together. But not in a rush. More like they were having a stroll.

I told them what had happened and they acted like I'd just shared an interesting but not terribly important fact with them.

"Are you listening? Someone threatened my life."

Officer Rowley had the kindness to get out her notebook. "Tell me about the call again. Did the voice sound familiar?"

"No, it was like it had been disguised."

"Could you tell if it was a man or a wo—"

"No, like I said, it sounded like it was disguised. Like it was coming through a voice changer."

"What about the sound quality? Could you tell if it was a cell phone or a landline?"

"A cell phone, I think. Can you trace it?"

She tapped the hospital phone next to my bed. "On an institutional system like this it would be nearly impossible to trace the call unless they called back. Possibly more than once. If they'd made the call to a cell phone—"

"In other words, no."

"That's correct. But nine times out of ten these kinds of calls turn out to be pranks."

"You see, darling," my mother said, smiling brightly. "There's absolutely nothing to worry about."

I stared at my mother. What was wrong with her? I knew she hated to be wrong. And if my caller *was* real, it meant I couldn't have been a victim of a ten fifty-seven by the convenience store robbers in their getaway vehicle. But this denial was extreme even for her.

"Are you crazy?"

"No. I just trust that the police know what they're doing. If someone called you, it was probably just an attention seeker."

"*If?*" I repeated. "You don't believe there was a call." I looked around the room desperately. The sinking feeling came back to the pit of my stomach. "None of you do. No one believes I actually got a call. I did."

She smiled at me, a smile I was sure was meant to be kind but felt like she was mocking me. "It doesn't matter one way or the other, darling."

"Yes, it does." Tears of frustration hung in my eyes. "I didn't make this up."

"No one is saying you made anything up. There's just a chance that not everything you experience right now is genuine."

I laughed without joy. "You are brilliant, Mother. I've never heard you do a better spin job."

"Don't be sarcastic, Jane."

When did she become this robot? What happened to the mom she used to be? The one who ran beside me at the park, hair bouncing around her face, saying, "You can do it, yes, that's it, keep going, keep going! Don't give up!" as I tried to get a kite up for the first time by myself. The one who, when I *did* get it up, stood by my side with her arm around my shoulders watching it, a fish with a long pink-and-blue tail that twisted and looped against the cloudy sky. I'd looked up at her and her hair was messy and her cheeks were pink and she had a smudge of dirt on her face and I thought she was the most beautiful woman in the world.

What happened to the mom who smelled of Jean Nate powder and shampoo and soap, who rushed to me when I fell and hurt my knee on the jungle gym, who crouched in the dirt next to me and held me against her and said in a voice that meant something, like it mattered to her, like she was really seeing me and feeling me and caring about me, "You're all right, sweetheart. I have you"?

I wanted my mom. I needed her. Where was she?

"I didn't make this up." Tears rolled down my cheeks. "Someone called and threatened me." I looked toward Pete imploringly. "You must have heard; you walked in right when I hung up." I needed an ally, just one person on my side.

Pete shook his head. "I heard you talking, but I wasn't paying attention. I was on my cell."

Loretta smiled soothingly and laid a warm soft palm on my shoulder. "There's someone coming up who can help you make sense of this."

"What kind of someone?"

"Dr. Tan is a psychologist. He specializes in trauma."

"I don't need a psychologist, I need a security detail." What was wrong with everyone? "Someone is trying to kill me. Why would I make that up? Why?" I looked around at all of them, demanding an explanation, but I was met with plastic smiles and blank looks.

"Why are you so sure you didn't hallucinate this?" my mother asked.

"I held the phone. I heard the voice. I did. I *did*."

"Whatever happened, no one is denying it felt real to you," Loretta assured me. It did nothing to make me feel better. But she was dauntless, going on to say, "While we're waiting for Dr. Tan, why don't you show everyone how you can open your present?"

Now I was a performing monkey. I started to rip the paper and my mother said, "Jane, that's wonderful. Your arms, your hands—" Her voice started to tremble. "You can move."

"It won't matter when someone kills me," I said, pulling the paper off a cardboard box. I think her eyes had tears in them, but I ignored it.

Inside the box there was a little ceramic figurine of an angel with bunny ears. A laser-printed gift card nestled next to it said, *Remember, you're never alone. Somebunny is always watching over you. Love, Your Secret Admirer.*

"Isn't that adorable," Loretta said, taking the statue and putting it on the table next to my bed.

"I think it's creepy. And the note. Someone is always watching me?"

"Jane, you're being a little paranoid," my mother said. "Please, darling, you need to relax."

"Now, now, I'll be the judge of that," said a man in a lab coat, who had to be Dr. Tan. Beneath the lab coat he wore a tan suit, and I wondered if he did that on purpose to match his name. He had a shiny head barely covered by a wispy comb-over and rimless glasses. He made straight for me. "I'm Dr. Keough Tan."

We shook hands.

"Its nice to see you surrounded by so many friends and family," he said. "You're a lucky girl."

I gave him a bright, fake smile. "Yes, I am. Except that someone just called to tell me they were planning to kill me."

He nodded, looking serious. "Tell me about that."

I described the call for the third time. He listened intently, his head cocked to one side, and I began to think that finally there was someone who believed me. When I was done, he said, "And nothing about the voice sounded familiar to you? Identifiable?"

"No, like I said, I think it was disguised."

"Have you had any other phone calls?"

"My boyfriend called yesterday."

"I answered the phone for that one," Loretta said. "Miss Freeman hadn't regained use of her hands yet."

"But you did for this call. You were able to answer it yourself?"

"Yes. So? The doctor said that my motor skills would come back."

Dr. Tan made a note on a paper. "I see from your file that you regained your voice after a similar incident."

"What are you talking about?" my mother said, but Dr. Tan ignored her.

"That was different. I was in the shower, I thought I saw some writing on the mirror. That was clearly something I made up. But this—

this *happened*. I heard it. You can't make up an entire phone call."

"So this felt more real?"

"No, they both felt the same amount real. But the other one—I mean, Loretta said with the medication—" I stopped. I could tell from his face how it sounded. "Maybe they were both real."

He looked at me for a beat. *Or maybe they were both fake.*

My God, had I hallucinated the call? No. It had happened. It had. *It had.*

He looked at Loretta. "And you had just administered an additional dose of pain medication?"

"Yes, there was a problem with the IV, so I had to give her a separate shot until we could restore the flow."

That was true. I had been on extra medication. But— "It felt so real."

Dr. Tan nodded. "Delusions often do, because they are projections straight from the most powerful part of our minds." He read my chart for a little and said, "I understand you have no memory of what happened to you?"

"Some pieces are starting to come back, but mostly no. The doctor said that was normal."

"It's not uncommon in traumatic situations for there to be selective memory loss. Frequently we repress things we aren't prepared to remember yet. But when that happens, it leaves gaps and the mind tries to fill them in, often with made-up stories. In this case, probably something happened that night that you aren't ready to think about, and the strain of keeping it hidden is causing your mind to generate fantasies. It's like a smoke screen, misdirection."

"What kind of thing? What would have happened?"

"That's for us to find out together. The harder something is for you to handle, the more deeply it will be buried. The fact that there's a link between these incidents and your regaining motor skills is immensely important. For example, I would speculate that the message you imagined seeing on the mirror was you giving voice to something deep in your psyche, which is why seeing it restored your actual voice."

"The message was 'You should have died, bitch.' So you're saying I wanted to be dead?"

Out of the corner of my eye I saw my mother half rise to her feet, but Joe put a hand on her shoulder and she slowly sat back down.

"It's not necessary to be so reductive. It could be a fear rather than a wish. All we know is that it is a profound impulse."

"And the phone call you say I hallucinated. In that the voice said it would come and kill me. So I want to kill myself?"

My mother did the half-rising thing again and now Dr. Tan spoke to her.

"I think Jane's subconscious has a lot of material to mull over. It may be not herself Jane wanted to kill but some *part* of herself." He returned to me. "Some part you don't like?"

"Or the phone call could have been *real* and someone is out to *kill* me. Isn't that the simpler, more rational explanation?"

"Simpler, yes. *Rational* is a sticky term." He patted my hand. "Let's talk about this morning. Did anything especially unusual happen today that could have triggered these episodes?"

"I'm in the hospital recovering from being hit by a car. Everything is unusual."

"Let me rephrase. Did you have an interaction with anyone that left you—surprised? Uncomfortable? Perhaps if we can locate the catalyst that sparked the delusion this morning, we can understand what it is you're repressing."

I didn't like that word, *delusion*. So I decided not to tell Dr. Tan about how strange David was or how upsetting it was that Nicky said

I drugged her or about Langley telling me how I'd apparently wanted to break up with David at the party, none of which I remembered and all of which felt strangely wrong to me, like an itch I couldn't find the right place to scratch. "No one thing I can think of," I said, not even lying.

"Okay. Well, keep working on that." He closed my chart. "And for the time being, relax. I'll come back and check in with you later. And if you get any more calls, try to remember what time it is."

"Will Jane have more of these hallucinations? I'd like to know what to expect," my mother asked.

"It depends on the presence of stressors and how Jane's mind works."

"Or if the killer decides to call me again," I put in.

Dr. Tan patted my hand. "Don't worry, you'll be fine."

How? I wanted to ask. If he was right, I was losing my mind. If *I* was right, someone was at that moment making plans to kill me. Neither of those seemed like scenarios that ended up with me being anything like fine.

When the doctor had gone, Joe cleared his throat. "You know, Rosie, I could get some of my guys to do a rotation, sit outside Jane's room, make sure no one goes in or out."

"Joe, you are a darling. As Dr. Tan just said, I should hope that's really not necessary. In fact"—her voice dropped a little—"it could be detrimental. We don't want to encourage Jane to have more hallucinations by adding stressors to the situation." Her phone rang. She looked at me with the smile she gave everyone else, said, "You'll see, Jane, everything will be fine," and then into the phone, "Hello, Perry, what can I do for you?"

I *did* see. It was back to work. Business as usual.

"Can you all please go," I said. In my ears my voice sounded brittle, defeated. "Loretta, would you wheel me into the bathroom. I want to be alone."

"I've got to deal with Mrs. North next door. Can't you hear that hollering? Pete, please help Miss Freeman into the wheelchair the way I taught you. Won't be a problem for a big guy like you."

He linked his fingers together and cracked his knuckles. "I live to please."

Before he left, Joe came over and patted me on the shoulder. "Don't worry, Jane. We won't let anything happen to you." His big dumb face looked earnest. "I've got your back."

Perfect. Shady Joe Garcetti and his crew had my back. That was just what I needed, I thought. But all I said was, "Thanks."

Chapter 18

*T*he door closed, leaving me alone with the guy named Pete. As he walked toward me, I gauged he was probably only a little older than me, with skin a shade past olive and close-cropped brown hair. He looked like he could be Indian or Pakistani, except that his eyes were very, very blue.

He stood by the side of my bed, looked at his watch, and said, "Oh well, it's over for you. Call the code at 2:03 p.m."

My eyes widened in shock. "That's what they say when someone dies."

"Exactly." He nodded. "Women have fallen in love with me after staring like that for only thirty seconds and I think you just took a full minute. You're doomed."

He said it completely seriously, deadpan, like it was a fact, but his eyes proclaimed he was joking. He was wearing jeans, Adidas, and a white T-shirt stenciled to look like a doctor's coat, complete with stethoscope and the name tag Dr. Feelgood. Really. I rolled my eyes. "You've got to be kidding."

"No. It's a curse."

"You're *bear*ing up beautifully."

"Bearing up. Good one." He pointed to the windowsill of flowers. "Have you considered that maybe you're OD'ing on all the pollen in here? This place is like a high-end funeral parlor."

"Wow, is that in poor taste. Besides, it's nice that people send me these things. Thoughtful."

Now his eyes got wide. "Sure. It means they really like you. That you're really popular and adored—" He tilted his head to read the card on the popcorn tin. "By Pontrain Motors."

"That's not fair. You don't know anything about me. There's a DVD my best friends made over there, right next to the two-dozen long-stemmed roses, and it has everyone from my high school saying how much they miss me. You should watch it and educate yourself."

"Oh sure. I'll get right on that," he said, taking the DVD out of its case and spinning it around on his finger. "But I already know one thing about you."

"What?"

"You're a lousy judge of people."

I turned my head away from him deliberately. "I think I want you and your hipster T-shirt to leave."

"I *know* I want to leave and my T-shirt thinks the company here stinks. But I can't go anywhere without violating the terms of my parole, so you're stuck with us."

"You're on *parole*?" Great. Not only did no one believe me but now they were leaving me with a convicted criminal.

"It was a figure of speech."

"If you're going to loiter, at least stop insulting me. And put down my DVD."

"I wasn't insulting you. *You* insulted *me*. I'm being frank with you. Is that so unusual in your pollen-drenched world that you can't distinguish between the two?" At least he slid the DVD back into its case.

"What is wrong with you?"

"You mean my unflinching honesty or my uncanny good looks?"

"Are you insane?"

"Are you?" He shook his head. "Never mind, don't answer that."

"I can't believe this," I said, more to myself than to him.

"Why don't you like that guy? Joe?"

I glared at him. "He's a barbarian."

"Nice word choice. Does he drag women by the hair and eat with his hands?"

"Nearly."

"I could tell he and I had a lot in common. Anyway, he seemed like he cared about you."

"It's an act."

"He certainly cares about your family. From what I hear, he hasn't left your mom's side since you've been here."

"That's called stalking and it's illegal in all fifty states."

"It's called being supportive and it's pretty rare. And—" Pete shook his head. "Never mind."

"What?"

"Nothing. You won't like it."

"*What?*"

"He *believes* you. That you got a threatening phone call."

"And you know this how?"

"I'm good at reading people." I snorted, but he ignored it. "What was the thing with the writing on the mirror?"

"Nothing. It doesn't matter."

"However you want to play it. But you should reconsider your opinion of Joe. He was the only one who wasn't buying what that psychiatrist was selling. Seems like a good guy."

"Why is everyone always trying to make me love Joe?" I yelled, surprising both of us with my vehemence.

He put up both hands in a peacemaking gesture. "Down, tiger. I was just trying to be nice."

I took a deep breath. "Sorry. I didn't mean to be so boisterous."

"Boisterous. I like the way you use words."

"My father was a poet," I said, startling myself again. Where did *that* come from? I never talked about my father.

"Would I have read any of his work?"

"Do you read poetry?"

"Occasionally. In the bathroom."

He said it solemnly, but his eyes were laughing and I found myself smiling at him. "My dad never published. He was a professor. The poetry was just a hobby."

"Obviously it rubbed off on you."

"Yeah." I stopped smiling. My throat went tight.

"Where is he?"

"He died. Three years ago." And then for no explicable reason, I started to cry. "I miss him."

Pete put his arms around me. "I bet. I bet you miss him right now especially. I know how lonely it can be when your view of reality doesn't match everyone else's."

I pulled away. "You do?"

"Actually, yeah." He used the sheet to wipe the tears from my cheek. "Now put your arms around my neck so I can get you into this chair and you can wash your face."

I did and he put an arm under me and lifted me out of the bed.

He went to put me in the chair, but it rolled backward. "This isn't as easy as Loretta made it look."

"Don't tell me it's the first time you've had a lady in your arms."

Grunt. "No, its just"—the chair moved another foot—"usually they're more complian—gotcha!" The wheelchair hit the back wall and he spilled me into it, trapping his arm behind me.

Which brought our noses right next to each other. We looked at each other like that, barely able to keep one another's two eyes from merging into one.

He smiled. His eyes got cute crinkles around them when he did that, and for the first time I noticed he had dimples.

His chin had a little growth of beard on it and he had really nice teeth and his lips looked soft and smooth, like a movie star's, curling up at the edges.

He raised his free hand to the back of my head. My heart started to pound. He was going to kiss me. He was going to kiss me and I wanted him to. I really wanted him to.

I wanted to feel his mouth against mine, feel the stubble of his chin against my neck, feel his tongue parting my lips. This boy in his ridiculous T-shirt with his blunt way of talking, I wanted him to want me, to like me. Because I liked *him*. He leaned in closer, urging my head forward, closer to his. My heart was racing. I closed my eyes and felt—

Him pulling his other arm from behind me. I opened my eyes.

"Sorry about that, I guess I need some practice," he said, taking a step backward. When I didn't answer, he bent down in front of me. "You okay? I didn't hurt you, did I?"

I swallowed. I was *not* disappointed, I told myself. "No, I'm fine. Just a little dizzy." Maybe I *was* crazy! I had a boyfriend I loved. I did not indulge in fantasies about other guys.

"Good. I'm pretty sure adding to patients' injuries isn't considered doing a good job as a volunteer." He started pushing me into the bathroom.

"What did you mean when you said you weren't quite a volunteer?"

He maneuvered me over the bathroom threshold. "My father is making me do this. It's penance."

"For what?"

"He's rescuing me from turning into a college dropout and a low-life deadbeat thug." I watched his face reflected in the mirror in front of me and saw a flash of something like disappointment flit across it. It disappeared and he winked at me. "Told you I was dangerous. You okay in here? Got everything you need?"

"Yes."

"I'll be outside when you want to come out. Just knock."

"Thanks."

He smiled and patted me on the head. "Don't let them make you doubt yourself. All the greatest visionaries in history have been told they were insane at some point."

The door closed behind him and I was left staring at myself in the mirror.

I knew it was me, but it didn't feel like me. The swelling had gone down a lot and the contours of my face were mostly back, but I still felt like I was seeing myself for the first time. Were those my eyes? Was that my nose? Were those my lips? I leaned across the sink and rested my hands on the cool glass of the mirror, covering up the parts that were still swollen with my palms to see if that made a difference.

A stranger looked back. A stranger with a black eye and a swollen lip. And now, as I remembered how I'd thought Pete was going to kiss me, a stranger who was blushing furiously. Was I out of my mind?

Why, yes, yes, I was. Everyone else thought so. And here was more proof.

I started to laugh, but not in a normal way. In a way that felt out of control, like I was hysterical. I was going out of my mind, losing my marbles: nuts, crazy, bonkers. I could have sworn the phone call was real, I could have sworn the writing was real. I thought Pete liked me.

I thought my mother loved me. She had, once.

On the day of my father's funeral I sat on the side of her bed—their bed—watching her get ready. She'd looked beautiful in her black suit, I thought. Perfect and polished and together. When I grew up, I wanted to look like that.

She'd reached for the pearl-and-gold chain necklace my father had given her for her last birthday. I had my nose buried in the puff of the Jean Nate powder she kept on her dressing table, the only thing she wore because my father didn't like perfume, so I didn't notice that the necklace had gotten tangled. Suddenly she held it out to me and said, "Jane, fix this, will you?" and I saw her hands were shaking. I looked up and she was crying.

I went to her, kneeling next to her, and she buried her face against my hair. We stayed like that for a long time, me comforting her, being comforted by it. I hadn't realized until that moment that it was hard for her too, hard maybe in a different way than I could understand. That he'd left her alone too.

When she pulled away, I handed her the unknotted necklace. She smiled at me, smoothing my hair, and said, "We're a good team, aren't we, darling? We can get out of any knotty situation if we just stick together."

I nodded.

"It's going to be hard in the months ahead. I'm going to have to work a lot to support us. I know you'll help me with Annie. I know you'll be brave." She'd smoothed the hair off my forehead. "You are such a good girl, my beautiful Jane. I love you."

"I love you too, Mommy."

The memory pierced me now. She loved me, she'd loved me then, and she still loved me. She did. We could get through anything if we stuck together. So if she said that the calls weren't real, that no one was trying to kill me, that had to be right. Didn't it?

I beseeched the stranger in the mirror. Didn't it?

Should I trust my gut? Even though everyone else said it was faulty?

Which was better, to be insane but safe or to be sane but have a killer after you?

I washed the face that belonged to me but didn't feel like my face and dried it on the rough institutional paper towels. I found myself wishing my mother's makeup were still there so I could do something to look better—*Not for Pete*, I rushed to tell myself. For who, then?

"So you've become a true stall sister," a voice said. "Worried about makeup when she should be worried about recovering."

I was alone. There was no one in the room. And yet it was Bonnie's voice, clear, laced with irony, back from the grave. And in my head. Where it belonged.

I knocked on the door to be let out.

"I think I must be immune," I said as it opened, working to keep my tone light. "I tested myself and I haven't fallen in love with you yet."

But it wasn't Pete standing there.

Chapter 19

"Oh, I'm all too aware of that, J. J.," Scott said. He'd been sitting in one of the blue nubbly chairs, but he jumped up when I opened the door and rushed toward me.

"Sorry, thought you were someone else."

"Someone *else* you're not in love with?" he joked. His tone was a little perplexing, but he was smiling as he leaned against the wall now, hands in his pockets. "Man, you're tough."

I didn't know if it was how close he was standing or just being in the chair, but I was acutely aware of how tall and buff he was. It was easy to see why he had such a hard time believing that I alone of all the women in the world wasn't in love with him and why he was routinely stopped by modeling agents. He was wearing black jeans and a linen shirt open at the neck. Scott's family was originally from Haiti, and he described his skin tone as being the color of polished teak. To me it registered as the perfect burnished tan. He had high cheekbones and a delicate mouth that was just full enough to miss being too feminine. His eyes were a light caramel brown that matched his curly hair and skin, making him look exotic and incredibly cool. Whenever anyone begged him—and it had come to that—to model, he always explained that his place was on the other side of the camera.

And he was a very talented photographer. He was very good at everything he undertook because he wouldn't let himself not be. He was intense that way.

"It's great to see you. If I'd known you were out here, I wouldn't have wasted so much time in the bathroom."

"I just got here." He wheeled me out and turned me to face him. His fingers lingered on my arms and he breathed deeply. "You look fantastic."

"For a girl who was run over." He always seemed like he was looking into me, through me. I wondered if he even saw how bad I looked.

"For anyone. Even someone who didn't get to use her favorite shampoo and who's not in love with me."

"Stop it!" I insisted. "It was just—"

"Nothing," he finished for me. "I know." He reached out to tuck a piece of hair behind my right ear. "Sorry I couldn't get here yesterday, I had to work," he explained. Scott was the oldest of four children being raised by his grandmother. She was a physician's assistant, which paid okay, but not well enough to support the family, so Scott helped out doing a bunch of different jobs. He never complained, but I knew he would rather have been taking pictures.

"You didn't miss anything. Not much goes on around here. The machines do all the work."

"I don't know, your mother certainly seemed busy when I saw her out there in the hallway." Scott sat down in one of the blue chairs and pulled me toward him. He picked a hair off my knee. "She was surrounded by a bunch of people plotting your recovery."

"More likely an intervention. Do you think I'm crazy?"

He frowned and was silent.

That wasn't good. "You have to ponder that?"

He grinned. "Naw, I'm playing. No, you're not crazy, why?"

I told him about the phone call and how everyone thought I'd made it up. Or at the very least, that I was taking it too seriously, that it was just a prank.

"I can see that," Scott said. "It being a prank."

"Why?" I demanded.

He shook his head. "Nice, J. J. Putting me to the metal. You're right, I have no reason to be sure. But I want to think that because I can't imagine anyone wanting to hurt you. I imagine that's true for everyone."

When school first started nine months ago, Scott and I talked every day, sometimes more than once. He'd call five or six times, text a bunch. But we hadn't been that close recently and I realized now I missed it.

I reached out and took his hand. "Thank you."

He shifted in his chair. "I don't want to insult you, but I don't think much of the decor here. Luckily I have an idea of how we can spice it up."

Without letting go of my hand, he reached down and I heard him rustling around in the messenger bag he'd propped next to the chair.

When he came up, he was holding a snow globe with the Statue of Liberty inside it. "It's even better than it looks. See—" He let go of my hand to wind something in the base and it started playing "New York, New York." "And there's no way to turn it off. Do you love it?"

"Yes." I held it up in front of me and looked at him through it. "I do."

"You have to get better so we can have a day like that again," he said.

The weekend after my first date with David, a brisk October

Saturday, Scott and I had gone to New York for what he called the Cloud Challenge. It was based on the concept that some people see faces in clouds, while other people see clouds in faces, that people's perspectives condition both how and what they see. His idea was that we would spend the day in New York taking photos of the same things and that by comparing them, we'd learn something about our individual styles.

"Should we buy a map?" I asked as we got off the train at Penn Station.

"We don't need one."

"But what if we get lost?"

Scott laughed. "There's no such thing as lost; there's just adjusting your perspective."

"I'm buying a map," I said.

"Suit yourself."

The air was crisp with a tangy bite like a good apple when we got off the train and made our way to the Met without the map. In Central Park the trees were starting to turn and we kicked leaves around as we walked over from the subway.

Inside the museum we got lost on our way to the photography section in a series of rooms filled with medieval altar paintings, saints, and Mary and angels all crouched together against lapis-blue or reddish-gold backgrounds, looking toward Jesus standing proud in the middle. That led us to a conversation about what it meant as an artist when you worked with really iconic subject matter. And I started to understand what Scott meant about never being lost.

From there we made our way downtown, without a plan, letting our feet and the traffic lights determine where we went. We ate roasted nuts from a cart on Fifth Avenue. We took self-portraits in the windows of Tiffany's and Barneys. We photographed manhole covers, solitary flowers in planters, and a dog tied next to a sign that said WILL WORK FOR FOOD. I never once took out the map.

Around Union Square, Scott said, "Keep your eye out for those," pointing to a black, red, and white sticker of a man's face looking very stern with the word OBEY beneath it. "They're all over the city, like an underground art show."

"Who put them up?"

"Anyone who wants to. The idea is to get people to think about how much they obey, follow the rules, in daily life."

"But the rules make civilization work. Without rules we'd all just kill each other."

"That's what everyone wants you to believe. But they've done these studies in Europe that show that in places with fewer traffic signs, people drive better. Because they pay attention to one another."

"I don't know. I feel like I already spend a lot of time thinking about other people."

"You think about what they think of you. It's different."

"Do you think I'm self-centered?"

"There you go again."

For our final set of photos we'd stopped at a stand on Canal Street where we'd each bought a snow globe with the most iconic thing about New York we could think of, the Statue of Liberty. We went away by ourselves to take pictures of it and agreed to meet half an hour later at a Chinese duck place in Chinatown Scott knew about.

I have to admit, I was feeling smug when I got to Great New York Noodletown. I thought my Liberty photos were smart and looked great.

I had taken the snow globe and put it near one of the OBEY posters that had a homeless man smoking a cigarette in front of it. The Statue of Liberty on one side and the word OBEY on the other were like a frame for the portrait of the homeless man. I named it Triptych of Modernity based on the altar paintings we'd seen at the Met that morning and I was really proud of how clever it was.

But Scott kicked my ass. He broke the snow globe open and photographed each piece separately. The statue, pieces of foam that faked snow, the music box, the black molded base, the empty plastic globe, the plaque that said LIBERTY and called it My Mistress at Her Bath or Patriotism Revealed.

Over duck and strong hot tea and water Scott told me about how he'd found Great New York Noodletown when he used to go visit his dad during his arraignment hearings at the courthouse nearby. Even though they both lived with their grandparents, I couldn't help think about how different he was from Langley. But they both shared a steely core, the kind of thing I decided that makes you a survivor. And a great observer.

"You're nervous about something," he said.

"Have you heard about the Getty Images internship?" I scrunched up my straw paper into a worm.

"Yeah. I would kill to apply, but I have to work. You should do it. Without me in the running, you're bound to win." He winked.

"Modesty so becomes you."

"Come on, I kicked your ass on this last photo."

"Maybe. Do you really think I should apply?"

"What I think doesn't matter. Don't you want it?"

"I guess. I don't know."

"Hold on." He got out his phone and held it toward me. "It's the cop-out hotline calling for you."

"I'm not copping out." I dropped water onto my worm so it started to grow.

"You're afraid. You're afraid of trying and not succeeding. What's the worst thing that happens if you apply and don't get it?"

"I'll be mortified."

"By whom?"

"I don't know. My friends?"

"Your friends will think it's cool you tried. Or don't tell them."

"Sure. You're right." I pushed a piece of rice around my plate with my chopsticks.

"Chicken."

"No, we're eating duck."

He pointed at me with his chopsticks. "You're always waiting for approval from someone else. Why don't you just do what you want?"

"It's not like that." He was getting that intense look.

"You know one thing that makes your pictures different than mine?"

I rolled my eyes. "Your hubris?"

"You use autofocus. You cede part of your vision to someone else."

"But it does a good job. And if I don't like it, I change it."

"Always?" He swigged the rest of his tea and poured us each some more.

"What does that mean?"

"I just think that once you begin to see things the way the camera says is the average way, the way most people want to see them, it can be hard to remember to go back and find your own focus, your own point of view."

"What are you now, the chair of the Extended Metaphor department? You sure seem to know a lot about me."

"I've watched you. I pay attention to everything you do." His voice had softened, but it got playful when he added, "Like I know you get sarcastic when you're pushed."

"And you get annoying when you're pushy."

He raised his eyebrows. "Maybe. But that's why you like me."

It wasn't at that moment. In fact, I was relieved when my phone buzzed with a text from Kate and Langley.

In the city shopping it said. *At Agent Provocateur then Intermix where ru?*

"Hey." I started gathering up my stuff. "Come meet Kate and Langley."

"Now?" He looked confused and a little disappointed.

"Yeah, they're in SoHo. This is perfect. I've been dying for you to meet them."

"Oh, me too. Elsa makes them sound great. What was it, the one with no soul and the one with a heart of darkness?"

"Shut up."

"So I guess this is it for the Cloud Challenge."

"For today. It's been amazing."

Scott and I paid for our food and walked up to SoHo, shooting a few more photos. But it was different and I was busy checking the map every block to make sure we were going the right way. He came into Intermix with me to meet Kate and Langley, and it was fun to watch the way all the women shopping there turned to stare at him.

After he left, Kate said, "He's even hotter than you said and he *so* has a crush on you."

"No way. We're just friends. And he thinks I live on autofocus."

"Whatever that means," Langley said.

"He's got a girlfriend."

"Have you seen her?" Langley asked.

"I've seen pictures of her."

"Anyone can fake a picture," Kate pointed out.

"Anyway, we're right and you're wrong," Langley said. She raised her eyebrow. "Did you tell him about your date with David?"

I hadn't. "It didn't come up."

"Right," Kate said. "That seems probable since it's the only thing you've been talking about all week."

"Ha. Maybe Scott and I just have more important things to talk about." I meant it as a joke, but it was also sort of true. I loved my friends, but I couldn't have imagined having a conversation with them about art and obedience and traffic signs in Europe.

"Speaking of David," Langley stepped in, "what are you going to wear when you see him next? If it's only a rebound thing, you'll have to make every date with him count."

I didn't think they were right about Scott having a crush on me or that Scott was right about me living on autofocus, but after that I was slower to respond to his calls and texts. In fact, I remembered, he'd called me the Thursday of the party more than once and I'd bounced it to voice mail.

"Scott, I'm so sorry I didn't get back to you the other day. I—"

"Yeah, that is why I'm here. To get an apology. I revise what I said before. You *are* crazy."

I laughed.

"Livingston High students certainly throw some party," he said. "Did you hear what happened to Elsa?"

"I heard she got into a car accident."

"And now she's in the psych ward here. I wanted to see her, but they said she couldn't have visitors."

"Wow. Maybe I'm not the only crazy one."

"I think it's just that you rich white people have too much time on your hands. Run out of things to do, decide to go nuts."

"Yeah, that's it."

"Assuming just for a second that you're not nuts, do the police have any idea how this happened? Any leads?"

I shook my head.

"They have no idea who could have hit you? There are no witnesses or anything?"

"No. And I'm useless. I can't remember anything."

"Not even leaving the party? What you were doing wandering around the streets of Deal?"

"No."

He was gazing at my hands. "Your ring. The friendship ring you and Kate and Langley all wear."

"What about it?"

He shook his head like he was trying to clear it. "Um, I was just thinking, didn't it used to be on the other hand?"

He was right, I realized. I always wore my friendship ring on my left hand, but now it was on my right. That was weird. "The hospital staff must have moved it. I can't believe you noticed."

"You know I pay attention to everything." There was a strange pause then, and I had the impression he wanted to stay something else, something more. But when he went on it was to say, "I'm sure you're right about the hospital staff." He stood up. "I'm afraid I have to take off. Those tables at Le Marcel don't bus themselves and I'm due there at four."

I smiled at him, rubbing the tip of my thumb against the ring. "Thanks for coming. I feel better right now than I have since I got here."

"Don't go getting any crazier."

"I won't."

Please, I thought, *let that be true.*

Sunday

Chapter 20

I didn't dream that night. When I woke up at ten in the morning, I felt better, more alert than I had in a long time. The Robert Frost dog was nestled beneath my chin.

Dr. Connolly had visited me the previous evening and declared my progress "nearly miraculous," and I hadn't had any more hallucinations. I dared to imagine I might really be on the mend.

When Loretta brought in my breakfast, I saw a box next to my bed. "Delivered this morning early," she said. I reached out and pulled it onto my lap, delighted by the simple act of using my arms. It wasn't wrapped, and when I opened it, there was a porcelain doll inside.

A doll with dark hair dressed like a fairy. Like I had been the night of the party. It was holding a rose in one hand. I lifted out the note:

A doll for a doll. Hope your simulacra brings you health. Love, Your Secret Admirer.

As I picked up the doll, her head rolled off onto the floor and cracked open.

My mother's perfectly lined lips were tight. "Jane, don't be absurd. Someone went to all the trouble of making a doll that looks like you. It was a lovely gesture, not a menacing one. There's no need to call in a security team."

"Really? A doll whose head falls off and breaks the minute I touch it? That's not lovely, that's voodoo."

Her blonde bob hardly moved as my mother shook her head. "I'm worried about this growing paranoia," she said to Joe, as though I wasn't there. "Maybe we should talk to Dr. Tan again."

"I can call him if you want," Joe offered.

My hands were clenched. "Yes, let's bring in someone to tell you what you want to hear rather than what I'm saying." I felt tears starting to prick my eyes. I was tired, so tired of being doubted, of not remembering. Of doubting myself. "Why can't you listen to me?" I demanded. "Why can't you believe in me? I mean, believe me."

My mother ignored my revision. "Of course I believe in you, Jane." She came over to stand next to me. "I know you can do anything you want. You're my brilliant, beautiful girl."

For a moment, a split second, I felt as though my mom—the one who put on Band-Aids and promised everything would be all right— was there again with me. I looked up and I saw her the same way I did the first day of kindergarten, the way I did when Amerigo the turtle died and we buried him, her face a map of love and concern and care. The mom who used to let me curl up and rock with her on the old hammock under the tree in the backyard while she read, until she dozed off and her glasses would slide down between us. We still had the hammock, but it wasn't out anymore. No one had time for it.

Gazing at her now, I whispered, "I'm scared, Mom. Everything is wrong. I'm scared of what I can't remember and I'm scared of what I will remember. Everyone seems discombobulated."

And like the mom of my memories, she said, "I know, darling."
She put her hand on mine and squeezed. It was a wonderful feeling.
"I know it's hard." We stayed like that for a minute and I felt a sense
of calm, of lightness growing inside of me that had been eluding me.
I didn't have to do this alone. She was here with me. For me. We'd
face this, whatever it was, together.

She said, "And that's why we should get Dr. Tan up here to help
you. So you can distinguish what is real and what isn't. And then
you'll be good as new."

She pulled her hand away to move toward the phone and I felt like
a weight had dropped onto my chest. My eyes went to my empty hand.

I don't need Dr. Tan, I need you, I wanted to say.

I said instead, "You don't have to call him. I'm fine."

"You will be." She dialed his extension on my room phone and from
the tone of her voice I could tell she'd gotten his voice mail. "Dr. Tan,
this is Rosalind Freeman. I was hoping you could come and have another chat with my daughter. She's a bit agitated this morning and I think a
talk with you would cheer her right up." She smiled at me as she spoke.

Yes, that was what I needed. To be cheered up. Because being
sad, feeling things, was some kind of sin.

She hung up with what sounded like a sigh of relief. "There,
now we have the experts working on it."

She'd just cradled the phone when Annie came barreling into the
room. "Jane, look." She rushed toward my bed, waving the porcelain
doll aloft like a trophy. "Loretta and I fixed her." The doll now had
a small bandage wrapped around her head, holding the two sides together, and a crack across her skull. "She's even more like you now."

"Great," I said. "That doesn't enhance her creepiness at all."

"Jane," my mother said warningly. She turned to Annie. "That's
adorable, darling."

"Her name is Robert," Annie announced, her face wreathed in proud smiles.

"Robert?" I asked. "She doesn't really look like a Robert to me. Are you sure?"

"Yes, she told me. And she says she comes in peace."

I laughed unexpectedly, suddenly realizing how much I'd missed having Annie around the day before.

"How was your time with Dora yesterday?" I asked her.

"It was fun. We played family vacation. Dora plays it different than I do."

"How do you play?"

"My way the family gets in a station wagon and goes to see the world's biggest ball of yarn and the dad reads out loud and the mother yells at the people on the radio even though they can't hear her and the sisters sit in the back and the big sister listens to music and the little sister tries to find license plates from every state on the cars they pass. And sometimes the big sister helps her."

Annie was describing the last family vacation we'd had before my father died, right down to the cursing at the political talk shows on the radio.

"And how does Dora play?"

"In Dora's they go to Casa del Campo, which is made of Kleenex boxes—but only the silver and gold ones. There's only Dora and Mother and Ollie, and Mother spends all day at the pool meeting people and Ollie is in charge of making sure Dora eats lunch and has things to do. And at night Dora offers her mother's guests cocktails. And sometimes Mother and Ollie fight about why Mother never spends any time with Dora."

"That *is* different. Where's Dora's father?"

"He died a long time ago. But it's okay because her brother is the Man of the House and takes really good care of her and they play great games. But when he fights with their mother, he gets sent home, where he hangs out with his nice girlfriend Angel Face."

"Oh." I'd had no idea that Ollie's father was dead or that like me, he had a single mom. Although his mom didn't sound exactly like mine. For that matter, the Ollie that played nicely with his sister and was the Man of the House didn't sound like the Ollie I knew at all. I wondered how much of this story was real and how much was make-believe.

Annie nodded. "But he and Angel Face are keeping it a secret because she says it's more exciting that way and why would they want the whole school knowing their business."

That, I guessed, was made up because Ollie was definitely not dating someone at our school.

I decided to change the subject. "What's it like at their house?"

"Mostly we just played by ourselves or with Rasheena—she's the nanny. But then at dinnertime Dora's mother came down from her nap. She is very worn out. She told us all about Charles Dickens, about how he was her favorite writer and that's why she named Oliver and Dora what she did because they were characters in a book by him. I pretended I didn't know about Charles Dickens even though of course I do because I'm not a baby."

Charles Dickens had been one of the authors Annie always wanted our father to read to her at story time, and in the year before he died, he'd finally acquiesced, telling her it was because she wasn't a baby anymore. Since then she'd read his entire set on her own.

"Sounds like quite a day."

"It was." She leaned in to whisper. "We did something naughty."

"What was it?"

Her cheeks got red and her eyes were huge behind the lenses of her glasses. "You have to promise not to tell."

"I promise."

"We snuck into Ollie's room."

I worked to match her solemn tone. "What was it like?"

"He has a picture of you on his dresser."

"Of me?"

"You with Kate and Langley and David."

"That makes sense. We're his friends."

"And he has girls' underwear. A whole drawer of it. All from that fancy store that Langley was talking about last time she came over. The one with the pink tags."

The weirdness of the revelation that Ollie collected Agent Provocateur underwear was overshadowed by the fact that somehow Annie could hear what went on in my bedroom. "Were you spying on us?"

"No. You didn't have the door closed. All the way."

I would have to remember that when I got home.

"And he had all these toys that you can use to listen to other people's conversations. Dora says it's because their family is in surveillance. They're really cool. One of them looks like a cigarette pack and one of them is a Diet Coke can and there's a plant and a stick of gum. There's one that looks just like the telescope in Joe's office."

It would not have surprised me at all if Joe had our entire house wired for security. And what she was telling me about Ollie and his surveillance toys didn't surprise me either.

Once in the early days of my dating David, Ollie had offered me a ride home in his car. I said yes because having my boyfriend's best friend like me seemed like a good idea. Even then Ollie made me a little uncomfortable, but I was determined to make a good impression. So when he said, "Want to hear something cool?" I was enthusiastic.

"It's a little out there," he added.

"That's good, I like out there."

He flipped through a few tracks on his iPod, hit play.

"Gimme a venti skim misto with light foam," a Brooklyn accent said. Behind it I made out a woman's voice saying, "No, the poodle gets the blow out, the Lab just needs ribbons," and someone playing the bongos.

"What is that?"

"The sound environment," he said. "Starbucks. Try this one."

"…so when someone thought to posit the possibility of the square root of negative one, it changed the face of…" said the voice of Dr. Reed, our calculus teacher.

"You recorded that at school."

"Everywhere." He smiled a little oddly. "Listen to this one."

"…hotter than you said and he *so* has a crush on you." It was Kate's voice.

"No way. We're just friends. And he thinks I live on autofocus." That was me.

"Whatever that means," I heard Langley's voice say.

I couldn't keep the shock out of my own voice. "That was last weekend. You taped us? In New York? How?"

Ollie hit stop quickly. "Technology. I tape everyone. I call them portraits. One day I'm going to put them together into a symphony."

I forgot about trying to make him like me. "That's spying."

"No, it's art. Louis Armstrong did it all the time. He was famous for it. Bellhops, people in his house, everyone."

"It's sick."

"That's a heavy word."

"If people knew you did this—" I started.

"They wouldn't care. People like to hear themselves. Plus I know you won't tell anyone; it would ruin the naturalness. I mean, listen."

He hit play again and I heard Langley saying, "Anyway, we're right and you're wrong. Did you tell him about your date with David?"

Me: It didn't come up.

Kate: Right. That seems probable since it's the only thing you've been talking about all week.

Me: Ha. Maybe Scott and I just have more important things to—

Ollie stopped the recording. "Incidentally, be careful with that Scott guy. He dated a friend of mine and she said he was weird. He had these little trophies he'd collected from one of his girlfriends and was generally a little creepy."

Takes one to know one, I thought.

He smiled at me and pointed to the tape. "Great stuff, right?"

"Yeah—great," I agreed. I had the uneasy feeling that I had just entered into a dangerous bargain.

"I knew you'd understand if you just thought about it," he said, patting me on the shoulder. His touch made me want to recoil. "I mean, really it's no different than you taking a picture of someone."

I couldn't believe he was comparing my work to his perverse hobby. I said stiffly, "People pose for my pictures."

"If you think people aren't posing when they're in public, you're more naive than I imagined, Jane Freeman."

In my hospital room Annie had climbed onto a chair next to my bed and was kneeling on it, holding Robert up to my face. "Want to know what was inside Robert's head?"

"Robert?"

"The doll."

"Oh, right. Yeah, what was inside?"

"Feathers."

I stared at the doll, tracing the cracks across its head with my finger, and thought how perfect that was. We were twins, both of us featherbrained and cracked.

Chapter 21

The ringing of the phone woke me up. I'd almost picked it up when I stopped myself, hand in the air. My eyes went to the clock to note the time. Five after one.

"Loretta," I called. I wanted a witness, someone to assure me that the phone was ringing. "Loretta!"

"What do you need, sweetheart?"

"Do you hear the—" was already out of my mouth before I realized it was Kate standing in the doorway, not Loretta. She was a really good mimic and she'd hit Loretta perfectly, the soft hint of a Jersey accent.

"Do I hear what?" she said in her normal voice now, coming toward me.

The phone had stopped ringing. *If it ever had been ringing*, a voice in my head said. "Nothing."

Kate always seemed calm, but now her movements were slower and her eyes a little glassy. Like she was unnaturally calm.

"Are you okay?"

"Oh yeah. Sorry I couldn't come visit yesterday; my mother and the girls got home from L.A. and brought a yogi with them? You have no idea how much time it takes to realign the chakras of a twenty-three-thousand-square-foot house."

"So the self-actualization went well?"

"Yeah. Especially if you like being told to breathe yourself out and feel the universe." Mrs. Valenti had been a lawyer before she stopped working to manage her husband's self-help empire. She'd redirected all her energy and acumen into a quest for self-knowledge that basically translated into wholeheartedly embracing a new religion every three to six months. I wasn't sure if she did it in earnest or because it was one of the things that kept the ratings on *Living Valenti* so high. If Kate was like a lightning rod, a passive instrument that created an electric atmosphere, her mother was lightning, fast moving, glamorous, and libel to hurt you if you got in her path. She said whatever was on her mind without softening it, which made her terrifying to me, but the flip side, as I'd learned last summer, was that she was very accepting.

Kate's gray eyes wandered around my hospital room and settled on my hands. A frown line appeared between her eyebrows.

"What's wrong?" I asked.

"N-nothing, I'm just tired?" Her eyes moved to the table next to my bed, where Annie had left the doll. "What's that?"

"According to Annie, her name is Robert. She's a present from my secret admirer."

"Any idea who sent it?"

"None."

"He certainly has a strange taste in gifts. A broken doll?"

"She wasn't broken when she got here; that's my fault. Her head fell off when I opened the box and that's when she got maimed."

She picked it up and turned it over. "Fancy."

"What do you mean?"

"It's one of those expensive dolls they had at the fund-raiser for the children's hospital? Remember the one that Langley's grandmother chaired? They auctioned them off. Elsa's stepmother went nuts for them?"

"Too bad I broke it or I could have sold it on eBay."

"I don't know. Someone once told me that flaws are what give people real beauty." Her words sent a chill through me. She ran her finger over the doll's face. "So how are you today? You look better."

"I can move my hands. But I'm going crazy."

"What do you mean?"

"I thought I got a phone call from someone threatening to kill me—"

Her fingers went to her mouth. "Jane, my God, that's awful."

"Seriously. But apparently I made it up."

"Why would you do that?" She set the doll aside. "And wouldn't you know if you'd gotten a phone call?"

"Did you hear the phone ringing when you came in?"

"No, I only heard you asking for Loretta. Why?"

I shook my head. "I guess the medicine I'm on makes me imagine things. And Dr. Tan says that sometimes when you can't remember stuff, the brain makes up stories to fill in the gaps."

"Stories about someone killing you?"

"I keep thinking if I could just remember everything that happened, I would be fine. The delusions would go away and I'd get better."

"Maybe," she said. Her fingers went to the cut on her otherwise perfect pink lip. "But maybe your mind is protecting you from something? Maybe it's better not to know?"

"What happened to your lip?"

"My lip?" She looked startled and moved her hand away, staring at it like she hadn't seen it before. "Oh, nothing. My sister stood up too fast and knocked her head into me." She smiled. "Why are you worrying about me? All you should be thinking about is getting better so we can spend the summer on the beach working on our tans." As though she wasn't already naturally the perfect golden hue. "Remember last summer when we saw that dolphin right in front of my house?"

"That was amazing. That whole week was amazing."

She ran her finger down the doll's arm. "Yeah, it really was."

Langley had been in Scotland all summer and Kate and I had spent a lot of time together, which was great. I learned about the wicked sense of fun that bubbled beneath her carefree surface and got a glimpse of her chaotic family life too. The entire household revolved around her father and his work, but he was only there on the weekends. So when he was in residence, it was like showtime! and everyone had their roles. When he wasn't there, everyone could be themselves. My first observation was to marvel at the fact that no one slipped up or acted out of character when the reverend was home. Unlike David's father, who made his displeasure known physically, the Valentis didn't beat their children. But if you displeased Reverend Valenti, he would freeze you out of his affections. You became invisible. It sounded painless, but the strain Kate was under to make sure that didn't happen suggested that it was a punishment far worse than I could imagine.

It finally helped me understand what I'd seen the first day we met in the bathroom, and it made me realize that she was an even better actress than anyone knew. I felt lucky to have the chance to learn all that but even luckier when her parents took her younger sisters away for the second-to-last week of summer and offered to let us stay in the beach house by ourselves.

I was especially glad because my mother and Joe had just gotten engaged despite my objections and it was the week we were moving into the Chatoo (also despite my objections). Or, as Joe liked to say, "Don't think of it as relocating, think of it as gaining a stepfather, a pool, a garden with a fountain, and a game room to entertain all your friends."

"What, no petting zoo?" I'd asked.

"Do you want one?" Joe said, meaning it. He started reaching for the blueprints. "Could be a space at the back of the garden."

My mother clenched her jaw. "Jane, please."

The less I had to be around for *that*, the better. No one seemed to care that I wasn't helping, wasn't being part of the family.

So for an entire week, Kate and I did nothing but lounge around the pool and lounge around the beach and watch TV. I saw a more relaxed Kate than I'd ever seen, and I felt more relaxed than *I'd* been since moving to New Jersey. Two nights before everyone was coming back, we took her dad's pride and joy, a '67 Cadillac Eldorado convertible, for a cruise through town, then went and parked it on a turnout with a great view of the ocean. It was a Wednesday, which meant it was deserted, just us and the huge sky and the full moon.

The radio was tuned to an eighties station and "You Shook Me All Night Long" came on. Kate grabbed the straw fedora we'd bought to share, climbed over the windshield, and stood on top of the hood. Feet apart, arms open, head back, she started to dance.

I got out my camera to take a picture.

"No, put down your security blanket and come dance with me." She held out her hand, letting go of the fedora, and the wind picked it up and whipped it off her head toward the beach.

Her mouth made a comical O and she laughed and said, "Finder's keepers," and took off after it. I jumped out of the car and sprinted to catch up. The hat wafted down the beach, rolling and flipping and bopping toward the water, and we followed, giggling the whole time. It kept going, just out of reach, and without realizing it, we'd waded into the surf. I had my fingers nearly on the hat when a freak wave pushed it toward Kate. We reached for it at the same time. Our shoulders collided, unbalancing us both, and we fell down, each hitting the sandy bottom in the waist-deep water with a splash. For a moment, shocked by the impact and the water, we just stared at each other.

Then we started to laugh. It was the kind of laughter that hurts your stomach and makes you gasp and forces you to cling together to keep from falling over. My head was resting on the shoulder of Kate's soaked T-shirt and hers was on the strap of my wet tank when we finally stopped laughing and were just gulping air.

"Honestly, I can't remember the last time I laughed like that," she said.

"Me either." It was certainly sometime before my mother abandoned me for Joe.

It was quiet for a minute.

"Do you ever feel like your head is going to explode? Like there's just so much inside pushing to get out?" Kate's face suddenly looked stormy in a thrilling, beautiful way.

I didn't. But I didn't want her to feel alone. "Totally," I answered, clutching my arms around my knees. It was chilly.

"I knew you did." She nodded. "What do you do when you feel that way?"

"Wait for it to pass," I guessed. "What do you do?"

She was watching me carefully. In the moonlight, hair hanging in wet tendrils down her shoulders with the sea glimmering behind her, she looked like a water nymph, something mythical and endangered. She reminded me of something, but I couldn't think of what. "I want to show you something. Come on." She got to her feet, tugging me up with her, and kept holding my hand as we squelched our way up the beach back to the car in our soggy jeans.

"What is it?"

"You must learn patience, young Jedi," she said with a mischievous half smile.

I stopped walking. That was the kind of thing Bonnie would have said. And that was who Kate had reminded me of, I realized.

For a moment I was seized with a feeling of missing Bonnie so profoundly it ached. Then Kate turned around and looked at me with concern. "Is something wrong, Jane?"

I shook Bonnie out of my head. "Nothing."

She smiled and tugged my hand. "Good."

We got to the car and she motioned me into the passenger side. "Open the glove compartment."

I did. A dozen containers of lipstick in horrible shades, five bottles of perfume, a pack of gum, a long pearl necklace, three Livingston High School IDs including the assistant principal's, a cell phone I recognized as Dom's, a box of nursing pads, and a pint of whiskey spilled out. "What is all this stuff?"

"I stole it."

"You steal stuff from"—I picked up one of the lipsticks and looked at the price tag—"CVS?"

"All over. I stole a fur coat once."

"How?"

"I just wore it out of the store. But it was weird; that wasn't as satisfying. Oh, and I stole a car. *That* was fun. But I put it back because how would I explain it?"

"Do your parents know about this?"

"Are you kidding? They'd go ballistic."

"But what if you get caught? Kate, you can't keep doing this."

She smiled at me. "That's what I wanted to tell you. That's what's so great." She took my hand.

"What?"

"Ever since we started hanging out this summer, I haven't felt that way. The exploding way." She traced the tendons up the inside of my arm, caressing them so lightly it felt like gossamer wings. "I haven't stolen anything at all since June."

I looked at her. She was glowing. "Really?" I didn't know what she was saying, why she was holding my arm like that. But I felt it was important. *I* was important. I was helping her somehow.

"Really." Her fingers brushed my hair like I was a doll. "I knew, since the first time we met, that you were special. Special for me. You make me feel like I'm okay. Better than okay."

Her words stirred something inside of me, something that had been knotted up since my mother and Joe announced their engagement. Made me feel like I *mattered* to someone.

She touched my cheek. "I want to kiss you."

"You do?" The only person I'd ever kissed, besides my parents, was Liam Marsh. I'd never really thought about kissing a girl.

Kate nodded. "I do." Her hair was starting to dry in loose wisps framing her face, making her look vulnerable. Making her look like Bonnie. Maybe this girl I *could* save. "A lot."

"Um. Okay," I said, my heart pounding.

I leaned toward her. She leaned toward me. We crashed together, our noses bumping, our teeth smacking, lips crushed. It was a horrible, awkward kiss. I wasn't sure if I was relieved or disappointed.

I leaned back. "Maybe this isn't such a good—"

She dragged my mouth back and held my head in place while her mouth brushed mine softly, like the lightest whisper. Her lips were chapped but smooth and tasted like seawater and cherry Blistex. We stayed that way, mouths barely touching, moving only a hair's breadth, for a long time. She came a little closer, increasing the pressure, and her lips opened against mine.

Her tongue slid into my mouth, sending shock waves through me. This wasn't like any kiss I'd ever had with Liam. I felt a surge of heat flutter from my lips to my toes, sending sparks down my spine. I wanted this, I wanted more. At least, my body felt like it did.

"Oh, Jane," she sighed against my mouth, and I felt her fingers moving down my arms again and my body ignited.

What are you doing? my mind demanded. *What would everyone at school say?*

I pulled away. I was breathing heavily. "We have to stop."

Her eyes were misty and sweet when she opened them, but when the mist cleared, I saw her normal aloofness. "Why do we have to stop?" she asked. "You can't tell me you didn't like it."

"I did," I admitted. "Like it."

"So what's the problem? We're just two friends experimenting. There's nothing wrong with that."

She made it sound so simple. Just two friends experimenting. And she wanted me.

So why was I so completely terrified?

"It's—I don't want to do anything to ruin our friendship."

"How could this ruin our friendship, silly?" She took a piece of my hair and began to wrap it around her finger. "But if you don't want to, we can stop."

Did I? I wasn't even sure.

"Do you want to stop?" I asked.

She shook her head slowly. "No."

"Then neither do I."

"Are you su—"

I put my hands on her shoulders and pulled her to me. Our kiss that time was fierce, hard, and breathless. I poured everything I'd been feeling, all my anger and rage and grief and fear, emotions whose origins I couldn't even recognize, into the kiss. I wished my mother could see me.

"Did you like that?" I asked, pulling away. I felt reckless. Bold. "Tell me you liked it."

Kate looked stunned. "It was—it was remarkable."

"Let's do it again. But all we can do is kiss. Okay?" *Who was this girl, speaking with my mouth, doing these things?*

I'd never felt so free, so feral, in my life. Was this what kissing was supposed to be like? This feeling of giddy wildness? Of not caring what else happened? These kisses didn't mean anything, they were just for now, barely even existed. We kissed like people kiss in movies, long and hot with tongues twisting together one second and then light little feathery touches at the corner of each other's mouths the next. Neither of us noticed our wet clothes or the cool breeze. She kissed my eyelids and made me sigh. I kissed her on her neck and gave her goose bumps.

"I like that," she said, giggling.

"Me too."

We moved into the backseat. Our hands clasped together, we kissed and laughed and told jokes and kissed some more. The kisses got longer until they were almost trancelike and I didn't know where her body began and mine ended. We made out for hours under the full moon with the sound of the waves and the sea grass shifting tenderly in the breeze. Kissing subsided into holding, and we lay twined together on the long leather seat of the Cadillac watching occasional puffs of cloud float slowly across the velvety night sky.

She said, "I love you, Jane."

It was what I wanted to hear. What I needed to hear. I realized that later. But when I said, "I love you too," I knew it meant different things to each of us. I loved her as a friend. I loved her needing me. Loving me, even. *That* was what I loved.

The next day we lay on a batik blanket on the beach in front of her house. Her head was on my shoulder and she was tracing droplets of water down the side of a Diet Coke can.

"What happens now?" she asked.

"What do you mean?"

"I mean when school starts. Will we see each other?"

My heart started to pound. "Of course, we'll see each other. We have most of our classes together. We see each other every day."

"That's not what I mean." She raised herself on one elbow. She was by far the prettiest person on the beach—maybe the prettiest person that I'd ever met. "Like this. Will we see each other like this."

"I don't know. I'm not sure—"

"Yeah, me either," she said, lying back down.

"Plus Langley would—"

"Oh, totally."

It was just an experiment. No one would know. Just fun.

That night, our last night there, we decided to try out what she called the Seventeen Headed Hydra, her parents' massive steam shower. It was amazing, the entire back wall lined with heated fog-proof mirrors. Kate was in the middle of styling a bubble mustache and beard for me, with strict orders that I keep my eyes closed, when all of a sudden she froze.

I opened my eyes to see why and was looking at her mother in the mirror. We weren't even doing anything, but we were both naked and I could imagine how it looked. How *my* mother would have reacted. How anyone would. My heart started to pound. For a moment the pulsing sound of the sixteen showerheads echoed through the room like a torrential downpour. Then Mrs. Valenti said, "Don't forget to mop up any water that gets on the marble; I don't want someone to slip and crack their head open."

We never discussed it. Summer ended and I started going out with David and Kate and I were never that close again. She tried to bring it up once, but I pretended like I didn't know what she meant.

But sometimes when I was at David's house, in his room, I looked over at Kate's window and remembered what it had been like to kiss her.

I wondered if I should tell her now. I looked at her but found that she was staring at my hand.

"Your ring," she said, pointing to the matching one on her left hand. "Where did you get it?"

"You gave it to me." Her eyes seemed to have gotten even glassier. Was she on something?

"I know, but—" She frowned. "Anyway, I forgot, I got you a present." She rifled through her Louis Vuitton tote and emerged with a long light-blue cotton scarf with golden threads woven into it. "I thought you could maybe wrap it around your head if you have to keep that bandage on. It would be sort of bohemian and chic."

"Thank you." I ran my fingers over the soft material, enjoying the fact that I could feel again, until I hit something hard and plastic. "Kate. It still has the security tag on it."

"Oh. They must have forgotten to take it off at the store." She looked scared. "I bought it. I did. I have the receipt in here somewhere."

She started pawing through her purse at first calmly, then more frantically, until it slid from her lap to the ground. The contents spilled out: a prescription bottle, denture adhesive, a bottle of Obsession with a tester sticker on it, a pair of bright-green reading glasses with the price tag still attached.

"Kate, what have you been doing?"

Her face was stricken. "I'm sorry. Oh God. I know I shouldn't have. It's just—I've just—I feel so guilty. What happened to you. All of this?" She waved her arm around the room. "In all honesty, I did it. This is all my fault."

"What? Why?"

"I should have stopped."

I couldn't believe she was actually saying what it sounded like. I felt goose bumps rise on my arms. "What?"

"Stopped you, I mean," she said quickly. "At the party. From going away. I should have known something was wrong with you, that you weren't yourself."

"Why?"

"You—I mean you were staggering. You needed a friend. And I wasn't there for you. I should have been. I should have known better. And I didn't."

"Kate. I don't know what happened that night, but I do know you, and I'm sure you would have been there if I'd asked."

She looked at me with an expression of complete horror, her hand over her mouth, her eyes wide.

A chill swept over me. "Kate, what's wrong?"

There were pink blotches on her face. "I—I have to go," she said, grabbed her bag, and ran out of the room.

Naturally, Pete chose that moment to come and bother me. "Wow, you weren't kidding. People really adore you," he said.

"I'm not in the mood." I tried to forget the scared look on Kate's face. "What just happened?"

"I have no idea." I looked at him. Today he was wearing a cowboy-cut shirt with pearl buttons and what looked like dancing chili peppers on it. "Where do you get your clothes?"

"Dazzling, right?"

"Does that mean makes one's eyes sting like poison?"

His face assumed its Serious expression, lips pursed, brow furrowed, which made him look unbelievably cute. "I do believe that's the etymology."

I couldn't help it. I laughed. "I am so tired of being cooped up in this place."

"Want to get away from it all?"

"Are you serious?"

He pointed at the wheelchair. "We've got wheels, baby."

Chapter 22

"**D**id you have any special destination in mind?" Pete bent near my ear to ask as he wheeled me over the threshold. The feel of his breath on the nape of my neck made my arms tingle.

Or maybe it was just because it was thrilling to be somewhere besides room 403. "I don't know. The cafeteria maybe?"

"You want to get sicker?"

"I hear the hot chocolate is really good."

"Someone who hates you deeply told you that," he said in a voice like he was very sorry to tell me the bad news, but.

"It was my little sister."

I could almost feel him shaking his head in mock resignation behind me. "Most murders *are* committed by family members."

"That's not true," I protested. I tried to turn around, but his hand on top of my head kept me facing forward. His grip was strong but gentle. "Is it?"

"Maybe, but you can't deny family members have the best cause." His fingers stayed in my hair for a moment and they felt wonderful.

He smoothed it, adding, "Although Annie seems pretty cool."

His thumb brushed my neck as he pulled his hand back, re-igniting the tingling in my arms I'd felt before and spreading it into my belly. *Stop that*, I told my mind, and made myself focus on the parts of the hospital we were passing through instead. The ICU was a warren of glassed-in rooms and nursing stations with a few areas with overstuffed but uncomfortable-looking couches and chairs scattered around. The walls were painted bright yellow, presumably for cheeriness, but I didn't think it was working. In the sitting area near my room a little girl with her hair in cornrows was sprawled on the floor coloring at the feet of an older woman who was thumbing through a Bible. Across from them a dark-haired husky-looking man in a leather jacket was drinking Gatorade and reading the *New York Post*.

Sickness made weird bedfellows.

"Do you have any siblings?" I asked Pete.

"A few assorted," he said lightly.

"What does that mean?"

"Some steps, some halves, one real. My parents enjoy marrying."

"But you live with your dad."

"Right now I do." We got into the elevator and Pete pushed a button marked *M*. "Live is sort of a strong word. I reside with my father. Live implies being able to breathe, which is not exactly what goes on in the stifling atmosphere of Dr. Malik's home."

In the polished interior brass of the doors I could see his reflection, slightly distorted, but clear enough to know that the expression on his face wasn't as blithe as his voice. He leaned against the back of the elevator, one shoulder higher than the other, staring down at me but not, I could tell, seeing me. There was a hollowness in his eyes, a sharpness in the dip of his shoulder that I recognized. Pete was lonely.

He glanced up, caught me looking at him, and smiled. Even in the imperfect mirror of the brass doors, his smile was movie-star white and dazzling. I just had time to smile back when the doors slid open.

M turned out to be the mezzanine, a sort of balcony that over-looked the main floor of the hospital. Here the walls were a bluish white punctuated by cheap prints of beach scenes and European capitals. But even as I took all that in, I was uncomfortably aware of Pete's presence behind me. When his fingertips grazed my shoulder, I shivered.

"Sorry," he said abruptly, for once not joking.

"No problem, you can do that anytime," I said. It was not what I'd meant to say *at all*, and I blushed furiously. "I mean, it's nothing. No harm, no foul. No—" I was making it worse. I needed to change the subject. I tugged at the threads of our earlier conversation. "So you two don't get along? You and your dad? Why don't you live with your mother?"

I expected him to make fun of me for being so tongue tied, but he seemed almost relieved. "Many reasons, but one good one is that she lives in Boise, Idaho." The tension between us evaporated.

"Couldn't you get an apartment around here? I mean, there must be other places you could stay than with your dad."

"You ask a lot of questions for a sick maiden."

"It's only my body that's sick, not my brain."

"That's not what I hear." He snickered.

I decided to retaliate. "Where do you go to school—oh wait, you said you were a deadbeat college dropout."

"Not yet. I haven't even started yet. That's just my father's prophecy. I got accepted to Columbia and if he's wrong, I'll go there in September. But he's rarely wrong."

"Why does he think you're a deadbeat?"

"Shhh," he said, pushing me down the linoleum corridor.

"What? What is it?"

"Listen."

"To what?"

"The harmony of the spheres."

"I think that's the climate-control system."

"I thought you said you had poetry in your DNA."

We went through a set of mahogany French doors and were in a wood-paneled corridor with thick green carpeting.

"What are you going to study at Columbia?"

"Has anyone ever told you that you should be a prosecutor? You're relentless."

"So?"

"Can you keep a secret?"

"No."

"At least you're honest. Okay, I'm going to study—"

A distinguished-looking man with olive skin a shade darker than Peter's, dark hair graying at the temples, and horn-rimmed glasses wearing a lab coat over an expensive-looking chalk-stripe suit walked by, did a double take, and came back to us. "Hello, Peter. What are you doing on this floor?" He spoke with a faint British accent.

Everything that had been loose about Pete now seemed to tighten. "Just taking our patient for some air, sir."

"Around the executive offices of the hospital?"

"She likes the plush carpeting."

Something in the man's jaw tightened for a moment, as though he suspected a joke and didn't like them, but he got it under control quickly. Then he bent slightly at the waist and held a hand toward me. "Hello, miss. What is your name?"

Pete did the introductions. "Jane Freeman, this is Dr. Sanjay Malik, the director of the hospital."

The distinguished man stood up, nodding to himself. "You're Rosalind's daughter. It's good to see you looking so fit. We've been proud to have you here. Your mother is a dynamo."

"Yes, she is."

He patted Pete on the shoulder. "Carry on, Peter."

"Thank you, sir."

I waited until we'd gone a bit down the corridor to ask, "That's your dad? He's the director of the hospital?"

"Yep." The shortest response on record from Pete ever.

"I don't get it. Why is he making you do, you know, this?"

"Long story." Second-shortest response. He really didn't want to talk about it. Which made me want to know more.

"Tell me. You know I'll just keep asking until you do."

He let out a sigh, a long one that felt real, not pretend. "It's a tedious story of a boy, a girl, a dog with a prosthetic leg, and justice gone wrong."

Now it was my turn to sigh. "No, it's not."

"You're right. He's just a tyrant and doesn't have anywhere else to stash me this summer." We'd come out of the executive offices and were back in the linoleum-corridor-with-bluish-white-walls mezzanine of the hospital with a railing overlooking the main floor. "Now on your left—"

"Shhh."

"Ha ha."

"No, I'm serious. That's a friend of mine and my boyfriend down there."

Beneath us, on the ground floor, I could see Kate talking to David. She looked angry and was using her hands a lot.

"Honestly, Kate…and chill."

"Don't even…nothing to say…why…just stay away…alone."

David said, "You know what. I'll let her tell me that herself," and started heading toward the elevators.

"Wait," Kate said. "I'm not—"

"Go go go," I told Pete. "Fast. If you've got any shortcuts back to my room, use them!"

"Do you know what that was about?"

"I'm not sure," I said. "But it was weird, right?"

He nodded, his impossibly blue eyes open wide, his expression solemn. "Oh yeah."

Kate and David had been friends before he and I started going out, from growing up next door to each other. But recently things had been strained. And at Langley's last riding event the week before, Kate had been really weird about him.

"I think I have to bag dinner tonight," I had said as we watched Langley ride. We were both leaning back with our elbows propped on the stands behind us and our toes on the seats in front of us, my black flats resting next to the toes of her new brown motorcycle boots. I felt the cool metal against my forearms where the navy-blue leather jacket I was wearing with jeans had ridden up. "How mad do you think Langley will be?" Her grandparents always took us to dinner after a competition.

"On a scale of angry to *très très* angry, I'd go for *très*," she said, punctuating each *très* with a tap of her boot. She was wearing them with leggings, a loose cotton button-down shirt, and an old tweed blazer of her father's with the sleeves rolled up.

"It's just that I really need to talk to David."

"Canceling on the girls for a guy is bad form. All for one and one for all."

"I know, but I don't have a choice. It's his only free night and the longer I put off telling him about the Getty internship, the more it's going to suck."

Kate appeared to be fascinated by the riding. "You mean the more you're going to have to suck to make up for it."

"Shut up!"

She raised her eyebrows but still didn't look at me. "Joking. But I'm sure he'll find a way to console himself."

There was something in her tone that was off. "What do you mean?"

Now she looked at me. Her gaze was appraising. "Nothing. Just that he may surprise you."

"Surprise me?"

"Don't you ever get tired of worrying about what David thinks and what David feels and what's okay with David?"

I sat forward, pulling the sleeves of my jacket over my wrists. I was suddenly chilly. "That's what relationships are about. Caring about the other person."

"Then I'm sure you'll be fine. Because if David cares about you, he must think about your needs as much as you think about his and he'll understand and be happy for you."

She was right. He did love me. He'd be happy for me. He *would*.

There was a snort from behind us. Turning around, I saw Nicky sitting there. "Sorry," she said. "I'm waiting for my brother's event to start and I just couldn't help overhearing. Very quaint." She put on a falsetto voice to mimic, "If he loves you, he'll understand." She rolled her eyes. "You must read a lot of bad novels."

"Just because you're bitter doesn't mean you have to make everyone else bitter too," Kate told her, sitting up.

"Does *bitter* mean 'living in the real world' now? I hadn't real-ized." Nicky stood up so she was towering above us. In her knit dress with skulls all over it, and green snakeskin cowboy boots, she looked pretty fierce, and fiercer when she put her hands on her hips and aimed her eyes directly at me. "Maybe you should try thinking for yourself once in awhile," she said. Then she leaned forward, tapped me on the nose and added, "Beware the counsel of false prophets–or their daughters."

Nicky walked away, leaving Kate and I to stare at each other.

"That was a little visit from the land of the very strange," Kate said finally, wide eyed.

"Uh-huh," I answered with the same expression. "I feel sort of bad. I mean, she's really nice."

Kate corralled her hair so it lay all on one shoulder and studied the ends. "Not to you."

Kate was right, but there was still a part of me that admired Nicky, admired the way she wasn't afraid to say things even if they weren't what people wanted to hear. Like she didn't worry about being nice to people she didn't care about.

Langley joined us then. In her beige riding breeches, black tai-lored jacket, and black riding cap with the blonde braids peeking out the bottom, she looked like something out of a Ralph Lauren catalog.

"It's a good thing you talked through my whole routine because otherwise I'd be mortified about how badly I'd done."

"Sorry," Kate said.

"Not your fault. I just had an off day."

"We meant about talking," I put in.

"No, honestly, it was a bust. Although Popo did give me this." She held up her right arm to show off a charm bracelet she'd been admiring the week before at Neiman Marcus. Then she turned to where her grandfather was sitting in his wheelchair with the nurse standing behind him and blew him a kiss. He gave a little wave.

"You two are so adorable," I said.

"I know. I can't imagine life without him. He's more than a grandfather to me. But back to the two of you, little baddies. Your punishment is that you have to tell me what you were talking so seriously about."

"Dinner tonight," Kate said.

I gave her a pleading look. I was nervous enough about telling Langley without her making it harder.

Langley looked from one of us to the other. "What about dinner tonight?"

"I can't come." I watched Langley's face for a sign of how angry she was, but it was impassive. "I would if I could, but I seriously have to go see David."

"To tell him about the Getty internship," Kate explained. "Where by 'tell' I mean use her mouth but not with words." She crossed her arms and leaned back as though waiting for fireworks.

Langley nodded slowly. "Keeping the course of true love running straight is more important than one dinner."

"Thank you," I said, hugging her. "I knew you'd understand."

"Of course, jelly bean." Over her shoulder I saw Kate's face register disbelief at how easily she'd taken the news.

Now as he pushed my wheelchair down the hospital corridors at an impressive speed, Pete said to me, "Are all your friends preparing to have their own reality shows? Because they certainly go in for drama."

"And yours don't?"

He swerved around a slow-moving gurney, eliciting a shout from the nurse. "Sorry," he said, waving over his shoulder. "Problem patient." Then to me, "My friends? They're not so much into the yelling at each other in lobbies and making out in stairwells, no."

I would have turned around at that news, but I was too busy gripping the armrests. "Who was making out in a stairwell?"

"Some of the people who were here yesterday."

"Some of the people?"

"Some girl and some guy. I just assumed they were friends of yours."

"What did they look like?"

"Hang on, I'll show you. I filmed it."

"You did?"

"No, doofus, that's the point." We were back on my floor. "When people are making out, you turn quietly and walk away. You don't note their distinguishing characteristics so you can relate them to the hot patient in room 403."

My pulse started to race at his words. "Is that me?"

Or maybe it was the fact that as he said it, we rounded a corner on two wheels, nearly knocked down orderly, and narrowly missed taking out a garbage can.

We zoomed past the sitting area outside my room. I caught a glimpse of the girl with the coloring book, but the dark-haired husky-looking man had been replaced with a bald husky-looking man reading the *Daily News* and drinking Tab.

"Yes, roughage. And speaking of room 403, here we are. Three fifteen p.m. and all is well. We beat that slowpoke boyfriend of yours by a mile." He pushed me through the door. "Would you like to be reinstalled in your bed or would you prefer the comforts of this delightful throne?"

"Bed, please," I said.

Pete wrapped me in his arms and picked me up. I nestled my nose into his neck. He smelled like blueberry pancakes.

"Do you really think I'm hot?"

"Right now," he grunted, "I just think you're heavy." He heaved me to the bed.

"Coward." Blueberry pancakes and smoky bacon and long breakfasts with lots of crumbs and sticky fingers that had to be—

"I never said I was brave," he told me, breaking into my daydream.

For a moment I was totally flustered—what was I doing, thinking about other guys when my boyfriend, my *awesome* boyfriend, was just about to show up—but then I remembered the drugs I was on. Probably this, like the hallucinations, was another side effect. Pete didn't mean anything to me.

"Do you have a girlfriend?" I asked.

"Yes."

And I didn't mean anything to him.

"Is she hot?"

"What"—grunt—"do you think?"

Pete was leaning over me to tuck me in when David got there.

"Uh, am I interrupting something?" he said, sounding tense.

"Just getting it on with your girlfriend," Pete told him. His face was a mask of innocence, but his eyes were very blue and very mischievous. "No, I'm joking, man. I'm the orderly here. Tucking her in. But she's quite a girl." He high-fived David. "See you later."

I watched him go. I did not, I told myself, feel a twinge of disappointment that he had a girlfriend. I looked at David. "How are you?"

"How are you?" he said. "You look even better than yesterday."

"I can move my arms."

"Nice." He nodded to himself, looking around. Today he was wearing his Snoopy 4 Pres T-shirt and dark-brown suede Vans. His pants were slung low on his hips and although I couldn't see them, I would have bet he was wearing his Captain America boxers. He liked to wear them with the Snoopy shirt, both of them being so patriotic, he'd explained. That was love, I reminded myself. Knowing what underwear someone is wearing without having to see it.

Knowing their every mood. Which was why I could tell there was something on David's mind.

"You seem distracted," I said.

"Me? No. Well—" He pulled up the chair and spun it around, then sat on it backward next to the bed. "I didn't get to say this the other day, lady-girl, but I'm truly sorry you didn't die."

Chapter 23

I **stared at him,** not sure that I'd heard him correctly.

"I mean, if that's what you wanted."

More staring.

"Langley told me—" he started to say, then stopped. His left leg bounced up and down. "You know, you're right about her. She's really great."

"I know. What did Langley say?"

"She told me how upset you were that night. About me and Sloan."

"Sloan?"

I leave David's lap and head for the stairs. I turn and see Elsa talking to him. I turn back and walk into—

Not the banister. A person. Sloan.

David said, "She told me how you were running around talking about how you wanted to end it all. She thought, you know, you meant break up with me. But I—well, I hear it different." His fingers started tapping on his thigh.

"What do you mean with Sloan?"

"I'm sorry" I say.

"No problem." Sloan smiles shyly. "Party foul."

My purse has flown open and she kneels and helps me get my cash and mascara and keys back into my bag. I'm still looking for my lip gloss when my phone buzzes again, Kate texting Where r u? 911 upstairs bathroom!!!!"

"If you find a lip gloss, you can keep it," I say.

Her face lights up. "Seriously? Wow."

David took my hand from the hospital bed and started stroking it. "Look, babe, we can get through this. For your sake, you've just got to breathe it out. All the pain. The anger. You need to choose what to stress about and what to chill about, right? Like sure, I was with Sloan at the party, but that was only because I was mad at you because of what Elsa said. I thought you were going behind my back, so I went behind yours."

Time, so much time has passed. I step into a room and see two bodies on a bed. One of them is David on top of a girl, kissing her, wearing only his boxers. He leaps up when he sees me. I'm shocked and afraid. He's coming toward me, with his hands out.

Someone is pushing—or are they pulling—me out of the room. I back away, stunned.

In my head I heard Dr. Tan saying, "We bury what we don't want to know. And sometimes it comes out in odd ways."

Yes, I'd definitely buried this.

But there was something missing. Something shady around the edges I wasn't seeing.

"You were with Sloan," I repeated, still looking for the flaw.

"Yes, but it was nothing, you know? I mean, it was only because of what you did. Or what I thought you did. You're my lady, you know that. And things had been rough between us." He leaned toward me, smiling and curling a piece of my hair in his fingers, his leg still vibrating. "I was really out of it. But being with her just made me appreciate you more. Plus it was better because you know how my temper is and if I'd seen you that night—" He shrugged.

I was looking at him, but I felt like I didn't even recognize him. "You didn't see me at all that night? After I got off your lap?"

"I mean I saw you when you walked in on me doing my thing. But not other than that."

What if that was a lie? What if he had lost his temper and tried to run me over? Was that possible? I didn't even know.

"Look, lady-girl, don't be mad. That's what I mean, about you being able to—"

"I think you should leave."

He slid his sunglasses down his nose to look at me with blood-shot eyes. "Don't do something you'll regret."

"That's why I want you to go now."

"Okay. You just get better and when you're out, everything will go back to being exactly how it was."

That had been what I wanted more than anything. But now—now I wasn't so sure.

"Stay soft," he said, flashing a peace sign.

"That doesn't mean anything. Why can't you just say goodbye?"

"Frisky," he said, nodding. "I like." He paused in the doorway, one big hand wrapped around the doorjamb. "Oh, and babe. I thought of 140."

I looked at him standing there. He was so handsome. His shirt rode up and I could see I'd been right about the Captain America boxers. I knew him so well. We were good together. And there were 140 things that he thought I was better than. "What is it?" I asked. I couldn't not.

"Cherry Slurpee." He pulled down his glasses to wink. "And that's a big one."

I managed to keep myself from crying until I heard his footsteps disappear down the hall. I wasn't crying about Sloan, although I probably should have been. I was crying about what he'd said. Number 140.

Because cherry Slurpees were something David loved. And he thought I did too because I always got one so he could finish mine even though I liked Coke better.

In a way, that said everything there was to say about our relationship.

I was still sniffling a little when the phone rang. At least I thought it did. But maybe I was just hallucinating it. Maybe the altercation with David had been—what did Dr. Tan call it?—a trigger and there was no phone ringing at all.

"Loretta!" I yelled.

"Yes, sweetheart. Why aren't you answering your phone?"

Aha! She heard it.

I reached for it.

Chapter 24

"*H*ello?"

"Jane Freeman? Is that you?" a voice whispered.

"Yes. Who's this?"

"It's Elsa. Hi!" She was still whispering.

"El—"

"Shhh. Don't say my name. They can't know I'm calling you."

"Who?"

"The Know-it-alls. They hear everything you say."

"What do you mean?"

"I heard them talking on the stairs. They're listening. They know if you've been bad or good so be good for goodness' sake. Or is it goodness's sake?"

Elsa had officially lost it. "Thank you for the warning. How are you? I heard about your accident."

"I'm not supposed to be doing this. I'm under the desk. It's so cozy here. Like a little mouse in a little mouse house. Isn't that right, Reginald?"

"Who's Reginald?"

"The mouse. Who's Reginald?" she repeated like it was the end point of hilarity, and started laughing so hard she snorted.

"Where are you?"

"At Reginald's, I told you."

"Is it nice?"

"If you like spiders. Which I don't."

"Oh."

"Shhh, someone is coming."

"Why did you call me?"

"I did? Why would I call you? You were so mad at me at the party."

"I was?"

"I couldn't help it. I didn't know what would happen."

"What do you mean?"

"Well, I shouldn't have taken the picture. But there's something else."

"What picture?"

"Shhh, I'm thinking. God, I don't know what they have me on here, but man, is it messing with my mind. Oh, I remember. At first I didn't see you there. And then there was nothing I could do. I tried. I tried to help you. To do what you would have wanted. To help you make the pain go away."

"Where? Where did you see me?"

"I have to go."

"Did you run over me?"

"Run over you? I wasn't wearing my running shoes!" I heard her laughing and then the sound of her hanging up.

My hand was shaking as I put the phone down. Had Elsa just confessed?

I picked up Officer Rowley's card and dialed her number and left a message on her voice mail.

As I waited for her to call back, I tried to make sense out of what Elsa said.

"You were so mad at me at the party."

I thought back, groping for a memory of her. I hadn't been mad when I saw her downstairs with David, I'd hardly—

As I stumble out of the room where Sloan and David are making out, I run into Elsa.

"Watch it, Freeman, wouldn't want anything to happen to you," she says, brushing past me.

I clutch at her. "It's David. He—"

"Why would I care about your boy problems?" She brings her hands up like she's going to strangle me, but instead she pushes me. "Get out of my way."

I stagger against the wall.

I have the sensation of moving—being moved?—from carpeting to something cool, but I can't see anything. It's dark, dark in my head. Slowly things start coming back into focus. I'm in a—

I'm surrounded by eyes. Everywhere I look, everywhere I turn, are eyes. Staring at me. I feel them above me, next to me, behind me. Watching me. Laughing at me.

Hating me.

"Goodbye, Jane," a voice says.

I have to get out of there.

I force myself to my feet. My palms tingle with the feel of the brocade wallpaper beneath them as I clutch at the wall to stay steady. I'm in a hallway and the Oriental carpet slithers up and down like a snake beneath my feet, making my ankles wobble with every step.

Keep going! I tell myself.

Behind me I hear people talking, laughing. Someone says my name.

"Stop, Jane!"

I shook my head out of the memory, but the feeling of being pursued—and watched—stayed with me. The eyes were so familiar. I knew them but couldn't place them.

My head echoed with a cacophony of voices, one flipping to the next like radio going haywire. Elsa: "They're listening. They know if you've been bad or good so be good for goodness' sake." Annie: "Ollie has all these toys that you can use to listen to other people's conversations." Officer Rowley: "You have a generous boyfriend." Me: "They're not from my boyfriend, they're from—" Elsa: "They're listening."

The wheelchair was next to the bed. If I could get myself into it, maybe I could use it to get me to the window, to get—

Loretta caught me as I was about to fall on the floor. "Sweetheart, what are you doing?"

"I have to get to the flowers," I said.

"What flowers?"

"The big ones. I have—I need to look at that big bouquet of flowers. It didn't make sense he sent such big flowers, but now I understand."

"Okay, you sit in bed and I'll bring them to you."

She picked them up and carried them to the table next to my bed. "They are beautif—what are you doing?"

"Hello!" I said into the flowers. "Are you listening?"

"Sweetheart." Loretta approached me obliquely.

"I hope you're listening because I want you to hear this, you bastard." I held the vase over the side of the bed and dropped it onto the floor. It made a glorious smack and shattered, flooding the floor with water and scattering flowers and pieces of glass.

"Happy now?" I yelled into the mess, and started to laugh. "I am!"

Loretta looked at me with horror. She put one hand on my chest, holding me against the bed, and pushed a button on the phone. "I need Dr. Tan up here stat."

I stared at her. "What are you doing? There was a bug in there. I was just getting rid of the bug." I was still giggling a little. "God, that felt good."

"Shhh. It will be okay soon," she said. "You just hold tight."

"No, I'm good. I took care of it. I'm better now."

"Quiet, sweetheart. It's going to be okay."

Her tone, the expression on her face, made me realize how what I had just done must look. First I'd talked into a bouquet of flowers like they could hear me. Then I destroyed them.

Insane. That was how it must look.

Oh God. Oh no. "I'm not crazy, Loretta," I said, the adrenaline of what I'd done beginning to wear off. I started to shiver. "I'm not."

"Shhh. It's okay, love."

"His family is in surveillance," I said. It was getting hard to breathe enough air. Was I crazy? Everyone thought I was crazy. "It makes sense," I assured her. "I can explain it. It all makes sense."

"Breathe, sweetheart," Loretta said, slipping an oxygen mask over my mouth. "You just breathe now."

"It does," I said, but the words were muffled. "I'm not crazy."

By the time Dr. Tan came in, I was breathing normally. "So, Miss Freeman, you've had quite a day," he said.

Loretta had sent Pete in to clean up the vase, which as far as I could see contained no bug. "Do you want me to leave?" he asked as he removed the oxygen mask.

I shook my head. "I don't care."

Dr. Tan settled himself in the chair next to my bed. "Tell me what just happened."

I told him about Elsa's phone call suggesting someone was

watching me and what Annie had said earlier about Ollie's surveillance toys and he nodded and made a few notes.

"And what else have you been up to today?"

"I met the head of the hospital."

"Nice."

"And I found out my boyfriend cheated on me."

"Ah."

I could tell what he was thinking, because it's what I'd thought before too. When I thought the phone call was made up. It hadn't been, but learning about David and Sloan could have been a catalyst toward paranoia.

Or I could have been justified.

"But that has nothing to do with me breaking that vase."

"Tell me what you were thinking when you did it."

"The guy who gave me those flowers? His family is in security. His hobby is bugging people. And he doesn't even like me, which means there was no reason for him to send flowers, especially such fancy ones. So you see, what I did wasn't as crazy as it looked."

"Most irrational beliefs have their basis in fact. The real question is why you so strongly wanted to believe that someone might have you under surveillance. And why instead of just having the vase removed, you felt you had to destroy it."

"I don't know," I said. "Everything that comes out of my mouth sounds crazy."

"Your mother phoned earlier. When she and I spoke, she said something about a doll?"

I pointed to Robert on the windowsill and Dr. Tan picked it up and brought it back to his seat.

He turned the doll over in his hands. "This was clearly made by someone who cares deeply about you," he said. "Do you have any idea who it is?"

"No. All the gifts, though, they're—just a little weird. Like sending me roses when I was found in a rosebush. And then a porcelain figurine with a note saying my secret admirer would always be watching me. This doll. When I took her out of the box, her head rolled off and onto the floor."

"Probably just broken in transit."

"Right. I know that. I know that none of it means anything sinister. That I can't trust my gut and I can't trust my eyes and I can't trust my ears. I don't even know what's real anymore."

"This will all get sorted out in time. Admitting that your experiences might not be what you think they are is a good step."

I'd been looking down at my hands and I saw my ring. "There's something weird about this ring too," I said.

"What do you mean?"

"I usually wear it on my left hand, but now it's on my right."

"Are you sure?"

"About the hand I wear it on? Of course I'm sure." I was. Wasn't I?

"You think your ring moved? On its own?"

"Maybe someone in the hospital moved it."

"Why would they do that?"

"I don't know. You think I'm being paranoid, don't you?"

 Instead of answering he made another note on my chart.

"What are you writing?" I demanded, straining to see.

"I'm making a note to remind myself to ask the nursing staff about your ring."

"Oh."

"You said you're no longer sure what is real and what isn't. I can tell you two things that are real. The first is that everyone in this hospital is sincerely concerned with one thing and one thing only: for you to get better. No one is out to get you. All we want to do is help."

"Thank you. What's the second?"

"The second is the shattered vase on the floor. This young man is doing a poor job of cleaning it up. If you want to get back into Loretta's good graces, I suggest you offer to help."

Chapter 25

*L*oretta sent Pete off to do something "he wouldn't dawdle at" and moved me into the wheelchair with a broom to help with the cleanup. It took me nearly an hour to sort through it and it was just after four thirty when I was ready to admit there was no bug. There were still a half-dozen pieces of vase scattered around when I heard footsteps and looked up to see Ollie himself in the doorway. He was wearing dark-wash jeans, a green-and-white-striped button-down, an aubergine corduroy blazer, and a matching corduroy cap.

"What are you doing here?" I might not have delivered it as nicely as I should have, but I was furious at him, furious because I'd suspected him and furious that I'd been wrong.

He took a step in, paused to look from the shattered glass to me, then said, "Officer Rowley asked me to come. What happened?"

"The vase with your flowers in it broke," I told him. From her place on the floor with the dustpan, Loretta shot me a look.

"Must have been defective or something. Sorry about the mess it made," Ollie said.

He didn't seem unduly concerned that the vase broke. Which he would have been if it had been some sophisticated bugging device, I reasoned. But that still didn't mean I'd been crazy to think he could be bugging me.

He got on his knees and started helping with the cleanup. It was Sunday, but he was wearing a shirt that required cuff links. The one I could see said LAW. I wondered if the other one said ORDER. Perfect for a surveillance junkie. As he bent over, I found myself checking his rear for panty lines that would indicate he was wearing girls' underwear.

Maybe I *was* insane.

"Thank you, dear," Loretta said to him, taking the trash can out when we'd finished the cleanup. She favored me with the evil eye. "I'll get someone with a mop in here soon to dispose of the remaining water."

Officer Rowley walked in then and closed the door behind Loretta.

"Mr. Montero, please tell Jane what you told me earlier today. Start with when Jane left the party."

"I saw Jane stumble out of the house and I followed her."

I tried to make my mind go back there.

The hallway is undulating, the carpet moving. I have my hands out, like a sleepwalker. If I could just get downstairs, I think. If I can get outside, I'll be safe.

Why?

Faces blur past me, faces that are familiar but now stretched, distorted with laughing mouths. I'm afraid to look in their eyes, afraid to see the hate I know will be there.

Keep going!

I make it down the stairs, into the living room. It's packed with sweaty bodies. People sway against me, but I have to keep moving, like a salmon going upstream for survival. I push and wriggle and—

I'm out.

I expect the air outside to be cool, but it isn't. It's hot and heavy like a blanket.

"I called to her," Ollie was saying to Officer Rowley and me.

In my memory I heard someone yell, "Jane, wait!" behind me. But it didn't sound like Ollie.

"When I finally caught up to you, you were swaying and you looked funny. I steered you onto the stairs and tried to look in your eyes to see if you had a concussion."

"From what?"

"Before you ran down the stairs, you got hit on the head by something and passed out for a little while."

"What hit me?"

"I don't know, I only saw you slumped against the floor. I checked your eyes and you looked okay to me."

I feel the warm stone of the steps through the fairy skirt and on my bare thighs. I'm sitting there, stunned, thinking about—

Suddenly Ollie is there, leaning into my face. He seems concerned, and sober. He grips my chin, turning my head from side to side.

"What are you doing?" I ask, pulling away.

"You hit your head."

"I'm fine," I say. "Leave me alone."

"Wait here and I'll drive you home."

"No."

"I'll be right back." He goes inside. I struggle to my feet.

Ollie shook his head when I told him what I remembered. "You're missing a part," he said, almost apologetically. He shifted from one foot to the other, like he was uncomfortable.

"What part?"

"The part where you said, 'You're just covering for your asshole friend. There's nothing wrong with me. I know what I saw.' And I said, 'David doesn't deserve you.' And—this is embarrassing—I tried to kiss you."

I had absolutely no memory of this. Nothing about it felt right or made sense. I would remember if someone tried to kiss me, wouldn't I? But Ollie had no reason to lie.

I wasn't sure I wanted to know, but I had to ask. "How did that go?"

"You pushed me away and said, 'What are you doing?' and I said, 'I thought this was what you wanted.' And you said, 'No. Not with you. Never.'"

I didn't remember any of that either, and although that probably would have been my reaction, I like to think I would have been nicer about it. "Harsh," I told him now. "Sorry."

He held up a hand to stop my apology. "You were just speaking your mind. Then you told me to go away and leave you alone. And I did." He put his hands in his pockets and jingled his keys nervously. "I was a little angry as I went back into the party. But then I felt bad. So I called your cell phone and apologized and tried to convince you to let me come get you. I asked where you were and you said, 'I'm on Dove Street.' And then—"

He paused and made a small circuit around the room, stopping in front of the windowsill with the flowers and presents on it, shifting them around, touching each of them in turn. With his back to me he said, "I was talking to you and I heard tires squealing and—and your phone went dead."

"You heard me get hit?"

"I didn't know what I heard. But that's what it sounded like."

He paused and turned around.

His face was bleak, his eyes haunted. "I'm sorry, Jane. I am truly sorry." The way he said it was different from anything else he'd said. This, alone, sounded true.

I stared at him hard. Not because he'd heard me get hit. But because so much of what he'd said didn't make sense.

"I'm on Dove Street." I said the words, testing them out in my mouth. That was the street I'd been found on, but the statement felt wrong. The bird part, that touched a chord, but Dove Street—

I'm holding on to the metal support of a street sign, leaning back to read it. It's dark, it's streaked in rain. It reads—

"Are you sure I didn't say Peregrine Road?"

"Positive. Weren't you found on Dove Street?"

"Yes. But that—it's not right. It doesn't feel right." How could I explain this?

"Peregrine Road is just around the corner from Dove Street," Officer Rowley said.

"You told me Dove Street," Ollie insisted, his voice rising and his face getting slightly flushed.

"Okay. I'll have to take your word for it." But how would I have come up with Peregrine Road if I hadn't seen it? Even though I'd been there the previous summer with Kate, I never paid any attention to the street names. Why would I imagine saying the wrong street name? And forget the right one?

"Your cell phone records confirm that Mr. Montero was the last person you spoke to," Officer Rowley said. "I was hoping this would jog your memory."

"It didn't." Now I'd gone from hearing phone calls no one else believed happened to *not* believing in phone calls that absolutely took place.

I stared at Ollie. Why didn't I remember?

"Are we done here?" Ollie asked Officer Rowley. "Can I go?"

She nodded.

"Take care of yourself, Jane," he said. "If I were you, I'd stop trying to remember and just concentrate on getting better."

"Thanks."

I was so distracted I forgot to look for panty lines again when he left.

"Did you call me earlier, Miss Freeman?" Officer Rowley jolted my attention back

"Yes. I got a very strange phone call." She sighed and put her hand on her hip. "A real one," I continued. "You can ask Loretta. It was from a girl in my class named Elsa. She had an accident the same night as mine."

"Elsa Blanchard. She phoned you? I was under the impression she was in the psych ward, and there are no phones in the rooms there."

"I don't know, she was very weird about it, talking about hiding and how she wasn't supposed to be on the phone. But she said something—odd."

I could tell that Officer Rowley was only barely believing me. "Yes."

"She said that she was only trying to help me make the pain go away. And there was something about the way she said it, and the fact that her car was then crashed, that made me wonder—I mean, could she have been the one to hit me? And then crashed into a post to cover it up?"

"We explored that idea two days ago, Miss Freeman. There's no question that all the damage on Elsa Blanchard's vehicle came from the impact with the post. And even if it hadn't, her car was of too low a profile to have caused your injuries. You were hit with something like a sedan."

If Elsa hadn't been confessing to hitting me, what the hell had she meant?

Officer Rowley left.

I was in the wheelchair still mulling that over, and searching every corner of my mind for some memory of Ollie trying to kiss me, when Sloan walked in half an hour later looking for my mother. Part of me wanted to be mad at her, hate her, but I couldn't. Her dark hair was glossy and she wore almost no makeup on her oval face with the wide-spaced eyes. Her outfit looked like something I would have worn.

When she saw I was alone, she tried to back out, but I stopped her.

"Hey. Can I ask you a question?"

She swallowed hard and stayed near the door. "I should really find your mom. She wanted me here at five fifteen and it's almost five thirty."

"Yeah, of course, I'll make it fast. I was just wondering, the night of the party, were you with someone?"

Her chin went up and she squared her shoulders. "I'm not sure that's really any of your business." God, she was already becoming a mini–my mother. And yet that answer kind of made me like her even more.

I smiled to let her know I wasn't the enemy. "Sorry, I did that wrong. I just want to know if you were with David."

"David?" she repeated, and although she was tense, she also seemed slightly relieved. "He drove me home."

I'd had all the hedges, evasions, shadowy half-truths I could take. I forced myself to ask what I really wanted to know. "Did you have sex with him?"

I was ready to hear anything. But I was still surprised by her answer.

Chapter 26

*S*loan said, "I don't know."

"What do you mean?"

She drew closer to my bed now, her eyes apprehensive and scared but kind, like an animal being tamed. "I don't know if you remember, but at the party you walked into me."

"I remember. My stuff dropped and you helped me pick it up."

"Right. Well, you put your drink down and you just left it there when you took off. So I drank it."

"And?"

"I think it must have had something in it because after that, everything kind of gets weird. I went looking for my friend and then I don't really remember what happened until David was on top of me waking me up and saying we had to get out of there."

"You woke up with David on top of you?" Her words took a moment to fully penetrate. "Oh, Sloan, are you okay? I mean, do you think something happened you didn't want to happen? Do you want to talk to a nurse?"

Her face registered surprise and gratitude. "You're so—That is really, really nice of you to ask. But I'm okay." She leaned toward me. "Plus—I have my period, so—"

I knew how David was about periods so I figured she was right. Nothing had happened. Not that I really thought David was capable of taking advantage of someone like that—when they were drugged—but then, I wasn't really sure of anything anymore.

"That still must have been upsetting. What happened after he woke you up?"

"He drove me home. I probably shouldn't have gone with him because I think he was pretty wasted, but I didn't realize that then. The next day he tried to talk to me, something about his car, but I ignored him. And I haven't seen him since…Well, except here."

At least David wasn't lying about that.

"And I solemnly swear I won't, ever," she added.

"If you want him, he's all yours."

"He's, um, not my type." Her pocket buzzed. "Oops, that's your mom. I've got to run."

She was at the door when she stopped and turned around. "There's one other thing. Remember how you couldn't find your lip gloss? And you told me if I found it, I could keep it?" She blushed and looked nervous. "This is kind of lame, but I've had, um, people say I look like you, and I thought maybe it would look good on me too." So I kept looking for it. I found it. The lip gloss, I mean. But you can totally have it back."

"No thanks." The last thing I was interested in at the moment was lip gloss. Which was a very new development for me. "I hope that, *um, people* like it on you."

She smiled and blushed. "Let me know if there's anything I can do to help."

I wished there were something she could have done to help. That anyone could. I fought back through the darkness to the party, to try to put this piece into place. If what Sloan said was true, then the red plastic cup had actually been drugged. But it wasn't how I got dosed.

I open the door and see Sloan and David together.

And someone else. There's someone else there. Someone—pushing me in? But why would someone push me into the room?

I'm confused and furious. "Why are you doing this?"

Langley? No, Langley was in front of the *bathroom* door, not the bedroom door, and she was trying to keep me from getting out, not pushing me in.

But—

I'm outside and it's raining.

I have to get Langley's shoes off. I'd promised her I wouldn't get them wet and it's pouring. Already they're getting drenched. Ruined. I lean over to undo the clasps and nearly fall over.

You don't have time for this! a voice in my head says. Keep moving.

I stagger back to my feet, giving up on saving the shoes. I'll buy her a new pair. I've got to keep going, get away.

The phone rings. It's dark and pouring and I have to squint at the screen to see the caller ID.

Ollie M.

Is that what it said? Or do I only think that because it's what people have told me?

I heard Nicky's voice from two weeks ago: "Maybe you should try thinking for yourself once in awhile"

Was I that easy? That spineless?

The phone rings again. And again.

If it was Ollie, why didn't I remember talking to him?

The phone was still ringing.

That's when I realized it wasn't ringing in my memory but ringing in my room.

"Loretta," I yelled. "My phone is ringing."

"Go answer it, sweetheart."

"Can you hear it?"

"Sure as apples."

My heart pounded. This could be the time I showed everyone I'm not crazy.

"Hello?"

"Hi, jelly bean," Langley said.

Loretta had come to stand in the doorway. I waved her away.

"Hey. How are you?"

"I'm okay, but I don't think I can make it there today. Popo—"

"Is he worse?"

"Well, he's not any better."

"I'm so sorry to hear that."

"Thanks. How are you?"

I stared at the balloon bouquet starting to dip slightly in the corner of my room. "Confused. David was here. He told me about Sloan."

Langley exhaled. "Oh."

"So when you blocked the door from letting me out of the bathroom—"

"Yes?"

"What did you hear me say again?"

"'I can't take it anymore. It's over. I'm done, it's done. I just want to end it.' Things like that."

"Are you sure it was about David?" My eyes roamed over the flower arrangements on my windowsill.

"I thought so. Why?"

"I—I don't know. I don't know anything anymore. Thanks."

"You sound low. I'm going to come over there."

"No, don't. Stay with your grandfather."

"Are you sure?"

"Positive."

"I love you, jelly bean."

"Love you too." I gave the receiver a kiss and hung up.

The phone started to ring again immediately. I answered it saying, "Seriously, I'm fine."

"Are you, Jane?"

I swallowed. It was the caller. Why hadn't I shouted for Loretta?

I moved the phone to the bed and stretched the cord as far as it would go. "Hi. How are you doing?"

"It's time."

"Time for what?" I asked. I held the phone away from me and leaned toward the door. "Loretta," I whispered. Finally someone else would hear.

"Don't play dumb. You just knelt there. In the middle of the road. You know you wanted it as much as I did. And you know why."

My entire body went cold.

Loretta rushed past me and grabbed the phone. She held it to her ear for a moment, then gently replaced it in the cradle.

You just knelt there. Only two people would have known that. Me. And the person who ran into me.

This wasn't a prank. This was a killer.

I looked at Loretta. "Why did you hang up? Why didn't you talk to him?"

"No one was there."

No. It wasn't possible. "But there had been someone there. He was talking right up until you took the phone out of my hand." I looked at her. "You have to believe me. He was talking."

Wasn't he?

I ran my hand over my hair, smashing it, trying to squeeze some reason out. "Somehow he must have known I'd handed the phone over."

"How? You said he was talking."

"I don't know. We must have made a noise." He'd been there. I heard him. I had.

Hadn't I? Oh God. I really was going mad.

You just knelt there. You know you wanted it as much as I did. And you know why. I could only imagine what Dr. Tan would make of that.

"What did he say this time, sweetheart?"

"What did who say?" my mother asked, breezing into the room. Joe lumbered after her, carrying a bag from the supermarket, with Officer Rowley, neat as always in her uniform, after him. Annie, today wearing a green dress, green leggings, and green sneakers, none of which were the same color green, brought up the rear.

My mother looked at me expectantly.

"My phone-caller," I told her. "He called again."

Instead of looking concerned or exasperated, my mother smiled. A warm, genuine smile. Clearly something had changed. "I don't think we'll need to worry about any more of those calls, will we, Officer Rowley?"

"I hope not," the policewoman said.

"Why?"

"Because the fine police of this city have apprehended the convenience store robbers," my mother announced. "Thanks in part to Joe's reward."

"Didn't have anything to do with it," he muttered, pawing around in his bag of snacks.

"Don't be so modest," my mother told him.

I said, "Did the robbers confess?"

My mother shook her head. "No, the Barney Brothers—that's what they're called—are refusing to speak. Lawyer's orders. But they didn't have to. The skid marks on the road are a good match to their tires, their car has dents on it that could be consistent with hitting a pedestrian, and they had your purse and your phone."

"They did? Can I get my phone back?" Any concrete link to that night would be welcome.

"When we're done processing it," Officer Rowley said.

"But don't you see," my mother said, beaming. "This means it's over. It's all over."

"It's good news, kid," Joe said.

"Tell that to the voices in my head."

"What did those voices in your head say this time?" my mother asked, like she was talking to a toddler.

"They said—" I knew if I told the truth, it would make me sound truly suicidal. "They said it was time. For it to be over."

"You see? We all agree. Me, you, and your subconscious."

I felt myself getting angry. I wanted to be alone. I looked at Loretta. "Could I take a shower? I think I could manage by myself if you'd just turn the water on for me."

"Of course, sweetheart."

"Bye, Jane," Annie said, coming over to give me a sticky kiss on the cheek.

"Eew," I said, wiping it off. "What did you just eat?"

"Jelly doughnut. And now you can have some too."

"Thanks but no thanks."

She kissed me again, laughed at my disgusted expression, and followed Joe and my mom out of the room.

I was just rolling into the bathroom in my wheelchair when my mother came back and put her hand on the armrest. "One more thing, Jane."

My jaw tightened. I looked at her over my shoulder. "Yes?"

"Dr. Malik told me he met you today. With his son, Peter."

"Yeah. Pete was letting me get some air."

"I'd rather you didn't spend too much time with him," she said.

"Don't worry, Dr. Malik didn't really look like my type."

"With his son, Peter. He dropped out of high school and he has a history of drug use. His father found him with quite a large quantity of something heavy and that's why he's here. So he can keep an eye on him."

The way my mother said "something heavy," like she was down with the peeps, yo, made me have to stifle a laugh. "Sure. Whatever you want. Can I go now?"

"I'd also like you to be a little more gracious with Joe."

"Why does everyone care about Joe so much?"

"He's a wonderful, kind man," my mother said.

"That's what I hear."

She pursed her lips together. "I don't—" I heard her swallow. "I'm not trying to replace your father, Jane."

"Maybe that's the problem," I said, and I could feel the tears quivering in my eyes. "Maybe you should be."

"Darling—"

"I need to go."

I don't know how long I sat under the shower, not moving, letting the hot water wash over me. *They caught the people who did this to you*, I thought. *They had your phone. How else would they have gotten your phone unless they were the ones who hit you? Let your doubts, let your fears, let all the gaps in your memory wash away.*

Let your feelings about Joe wash away. Stop feeling stop missing stop caring stop worrying. None of that matters now. Everything is fine. Everything is safe. Your life as you knew it is intact. Just admit you're crazy and everything will be okay.

When I got out, the mirror was steamed up. The palm prints I'd left the day before when I was trying to block out my hair came up, leaving an empty face-sized shape in the middle.

That was me. A blank space. Who was I? Who was Jane Freeman?

I cleared a space across the mirror so I could see only my eyes and stared at them, but they held no answers.

Chapter 27

*T*hat evening Joe took my mother and Annie to Annie's favorite pizza place for dinner while I enjoyed a selection of beige food in my bed with the TV. It was a dark rainy night and the sound outside my window reminded me of the rain the night of the party.

Patter patter patter patter.

The rain is falling softer now, on my arms and legs and face, and it's colder. Each drop brings pain with it; my whole body aches. There's something poking me everywhere, piercing my skin.

Someone says, "Yoo-hoo, Jane."

I'm here, I want to cry. Right here. Come find me. Rescue me. Please. I can't fight anymore. I'm so tired. Please, please help me. But I can't make my mouth work.

"Yoo-hoo," the voice says again. Then it's right over my face; I can feel breath against my cheek and a hand on my neck. Thank God. Someone will save me. I want to reach for the hand, but I can't.

The voice says, "Jane Freeman, you're a goner."

My eyes flipped open. I was in my hospital room alone. There was no one there, no one whispering next to my face.

Had it been a dream? Or was it a memory? Had someone really stood over me as I lay in the rosebush and said, "Jane Freeman, you're a goner"?

Because if someone had, it meant that my getting hit was no random accident perpetrated by the Barney Brothers. It meant that I'd been run down by someone I knew. Someone who knew my name.

My heart started to pound. If that was true, it meant the killer had to be one of my friends.

I jumped at the sound of Scott's voice.

"You look like someone in the middle of an existential crisis," he said. "Or they're not giving you enough fiber."

It had to be one of my friends, my mind repeated. One of my friends who had been at the party. Which meant anyone *but* Scott.

"I am so glad to see you," I said. "And it's probably both."

"Which existential crisis are we dealing with? The 'Why are we here' one? Or the 'What should I do with my life' one?"

"More basic. The 'Who am I' one."

"Uh-oh, that's a bad one. What brought it on right now at"—he squinted at the clock—"seven forty-five on a Sunday?" He slid into the chair next to my bed and leaned forward. His white shirt was rolled up at the sleeves, revealing a tantalizing glimpse of his strong forearms.

"I got another call from the killer today."

"Ah."

"Only as much as no one believed me before, now that they have the convenience store robbers—I'm sorry, the Barney Brothers—in custody, they *really* don't believe me."

"Oh."

"And this time the killer said, 'You just knelt there. You wanted it as much as I did.'"

His eyes crinkled and he sucked in his cheeks. "Ugh."

"Which means that either it's the real killer—because how else would anyone know that? Or else I made it up and it's a sign from my subconscious that I wanted to die."

Now his eyes got wide. "Uh-oh."

"Exactly. So I'm left with two bad options. But it doesn't really matter because my mother would rather think I'm crazy than entertain the idea that this wasn't the Barney Brothers."

He leaned back. "That's a really bad name. I mean, it wouldn't even make a good band name."

I laughed. "You're right. At least they didn't succeed. I wouldn't want to have that in my obituary."

"I like your attitude. And I've got a diagnosis for your existential crisis. You're a victim of shutter-click syndrome."

"What's that?"

"You know how on digital cameras the shutter still makes a sound when it clicks? Even though that sound was originally the mechanical noise the lens made opening and closing and on digital cameras it's just programmed in?"

"Yeah."

"It's because people like to have markers. They like to maintain their expectations, not question things. It sounds like that's what your mother's doing. For some reason, it's really important for her that this is an accident perpetrated by strangers. Even if they have an unfortunate name."

"Why?"

"Why don't you ask her?"

"That's a novel approach." I thought about it. "I wish I just had one thing, one solid fact that contradicted the stranger-accident theory."

"To bolster your case or simply to annoy your mother?" I shot him a mean look. He shrugged. "Just asking. What about the car that hit you? There had to be damage, right?"

"There's damage on the convenience store getaway car that 'could be consistent' with what they found."

"But they stopped looking at other cars." He thought for a moment. I was struck for the millionth time by how handsome he was—especially when thinking deeply, a favorite pastime of his. "Listen, do you really think it was someone at the party?" he said now.

"I remember someone saying, 'You're a goner, Jane Freeman,' when I was in the rosebush. So if we assume that was true, it would have to be someone who knew me, and the only people on the Jersey shore who knew me were at the party. Why?"

"I did a story for the school paper about auto-repair places—a lot of our 'graduates' end up working in that field. I could ask around at some of the places and see if any Livingston High kids have brought in cars for work this weekend. It might be a stretch, but—"

Here was someone who believed in me. Someone who would stand by me. Or, at this moment, sit by me.

In the chair next to my bed, his head was at the same level as mine. I pulled his mouth toward me and kissed him.

"Was that just to say thank you?" His confidence seemed to have evaporated and suddenly he was shy. Even timid.

"I don't know. Do you want it to be just thank you?" Somewhere in my mind a warning bell went off. But how did I know that wasn't the same part of my mind that was going crazy?

He gazed at me. "You'd have to be a fool not to know how I feel about you, Jane. How I—how much I like you."

"Tell me." At that moment, I needed all the reassurance I could get.

"Let's just say I think you're neat."

"That's it?"

"I'm holding my A material. I want you to be sure."

"Sure of what?"

"Sure that you want to be with me because it's your thing, not because it will make me happy."

"I'm not like that."

"Jane Freeman, you are the biggest people pleaser I know. You'd order popcorn at the movies even though you like peanut M&M's better if you think the person you're with would rather have popcorn and might want to share yours."

I stared at him. "Are you a mind reader? Peanut M&M's *are* my favorite."

"I know a few thousand things about you," he said teasingly.

"Then you'll know that this will make me happy." I kissed him again.

He kissed me back. Then he *really* kissed me back. His lips were warm. He smelled like sandalwood and baby powder. He kissed me long and soft and expertly with his hands cradling my head in a way that made my toes wriggle.

I pulled away, panting. "My toes wriggled! You made my toes wriggle."

It took a moment for his eyes to focus, but then he grinned. "Really? Or do you say that to all the guys?"

"No, really. Look." We both watched as first the toes of my left foot and then the toes of my right foot wriggled. "Kiss me again, let's see if I can't get all the way up to my knees back."

"Are you just using me for my medicinal lips?"

"Yes." I nodded, trying to keep my face serious.

"As long as we're straight on that," he said. This time his kiss was slower, deeper, and more detailed. It was clear that Scott had a lot of practice kissing and, like everything he undertook, he did it masterfully and with control.

"Anything in the calves?" he asked, forehead leaned against mine.

"Not yet. We'll have to keep trying." I ran my hands down his chest, enjoying the feel of his muscles under my fingertips.

He looked at me like I was something precious, valuable. "Do you know how long I've wanted to do that?"

The question made something in my chest a little tight so I just smiled at him.

"I wish we could have a little more privacy," he said.

"Me too." There was the warning bell again. Quiet, you! God, his abs were nice. "I would love to see you without your shirt on."

He swallowed hard. "Um, let me see what I can do for tomorrow."

"What do you mean? I know you're magic, you made my toes wriggle, but how could we have more privacy?"

"I have my ways."

Looking into his eyes was like the opposite of the eyes in my memory. No hate, no mockery. They were all openness and adoration. I might not know who I was, but I knew how I wanted to be seen.

We were about to embark on another round of physical therapy when the sound of Annie's voice reciting "Peter Piper Put a Peck of Pickled Peppers on His Pocket" echoed from the hallway. Evidently Pete had been teaching her a new version of the tongue twister.

Scott leaped up and was an appropriate and innocent distance away by the time Annie led my mother and Joe into the room.

"Oh hello, Scott," my mother said, and patted her hair. Like all women, she got a bit preeny in his presence.

"Hi, Mrs. Freeman. Annie. Hello, sir." He shook Joe's hand. "I was just, um, checking on Jane."

"And how do you find her?" my mother asked with real concern, like we were taking a focus group poll.

His eyes locked on mine. "I find her marvelous. I always find her marvelous." He made a big show of looking at the clock. "Eight thirty? I've got to run. Goodbye," he said to everyone. To me, "I'll work on both those projects we talked about."

I'd forgotten about him visiting the auto-body stores. "Great."

He grinned. "See you tomorrow."

"I can't wait."

When he was gone, Annie said, "Were you and Scott making out?"

My mother said, "Don't be ridiculous, Annie. Jane is dating David."

"Not anymore," I announced.

"Why not?"

"Because I think I only liked David because he liked me. I never bothered to ask myself if I liked him."

"Do you like Scott?" Annie asked.

"He's a really good friend." I wanted to change the subject. "And unlike some people, he doesn't think I'm crazy."

"Unlike some people, he may not have all the facts," my mother said.

"How did you become so sure of yourself, Mother? How do you know you're right and I'm nuts?"

"I've listened to the experts, Jane, and they say—"

"What about me? I'm the expert on me. What do you really know about me?"

My mother got very still and when she looked at me, it was like she was looking at me with her entire soul. "You're right, Jane. I feel like I don't know you anymore. I don't understand what's happened to us. Between us. I—I feel like I've failed you. Ever since Bonnie killed herself, there's been this gap I haven't known how to bridge.

Oh, Jane, I'm so sorry."

She was standing by the side of my bed, head hanging down, crying and holding my hand. This time I could feel the tears.

"Bonnie didn't kill herself," I said. I was done being the girl who ordered the cherry Slurpee.

"What?" My mother looked up at me, shocked. "Of course she did."

"No. I have to tell you something. Something I should have told you a long time ago."

Chapter 28

I remembered Bonnie's funeral. It took place in the same chapel my father's funeral had taken place in six months before, but it had been early summer then and now it was winter.

"Why would you go into a hot tub in the winter?" I heard the echo of my words to Bonnie.

"Stop trying to control me."

The church was full when my mother and I got there. I remember my mother reaching for my hand, but I kept it clenched in a fist at my side and after two attempts she stopped. "I know you weren't as close this year as you had been," my mother leaned toward me to say, "but I know this is hard—"

"Stop it." *You don't know. How can you? How can anyone.*

"Jane, please, it's—"

"I told you not to come."

"Sweetheart, sometimes you want someone to lean on. Even when you don't know it." I could just spill it, I realized then. Just turn to my mother and tell her I'd been at the party and I didn't think

Bonnie committed suicide. That it just didn't make sense. I had no proof, but—

A voice next to me on the pew said, "Jane. How are you?" and I was looking up into Liam's handsome face. "I know you and Bonnie were friends," he said, like we were just casual acquaintances, like we hadn't ever kissed in the back of his car, "and I wanted to tell you how sorry I am."

"Hello, I'm Rosalind Freeman, Jane's mother," my mother introduced herself to him.

"Liam Marsh." They shook hands.

My mother rifled her mental Rolodex. "Dudley Marsh's son?"

"The one and only."

"Your father is a very upstanding member of the community."

"Upstanding enough that you would let me take your daughter out?" Liam asked. He winked at me. "If Jane doesn't object, of course."

My mother smiled. "If Jane doesn't object."

"In fact, a group of us are sitting up front. Then afterward we thought we'd have a sort of memorial. Jane, if you want to come—?"

"Go on," my mother had said, almost excited. "Don't worry about me, I'll be fine. A change is what you need. It will be good for you."

I still could have done it then, come clean. It wouldn't have been too late. Bonnie hadn't even been buried.

But my mother smiled her brave smile and seemed so eager for me to go with Liam. He was a nice boy from a good family. Maybe what he'd told me was true. Maybe Bonnie did OD on her own.

And maybe it didn't matter. Because looking from him to my mother, who was nodding and gesturing to me to go, now he was all I had. Bonnie was gone. It was time for me to start over.

Besides, wasn't this what I wanted? Why I'd gone to all the trouble of doing the make over that had gotten us invited to Trish's party?

My mind veered dangerously back to the afternoon before the party, when I'd been bothering Bonnie about her appearance. She had a lot going for her in the looks department, including big boobs, but she never did anything with it. That day I tried to give her suggestions about outfits, but she ignored me. "It doesn't matter what I wear because I don't care what these people think and I don't want to be friends with people who judge me based on my clothes," she said as she stepped into the pair of overalls she wore every weekend. Her one concession was to wear a tank top under them and one of my new cardigans over them instead of her oversized unicorn T-shirt underneath and a sweatshirt on top. But that wasn't much.

"At least let me tweeze your eyebrows."

"You're nuts," she said. "You've gone totally around the bend. You leave my eyebrows alone. Plus I doubt I'll stay long enough for anyone to notice. You're sure you want to do this?"

"Bonnie, it's our big chance."

"Why, are they outlawing boredom at all other times?"

"Come on," I pleaded. "You'll have fun."

She hesitated for a moment, then her shoulders slumped and she shook her head. "You and your Jedi mind tricks."

Mark Ellis, the bait I'd used to lure her there, was the first person we saw when we arrived at the popular kids' party. He was the principal's son, which gave him an air of authority. With ice-blue eyes, eyebrows and eyelashes so blond they were almost invisible, and lips that were always chapped during the winter from snowboarding, he looked rugged and a little older than his seventeen years. I don't know if it was because his eyes were so cold or if it was just instinct, but Mark gave me the creeps.

Not Bonnie, though. She'd been in love with him since school started, even though he was two years older. As we walked through the door, he said to her, "Hey, aren't you a lifeguard at the pool in the summer? I remember seeing you there."

Bonnie slid from my mind after that because that's when Liam Marsh, Mark's best friend and my personal pick for hottest guy in the junior class, came over and started talking to me. The next time I saw Bonnie, it was much later in the night and she was grabbing me and pulling me into the bathroom. She started taking off her clothes.

"Isn't this fantastic?"

"What are you doing?" I asked.

"Mark wants us to go skinny dipping with him in the Jacuzzi."

"No," I said, stopping her as she pulled off her shirt. "That's a bad idea."

She looked at me and hiccuped. "Why?"

"Because you've had a lot to drink and it's cold out there and you don't know what will happen."

"I thought the reason we came here was to have experiences we'd never had. With boys." She was pulling off her pants then.

"It is. It was. But not like that." Her eyes were unfocused, and as I watched, she tripped over her pant leg and almost fell down. I reached out to steady her, but she pushed my hands away.

"Don't touch me," she said, glaring at me. She stood up and steadied herself on the side of the sink. "Why are you staring at me? Huh?" Her expression was challenging, her jaw tight. "Wait, I know. You're jealous." She laughed maliciously. "You're jealous because I'm going to be kissed before you are."

"That's not true. I just don't think what you're doing—"

"Jane is jealous, Jane is jealous," she sang, weaving her head back and forth. "Well, let me tell you something, Jane, you may end up a prude stick-in-the-mud, but I don't want to be one."

"Bonnie, you're not acting like yourself."

She sneered. "You mean I'm not acting the way *you* want me to. Letting you control me."

My face burned like I'd been slapped. Before I could say anything, Bonnie was going on, saying, "Everyone else seems to like the way I'm acting just fine. Especially Mark."

I found my voice. "If he really likes you, he'll still want to kiss you tomorrow."

"Why put off until tomorrow what you can do today? That's what my mom always says. Step aside, Jane. I told you it wouldn't matter what I wore." She was naked except for a towel now.

"Why would you want to go in a Jacuzzi in the winter?"

"Stop trying to control me."

I stood in front of the door.

She stepped up to me and stood with her nose touching mine. "Get out of the way, you jealous bitch, or I'll make you."

"What's wrong with you? What have you been—"

She slapped me.

"Now will you get the fuck out of the way?"

I did. I knew she was very out of it, the girl who slapped me wasn't a girl I recognized, but I was too mad to realize what that meant. I spent the rest of the night upstairs just talking with Liam and listening to songs on his iPod and being upset in ways I didn't understand about what Bonnie had said. I was *not* controlling. I was just trying to help her. Help us. Wasn't I? I must have dozed off because the next thing I remember is Liam rubbing my shoulder and saying, "We need to get you home."

"Where's Bonnie?"

"There's been an accident. Come on, get your shoes on and we'll get you out of here."

I was completely awake then. "What kind of accident?"

"The kind where the police come. You don't need to be here for that."

"But—"

"Listen, Jane. This is going to be hard for you, but Bonnie—Bonnie died. She took too many drugs and she killed herself."

I laughed. I had to laugh. Because it was impossible. He had to be joking.

"I'm serious. And the police are coming soon. And there's no reason for anyone to know you were here."

"But Bonnie wouldn't kill herself."

"Trust me. This is what happened. But you won't have to tell anyone about it if you just let me take you home now. Otherwise there could be a lot of trouble."

He was looking down into my eyes with his big brown soulful ones and I knew he had only my best interest at heart. I nodded and we left.

"I want to see her," I said.

"No, you don't."

"Yes. I have to."

He said, "Fine," and pointed to the door that led to the deck.

She lay at an angle in the Jacuzzi, her head bobbing on the surface of the water, hair splayed out around her, her body beneath it. Her arms floated peacefully at her sides. Her eyes were open, lifeless pools.

Even with the heat turned up full blast in Liam's red Jeep, I shivered the entire way home. Before he let me out at the end of the block, he said, "You okay?"

I nodded.

"Good girl." He grinned at me and cupped my cheek in his hand. His lips came over mine, soft, then harder and demanding, pushing me against the door until the handle gouged my back. I knew there was something I was supposed to be remembering, that something had just happened, but all I could think about at that moment was that Liam Marsh was kissing me.

"Remember, you were home all night tonight. You didn't see your friend, and you didn't sneak out to go to a party."

I nodded. How could I think of anything except his kisses?

"I'll call you and we'll go out."

He did. We went out almost every night for the rest of my freshman year. Under his wing I became popular. I had everything I'd ever wanted.

Bonnie's suicide shocked everyone. "How—what? Why? Jane, why would she take her own life?" her mother said, pleading with me for answers.

"I don't know," I told her.

"A godforsaken party." Her father paced their kitchen, wearing new grooves in the yellow linoleum. "Bonnie never went to a party in her life."

"Who were those people she was with?" her mother wanted to know. "I know you girls weren't as close recently, but who were they? Why did she want to be with them?"

Her father raked his hand back and forth over his hair, leaving it standing up in patches. "She said she was going to your house. Why would she lie to us? Why would she do this?"

"I feel like I didn't even know her anymore, my own daughter," her mother sobbed. "Oh dear, I'm sorry, Jane, I know this must be hard for you too."

I was numb. I pushed the pain down and the confusion down and I chose to believe what Liam had told me and what I had told everyone. I became the girl who hadn't been at the party, the girl who dated Liam Marsh. The girl who was popular. Who everyone loved. The girl who forgot the truth about Bonnie.

I'd traded my best friend for a few kisses and a place at the popular lunch table. Because after my dad died, I was too scared to be left alone. I didn't see that I wasn't alone at all. I had Bonnie and my mom and Annie. And myself.

I'd been a coward. But I was done with that now.

"Bonnie didn't commit suicide," I repeated in my hospital room, saying it to my mother and Joe and Annie.

"What are you talking about, Jane?

"I was at that party. Bonnie wasn't alone in the corner with her book like they said. She was with Mark Ellis. I think he gave her something, some kind of drugs. I tried to get her to stop, but she wouldn't. I think he must have given her too much. She OD'd, but not on purpose, I know not on purpose. She died in the Jacuzzi and they must have moved her afterward. I saw her, there in the water. She looked—peaceful. Like a princess." I gasped when the word *princess* came out of my mouth. A dead princess. How had I not realized what I'd been photographing all these years? "I tried to get her to stop, but she wouldn't. She slapped me and told me to get out of the way. I tried to get her to stop, I did, but—" I couldn't stop the tears from rolling down my face.

"Jane, what are you saying?" my mother demanded. "You weren't at the party. You were at home. In bed."

"I snuck out. That's where I met Liam. And—" It was time for me to come clean about this to myself as much as everyone else. "I think he only dated me to keep me quiet. It's hard to talk when you're being kissed."

My mother was frozen. "All these years, all this time. Why didn't you tell anyone?"

"I didn't know anything definite. I just had a hunch. And I guess it seemed like it didn't matter. Whether she'd tried to kill herself or overdosed accidentally, she would still be dead."

"There's a huge difference." My mother's hands were clenched. "An enormous difference."

"I know that now," I said miserably. Bonnie mattered. Her parents mattered. And the fact that someone got away with murder definitely mattered. "I almost did tell you at the funeral. But then Liam came over and you gave permission for me to go with him. How could I after that? You seemed so happy to be rid of me."

"Rid of you? Darling, I just wanted you to be happy. I knew what Bonnie meant to you; you two had been inseparable and I thought maybe if you had new friends, it would help ease your grieving. I was trying to let you know you didn't have to stay to take care of me." My mother sank down into a chair with her head in her hands. Joe put his arm around her. "My God, her parents."

I swallowed, gulping back tears. "I want to call them. To tell them."

My mother looked up. "No, darling, I'll do that. You need to focus on getting better. It's too hard."

"Doing something hard will help me get better." I'd been sitting on the sidelines of my own life, watching it all through autofocus, for too long.

Joe had been completely silent through my story. Now he came toward me and stood at the side of the bed. His face was set, almost angry. He said, "That was a brave thing you just did, kid. And a brave offer. I'm impressed. Shake hands."

He held out a hand. I held out my hand. We shook. I felt more tears prick my eyes.

"Good. Now I think we'll both agree I should get your mother and sister home."

I looked at them. My mother looked shattered, fragile. And old.

"Thank you," I said, with genuine gratitude. "Thank you, Joe."

They left the room, her arm around his waist, his over her shoulders.

Annie came over and kissed me on the cheek. "I thought it was brave too. I have the best big sister in the world."

"I have the best little sister," I whispered. Tears hovered at the corner of my eyes.

"What kind of cake do you think you will have for your welcome-home cake?"

"I don't know. What do you think?"

"Ice-cream cake."

"That sounds like an excellent choice."

She left and I was alone.

I waited until I heard the elevator doors open and close before reaching over and pressing Robert Frost's toe.

My father's voice, low and sweet, came to me, wrapping me in its honey.

"Two roads diverged in a yellow wood…"

The tears poured out of me in a torrent, like a cleansing stream. When they were done, I was spent, exhausted. I dozed off. Through half-closed eyes I had the impression of someone peering into my room, but it must have been a dream because it stayed quiet.

The phone rang. "Hello," I answered, half in a dream. I glanced at the clock and saw it was ten minutes to ten. "Scott?"

But it wasn't Scott's voice that said, "Good night, Jane."

I was awake now. Awake, alert, and sure of what I was hearing. I thought. "Stop calling me. You're not my friend, you're a murderer,"

"I know you are, but what am I?"

"What are you talking about?"

"You hurt everyone who cares about you, don't you, Jane?"

"No, that's not true."

"With your secrets and your lies. Everyone is just a pawn in your little game."

A chill ran through me. This had to be a real phone call. It couldn't be in my head. Because I didn't believe that. "I'm not like that. I'm not." *Was I?*

A slide show of faces flashed through my mind. Bonnie. My mother. Kate.

No!

I couldn't take any more of this. "It's time for this to be over."

"I agree. See you tomorrow. Sweet dreams." The line went dead.

I was hyperventilating. I clutched Robert Frost to me as my father's voice intoned, "Oh, I kept the first for another day! Yet knowing how way leads on to way, I doubted if I should ever come back."

See you tomorrow.

Whether the killer was in my head or outside it, this was going to end.

Monday

_____

Chapter 29

he dock jutted over the smooth water of the lake like the tongue
of a mouth open to scream, the yellowed trees surrounding it like teeth.
Beneath my feet the worn boards were hot and uneven and splinters
poked me. My toes tingled.

"What are you waiting for, Jane?" the pretty camp counselor said,
floating in the water three feet in front of me. "Come in, it feels great."

I jumped. At first the water felt fantastic, cool and welcoming. The
weeds Bonnie warned me about just brushed past like friendly tongues
lapping at me, welcoming me. I turned on my side and started to swim
toward the float in the middle of the lake.

The tongues got friskier, less gentle. Now they were lashing me,
each stroke harder, more biting. They wrapped around me, engulfing
me, and tugged me down toward them. "You're ours now," they seemed
to say. "You can't escape us." I feel like I hear a hundred voices com-
menting on me, mocking me. "What happened to your bangs? Look at
the runs in her tights."

Voices all around me, pressing on me, making me lose my resolve.

I'm so tired. I want them to stop. Just relax, just give in, you'll be fine, they tell me.

Lies. I knew these were lies. I swam with all my strength, fatiguing every muscle, using every breath in my body. Up ahead, through the weeds, I saw a hand. Someone was reaching in to save me.

But as hard as I swam, I couldn't get to it. Every stroke took me closer, but not close enough. I felt like my lungs were going to explode, like I couldn't go on. And in that moment I saw her, through the tangle of weeds. She was staring at me, eyes locked on mine.

Eyes filled with hate and malice and loathing. Eyes that wanted me dead. Eyes I recognized.

"You can say that again," Loretta said, coming into my room.

"What did I say?" I was just waking up and must have been talking in my sleep. I looked at the clock. It was eight thirty in the morning.

"It sounded like 'my eyes.' Will you look at this thing?"

I propped myself up and saw that Loretta was carrying a massive floral wreath. "This is about the limit," she said. "You'd better get well soon and check out of here or we're going to run out of space." She handed me the card.

The wreath was made of red and yellow roses in two entwined hearts and had a white satin bow across it imprinted with WE'LL MISS YOU! in gold.

"Didn't they get the message wrong?" Loretta asked.

I opened the card. *Don't worry, Jane, our destinies are linked. I'll take care of you anywhere you go. Love, Your Secret Admirer.*

Something must have shown in my face because Loretta shook her head. "Don't go trying to say this is a threat. It's hearts. Hearts aren't a threat. Two interlocking hearts means love."

"Of course. You're right."

My mother called to say she and Joe wouldn't be in until later because Annie was running a slight fever. As I hung up, Dr. Tan, in yet another tan suit, appeared.

He was jolliness in person. "Good morning, Miss Freeman. I hear they've caught the driver of the car that ran you down."

"If you believe it."

He appeared to work hard to stifle a sigh. "You don't?"

"I remembered someone leaning over me while I was trapped in the rosebush and saying, 'You're a goner, Jane Freeman.' The Barney Brothers—the convenience store robbers—didn't know my name, so it couldn't have been them."

"Or perhaps this is another fictional memory. Another clue in our arsenal."

"Why wouldn't I want it to be the Barney Brothers?"

"We're still working on that. Any more delusions? Hallucinations?"

"The killer called last night and told me I would meet him today."

"That's interesting," he said. Pretending like he believed me. "When?"

"He called at ten minutes to ten."

"Well, then, we'll have to keep an especially close eye on you. Ten minutes to ten. Does the number ten have any significance to you?"

Oh, that was bad. How had I not thought of it? "My birthday is on October 10."

He looked at me with surprise for a moment, then went back to his notes. "And how do you feel today? Do you feel like today is momentous in any way?"

"Apart from meeting my killer? No."

"What about the ring? Has it given you any more trouble? Moving from one finger to the other?"

"No. Because I'm not crazy." I wasn't. *I wasn't.*

"Of course not." He closed the chart and left, promising to come back later.

Officer Rowley was my next visitor.

"Have the convenience store robbers confessed yet?" I asked.

"No. But they've changed their story somewhat. They claim they saw your purse and phone lying by the road and that's why they stopped. According to them, they didn't even see you. And our forensics team found this in a gutter near the rosebush." She handed me a photo. "It appears to be a clasp from something. Is it yours?" It was a picture of interlocking jeweled Cs.

"It's definitely not mine."

"Have you seen it before?" she asked.

"Yes."

"Where?"

"On a mannequin in the window of the Chanel store in the Short Hills mall," I supplied helpfully.

It was true. She hadn't asked where I'd seen it *last*. I'd learned that cooperating didn't help me. And the clasp had triggered an idea.

Yoo-hoo, Jane.

An idea that might just solve everything. But I needed to ask some questions first.

"I've been authorized to give you this," she said, handing me an evidence bag with my phone inside.

It was weird seeing it like that. For so long I'd felt tethered to my phone, as though I was nothing without it. Now it was just an object.

But seeing it in the evidence bag gave me another idea. "Do you have a photo of the scene? From when I was still in the rosebush? I'd like to see what it looked like."

"Why?"

"I guess I'm kind of vain," I said, figuring she'd believe it. "And I'm a photographer."

"I'll see if I can get you a copy." She stood.

"Thanks. And could you ask Pete to come help me if you see him?"

By the time Pete appeared fifteen minutes later, it was after ten and I was almost ready to try getting myself into the wheelchair. "Where have you been? I've been waiting."

He was squinting at the light from the windows, and if it wasn't for the unwrinkled quality of the wood-grain-patterned button-down he was wearing, I would have thought he'd slept in his car. There were dark smudges beneath his eyes and he had a light sprinkling of stubble on his chin and cheeks.

"I didn't know we had a date."

"Your shirt's really groovy," I said.

He eyed me narrowly. "What's wrong with you?"

"Nothing. I'm just looking forward to our time together."

"No, you're not. Neither am I."

"Will you take me to see a friend of mine who's a patient here?"

"No."

"Are you hung over?"

"No."

"Because you seem like you might be. The way your eyes are all tiny and bloodshot. And you're sort of touchy."

"I'm not. My eyes aren't tiny and bloodshot."

"Like a little rabbit. Or maybe it's a pig. What has really small beady red eyes?" I goaded him.

"Why are you talking?"

"I'm just trying to be friendly." I smiled, which hurt the cuts on my face.

"Be less friendly."

"I will if you take me to see Elsa Blanchard. You never told me where you get your shirts. Do you shop for them in Manhattan?"

"Is this a bribe? If I do what you want, you'll be quiet?"

"Smart boy."

"Fine." He maneuvered me into the wheelchair. "We'll go see Elsa Blanchard."

"You're getting—"

"Shhh."

"I was just going to give you a compliment," I whispered.

"The best compliments are conveyed in the form of silence."

He started wheeling me down the hall toward the elevator. The girl with the braids and the coloring book and her grandmother were gone, but the husky man with the Gatorade was back. He was reading the *Post*, but I had the sensation that he was watching us as we went by.

"What room is Elsa in?" Pete asked.

"I don't know. I thought you could find out."

He parked me in the middle of traffic and lumbered over to a computer. When he came back, he turned the chair around and started steering me back to my room.

"Where are we going?"

"Your friend is in the psych ward. The locked part."

"So? Doesn't that just make it more exciting?"

"No. It makes it impossible."

"*Impossible* is just another word for 'loser who gives up.'"

He kept pushing me toward my room.

"Did you really drop out of high school?"

"Yes."

"Why?"

"To join the pro-Frisbee tour."

I burst out laughing. I couldn't help it, it was just too random. "Don't make me laugh, it hurts my face."

"Believe me, it wasn't intentional. Hearing you laugh hurts my head."

"So what's the real reason you're not in school?"

He came around and bent to get his eyes at my level and with his hands on the arms of my chair said, "Beautiful, are you doing this just to be annoying, this conversational hit man act, or is seeing this person actually important to you?"

My heart started to pound. *Beautiful? Do you really think I'm beautiful?* I wanted to ask. *Don't be ridiculous,* I told myself. *He probably says that to everyone. You're making a fool of yourself.*

Instead I asked, "What's a conversational hit man?"

"You know, hit man protocol?"

I shook my head.

"When a hit man is aiming for something behind a window, he needs two bullets. One to drill a hole in the glass and then another to go through the hole and hit the target."

"That's like me how?"

"You ask easy questions until boom! a hard one sneaks through and gets me where it counts." He pointed to his forehead. "Which today is right here. So, are you just trying to torment me or does this Elsa matter to you somehow?" He was looking at me so seriously, his blue eyes moving slowly over my face. He smelled like fabric softener and soap and something ineffable that had to be just him. Both his gaze on mine and his effect on my pulse were serious.

What are you thinking? I demanded of myself. *He has no interest in you. You have a date with Scott. And a killer possibly after you.* I blinked to clear my mind. "She matters."

He took a deep breath, muttered, "I'm going to regret this," stepped back around the chair, and pushed me back toward the elevator.

"Then—"

"Silence."

The silence continued up to the eighth floor.

There was a formidable nurse on duty just in front of the elevator, sitting next to a locked and secured door.

"My father asked me to bring this patient up so she could see a friend? Elsa Blanchard, room 808?" he said with an ingratiating smile.

"Miss Blanchard's protocol is no visitors."

"I'm just doing what my father asked. You can call him if you want." Pete looked at his wrist. "Ten twenty-five. He should be on the eighth hole right now."

The nurse pursed her lips, thinking, then made up her mind. "Go ahead, dear."

"Thanks."

When the door closed behind us, I said, "You're good."

"I told you, women just fall in love with me."

"What do you want to be when you grow up?"

"A lawyer."

"My mother says you were caught with drugs and that's why you're under house arrest."

"I thought you were being silen—ah, here we are. The end of our tour."

Elsa's room was like mine except it had no windows and everything was bolted down, including her, onto the bed. She looked up when Pete pushed me in and I was shocked. I'd never seen Elsa without thick eyeliner and red lipstick on before, but now she was wearing no makeup and it made her look incredibly young and innocent. Her cheeks seemed soft like a baby's and her eyes were immense. Ignoring the white bandage that secured two electrodes to her forehead, she looked better now than I'd seen her in ages.

She studied us and finally said, "Are you real or are you a hallucination? They've got me on so much stuff, I can't tell anymore."

I almost hugged her.

"I'm real."

She was a little twitchy. "Are you sure? Your face looks nuts."

Pete cleared his throat. "I don't know how long we have before Nurse Nosy out there decides to try my father—"

"—but you said he was playing golf."

"My father loathes golf. He's in his office. Which is why you might want to cut the meet and greet short and do whatever you came here for."

I looked at Elsa. "What happened after the party? How did you get here?"

Her eyes went to the corner of the room and her head bopped back and forth. In a singsongy voice she said, "What do you call a plant that's out of place?"

She wasn't looking at me, so I didn't answer. Then her eyes zipped toward me. "What do you call it?" she demanded.

"I don't know."

"A weed. Same thing with thoughts. Thoughts out of place, they call them crazy." Her gaze was intense. "But I'm not crazy, Freeman."

"I know that."

She started nodding to herself. "I'm not crazy. It's the drugs. They make me a little loco in the coco if you know what I mean."

I heard Pete stifle a laugh.

"I'm not kidding, man."

"What happened after the party?" I asked.

"Party. More like a meeting of the drama club. Everyone yelling and crying. *That* was crazy. I had to get out of there. Had to ease on down, ease on down the road." She started humming, her head bopping. "Ease on down—did you know my uncle wrote that song?"

"No," I said.

Pete tapped his wrist where a watch would be.

"You got in your car," I prompted.

In one big breath she said, "I got in my car and I drove away and I saw something by the side of the road so I pulled over and went to look." She inhaled. "It was you, Freeman. In that bush. Freeman freeman freeman," she repeated. "You weren't free then, were you?" She started to laugh.

"And then?"

"You looked kind of cute snuggled up there all cozy, but I thought you should probably move. So I bent down to try to wake you up."

"Did you say, 'Yoo-hoo, Jane'?"

"Yes!" She brightened up and her eyes focused for the first time. "I totally did. I remember that."

"And, 'You're a goner'?"

"I said that too!" She looked pleased, like a child discovering a new toy. "When I couldn't wake you up. You were kind of moaning and saying, 'It hurts, please help,' so I knew you needed help but not my kind of help, oh no. Big strong help. From manly men." She looked at Pete. "You wouldn't have done at all. Not strong enough."

"Thanks."

"Did you call for help?" I asked.

"I tried, right? I looked for my cell phone, but I couldn't find it, so I started driving. And driving. I was looking for something, but it was raining and so hard to see and then—" She focused again. "A pay phone. That's what I was looking for. But I found a post instead. Ran right into it. Oops, my bad." She laughed. "But it worked, right? Because then all these manly men came, all these par-a-medics." She sounded out the word, then stopped. "Does that mean they are paranormal medics? Like vampires?"

"No," Pete said.

She took that in for a moment. "Well, I told the par-a-medics that they should go help you and not me. I kept telling them over and over, 'Go help my friend, go help my friend.' But they didn't understand." She looked at Pete again. "You're sure they're not vampires?"

"Yes."

One of her legs had started to vibrate a little. "Because they didn't understand at all. They kept saying, 'There's no one else in the car with you, ma'am,' and I said, 'I know that, silly, it's my friend who needs help,' back and forth like that over and over and over." She lolled her head around in circles as she said the last part. Then it snapped to attention. "They wouldn't listen, so I slapped one of them." She wrinkled up her nose. "Not even hard, just a teensy slap. Like you would give a Chihuahua. Hee hee. But he didn't like that. He was such a bully, he locked me up. I think he also must have taken my pearl necklace."

"It broke. The police found the clasp by the rosebush."

"Tell them to give it back. It was custom made for me by Karl." She looked at Pete, flirtatious now. "Karl is a personal friend of mine."

"Ah."

"Aha!" she said, and looked at him expectantly. "Now you say 'ah ha ha ha.' Like a game."

Pete said to me instead, "We should be moving along."

"Don't go!" Elsa looked panicked. "Stay awhile. Have some tea and crumpets."

It was a little scary to see her like this, so out of it. I hoped like hell it wasn't how I looked to other people. "We really have to leave," I told her. "But you've been super-helpful."

Despite her craziness, that was more true than she could know. Because now I knew who had said I was a goner. And I knew it wasn't someone trying to kill me. Which meant the Barney Brothers could be the ones who hit me. And even though it also meant I'd made up the calls—no doubt because of my medication—I felt a huge sense of relief.

"But—you haven't seen my photos yet."

"What photos?"

"The pictures from the parrrrteee," she sang. She cocked her head toward Pete. "I know you want to see them, don't you, bad boy."

"Peter would love to see your pictures," I answered for him.

He looked at the clock. It was one minute to eleven. "Quickly."

Elsa leered at him and pointed with her right hand to a camera sitting on a shelf by the wall. "Bring it to me."

He did and she started flipping one handed through the images on the screen in the back. "These are all the ones from the party." She made a coy face. "Don't show that to Jane."

"What?" I asked.

Peter held the camera for me to see. It showed David with Sloan on his lap. Her eyes looked glazed and her head was lolling back like she was unconscious. Charming.

Elsa took the camera back and flipped some more, humming to herself as she did. "Ooh, this is a good one."

Pete tilted the screen so I could see it. It showed Langley on her hands and knees on the floor looking like a dog searching for a bone.

"Woof woof," Elsa said.

"What was she doing?" I asked.

"Reverting to her true self?" Elsa laughed at her joke but suddenly went somber. She looked more sane, more focused than she had since we'd come in. "I'm sorry I took this one. I shouldn't have." Pete held the camera toward me.

The screen was with me sprawled against a wall with my eyes only partially open. My forehead was propped on my left hand and my right was held up toward the camera to ward it off.

My friendship ring wasn't on either hand.

Apparently this wasn't the end of my questions after all.

"That was unusual," Pete said as he wheeled me back to my room. "You really have some very interesting friends. I'll have to watch that DVD your pals made after all."

"She's not normally like that."

"That's a relief. Did you learn what you wanted to?"

"I don't know." How could a ring vanish and then reappear on the wrong finger? "Have you ever felt like you're losing your mind? Or like everyone else around you is?"

"Yep."

I took a long ragged breath as he maneuvered my chair into the elevator.

He cleared his throat. As the doors of the elevator closed, he said, "The drugs I was found with, the ones your mom mentioned, belonged to a girl I knew."

"You don't have to tell me this. It was none of my business."

"I want to. Besides, it's relevant. This girl was trying to get clean and she asked me to go through her place and find all her stashes so she couldn't relapse. I went through everything, you name it, and even though I found a pharmacy worth of crap, I knew I kept missing something. Finally I found it, her last two grams of coke. She'd hidden it in her dog's prosthetic leg."

I craned my neck around to look at him. His jaw was tight and his hair was a little ruffled and for a moment I was distracted by how hot he was. Then I remembered what I meant to say. "You weren't kidding about that story?"

He put his hand on my head and turned it back around. "Eyes forward. No twisting in the chair. And nope, I wasn't kidding. Totally true. And you didn't believe me." He sounded hurt.

"That's not fair," I protested. "It sounded—specious."

The elevator doors opened and he pushed me out. "I'm kidding. But my father doesn't believe me about the drugs. He thinks I'm trying to pull the proverbial 'just holding them for a friend.'"

"But you really were."

"Impossible to prove."

"Why can't you have her tell your dad?"

"Him take the word of a junkie? You've got to be kidding. Besides, she's not around anymore."

"What happened? Did she get clean and move?"

"She was clean for three months. Then she disappeared and I sort of doubt it was to live a clean awesome life."

"I'm sorry."

"Yeah, me too." His voice had a note of strain in it that was different than his usual self-mockery, and incredibly touching.

"And now you're the one who's in trouble. So it wasn't worth it."

"It's always worth it to do the right thing, even if you don't succeed." He laughed, deep and sexy. The strain was gone. "God, I sound like an asshole. Plus without that, what excuse would I have for my lousy relationship with my father?"

"Are you saying you like your bad relationship with your dad?"

"People find patterns—the familiar—comforting, even if it's unhealthy. It takes someone really brave to confess they're wrong and try to make it right."

I let that sink in for a moment. "So is that why you want to go to law school? To make sure people get heard properly?"

"Could be. Or maybe I'm just a bastard and I want to make an obscene amount of money by milking other people's misery."

"I'm frightened by how excited you sound when you say that." I couldn't help but smile, no matter how much it hurt.

Chapter 30

Scott was pacing my room when we got back. "Where were you? I was so worried." He glanced at the clock. It was a quarter after eleven.

"No way," Pete said, stopping at the door and pulling me back. "No way am I leaving you alone with this guy."

"He's my friend. He's fine." I grinned at Scott and gave him a little wave.

"Are you nuts? He's way too good looking. Get lost, buddy."

Scott laughed. "He's kidding, right?" he said to me.

"I assume so. You never know. Pete," I said over my shoulder, "it's okay, you can go."

He shook his head ruefully, said, "And I thought *I* was handsome," leaned down to whisper to me, "Don't say I didn't warn you," brushed his hands as if washing them of the matter, and disappeared.

Scott watched him go. "Who is that guy?" He started walking toward me, slowly, as a smile spread over his face. "Never mind, I don't care. God, I'm crazy about you. Even looking so perfectly imperfect, like this."

"I'm glad," I said. I smiled, but I was momentarily aware of something very slight tugging it down in the corners.

Scott bent over and put his hands on the arms of the wheelchair and brought his lips to mine. "And you taste good too." The mental tugging vanished.

After a little while he pulled away. "How are your toes?"

"Tingly," I reported. "Also wriggly."

"Outstanding. Think you're ready for an outing?"

"Sure. Where are we going?"

"There's a small executive dining room on the second floor that's not in use today since it's a holiday," he said. "It happens to be perfect for a picnic."

"How did you swing that?"

He winked. "I have my ways." I could imagine the entire scheduling staff of the hospital capitulating to his ways. "I've already gotten the okay from Loretta as long as you take your cell phone. If you're ready, we can go."

"I wish I had something a little less hospital chic to wear."

"Don't worry, I love you for your mind." Something about him saying "I love you," even just as a joke, sent a weird twinge through my body. I mean, we were friends, and maybe Kate had been right about him having a thing for me all the way back in the fall, but we'd only kissed for the first time *yesterday*. It wasn't like either of us knew what this was.

Scott installed me in the posh executive dining room and went to the kitchen down the hall to get what he called "provisions." While he was gone, my cell phone rang.

The caller ID flashed David. My heart leaped up for a second, out of habit, and then thudded. I debated about answering it, remembered how he had looked in the doorway, and finally gave in.

"Hey, babe. How are you feeling today?"

"Better."

"Listen, I know things got rough yesterday, but I wanted to tell you, I forgive you. I know you're just stressed. But we're too good together to let this fade."

"You forgive me?"

"Of course, babe."

The old me would have let that slide, not wanted to say something upsetting. The new me was angry. "I didn't do anything wrong. I can't believe you got together with Sloan just because Elsa told you about the internship."

"Internship? What are you talking about?'

"My internship this summer? In the city."

"Are you on some new meds?"

"What did Elsa tell you? That made you ditch me and get together with someone else?"

"Why are you still harping on that? Water under the bridge, babe."

"I just want to know."

"She came to find you because your little buddy Scott was outside waiting for you. I couldn't just sit there and be humiliated, could I?"

He went on, but I wasn't listening. *Scott* had been at the party? *That* was why David was so upset—he thought I'd been sneaking around with Scott behind his back.

Wait. If Scott was at the party, why hadn't he told me? Why had he pretended he wasn't there? Why—

Scott had somehow managed to come up behind me silently. He took the cell phone from my hand and ended the call.

"I know you had to bring it, but I don't think we'll be wanting any intrusions."

His voice sounded different to me. Tighter. "I want it to be just you and me. All alone."

He turned my wheelchair so it was facing him and put his hands on my legs. I realized I was starting to regain feeling. I couldn't move them, but I could feel the slight pressure of his palms.

His deep-brown eyes were glittering strangely. "I've been waiting so long for this, Jane. So long to have you all to myself. Look, I have a surprise for you."

He pointed to a series of photos arrayed on the table. One of them showed a Kleenex, another a straw wrapper. There was a lipstick kiss blotted on a Spanish flash card, a sock with a hole in the toe, and a wilted rose. "Do you know what those are?"

I shook my head.

His breathing was uneven. "They're my trophies. Of you."

I remembered what Ollie had said about Scott. That he kept creepy trophies of one of his girlfriends. Had that been me?

"This one"—Scott pointed to the photo of the white paper tube—"is the paper from your straw that you squished the day we were in New York. This"—pointing at the one of the Spanish flash cards—"you dropped one day when you had coffee with friends at Starbucks. Some of this I had to get from your trash."

"You went through my trash?" I felt like I was going to throw up. How had I not seen this? How had I ignored all those warnings? Scott. Scott had been at the party.

He cocked his head. "Why don't you look happy?"

"Why did you try to kill me?"

"Kill you? I love you. You're—you're everything. Look at all the time and effort I've put into learning about you. I know everything about you." He reached for me.

"Don't touch me. If you come any closer, I'll scream."

He laughed at that, a laugh with a cold edge. "Who would hear? As you've noticed, it's pretty isolated here."

"You were there that night. At the party. You lied to me."

"You mean the night you wouldn't return my calls." His voice got tight. "The night I called you four times, but you couldn't bother to get back to me?"

"I'm sorry, I didn't know it was important."

In an instant the tension eased. "That's okay. I know it was hard then. With loser David still in the picture. Do you know what it was like those nights sitting outside your house knowing he was in your room with you? But that won't happen again." His eyes burned into mine with all his wonted intensity. But now instead of being intriguing, it was unnerving. Very.

"No." *Keep him calm,* I told myself. "Of course not. Why were you calling me?"

"I'd heard some Livingston guys trying to score roofies for the party to spike girls' drinks, that there was going to be some kind of competition over who could hit the most girls, and I wanted to warn you to be careful."

"Why didn't you leave me a voice mail about that?"

He smiled sheepishly. "I guess I also wanted to hear your voice. But you wouldn't call me back or reply to my texts. I was going to your house when you passed me in the back of Langley's red car."

"How did you know what kind of car Langley drives?"

"I know all about you. Everything. You and photography are my main fields of study. And I'm a very quick study. I know that you don't like it when David kisses you on the neck, even though you pretend you do. Especially at the movies."

Scott's eyes went to my neck and then back to my mouth. I felt completely nauseous. "You see. I am an expert on Jane Freeman. Which means I know exactly how to make you happy."

I pushed my disgust down. The only important thing to do now was find out what else he knew. "I'm impressed," I said, hoping my voice didn't sound as fake as it felt. "What did you do when you saw Langley's car?"

"I did a U-turn, followed you out to Deal, and parked outside the party, trying to decide what to do."

"Why didn't you just come in?"

"Not really my scene, J. J., you know that. But then Elsa came out and tried to get me to make out with her."

"Elsa?"

"She's been hitting on me since camp. Gotten to the ugly stage where she says, 'You're waiting for Jane, but you'll never have her,' and shit like that. I knew she'd be wrong." He reached out to stroke my hair.

I stopped his hand. "What happened then?"

He looked at me quizzically. "But you love having your hair stroked."

I felt like my stomach was trying to crawl up my throat. I swallowed, hard. "In a little while. Tell me, what happened with Elsa?"

"I told her to tell you I was outside and wanted to talk to you, but you didn't come back. I was just about to storm the battlements myself when I saw you come out with one of your girlfriends, so I assumed you were okay and I took off. But man, I felt bad the next day when I heard what happened. I knew I should have stayed. That you needed me."

"What girlfriend did I come out with?"

"One of the ones wearing wings. Why do you rich people dress up so weird anyway?"

"But which one?"

"I couldn't see. It was dark and raining." He got up and started pacing. "Why are you giving me the third degree? I left after that. And I've done nothing but help you. I care for you so much." He bent to kiss me and I pulled away.

"What's wrong, J. J.?"

"This. What we're doing. I can't go through with it."

"What are you talking about?"

"I'm not going out with you. It was a mistake. I was doing it for the wrong reasons. Whatever there is between us is better as friends."

He looked like he'd been slapped, even started to rub his cheek. "You don't mean that. You can't mean that. We're perfect together." He paused and got a wild expression in his eye. "Wait a second." Grabbing my phone, he checked the caller ID. "I knew it. That bastard, David. The 'stay soft' man. He called you and you're getting back together with him."

"No. It has nothing to do with him. You—you stalked me."

He laughed. "Stalked you? I tried to *protect* you. I memorized you, learned everything I could about you so I could love you. It's exactly what a good photographer does for his subject. Is that a crime?"

"I just don't feel the same way about you as you do about me."

His chiseled handsome face showed incredulity and something else. I saw a bead of sweat starting to form at his temple. "No. You don't feel, period. You're terrified of feeling, aren't you?" He bent and put his face near mine. His expression was mean. "Scared of getting carried away. That's why everything in your photos is cold and dead. Because *you're* cold and dead. Or close enough."

"I'm sorry, Scott. It's just not right."

"Not right? Do you want to know what's not right?"

He was really sweating now and his eyes were bulging out. He was no longer handsome at all. He went to a big backpack he'd propped in a chair and pushed things around inside it until he found what he was looking for. "I'm not the bad guy here. I'm the good guy. You want to know who the bad guy is? Look at that."

He threw a piece of paper on the table. "I hope you're happy," he said, storming out. Leaving me alone with a Xerox copy of an auto-body repair estimate from the day after the party for an Audi A4 bumper registered to David Tisch.

Vehicle hit a post is what it said. I realized it was true. I'd been dumb as a post anyway.

"It looks like you were kneeling in the middle of the street, waiting for the car to hit you," Officer Rowley said the first day I met her. "There are generally only two explanations for that kind of behavior."

But she was wrong. There was a third. You might kneel in the street without moving if you knew the person driving the car and had every reason to believe they'd stop.

Chapter 31

I **knew I should** call for help. Reach out and push any of the buttons on the phone in the middle of the conference table and ask for Officer Rowley or Loretta or anyone. The news about David's car—no wonder he'd come with Ollie that first day—made the whole convenience store theory impossible. And the other thing Scott had said, about me being outside with one of the girls I'd come with. "Girls with wings." That could only be Langley or Kate.

If Scott saw me come out of the house with one of them, it meant that Ollie had lied. He didn't follow me out of the house. But someone else did.

The harder something is for you to handle, the more deeply it will be buried, Dr. Tan had said.

I'm at the door of the bedroom. It's blocked by someone, someone is standing in front of it.

But not blocking it. Holding it open. It's Kate, Kate who is holding it open, Kate who says, "You want to find your precious David? Look, there he is." Kate who points to David and Sloan on the bed.

I'm stunned. "How could you do this?" I ask.

"I thought you'd want to know."

"Like this? Really?"

I take off the friendship ring she'd given me and throw it in her face.

The floor of the hallway writhes beneath me. Somehow I make it outside.

"Jane, wait."

Kate is following me. She has mascara in streaks down her face like she's been crying and there is a rip at the neck of her fairy costume. Kate is now saying, "I'm sorry. That was brutal. I shouldn't have done that. You're not the only one who got hurt tonight."

"Don't lie." I'm furious. Furious with David. Furious with myself. But I blame her. "You've been trying to break us up all along. Well, you succeeded. Nice work."

"That's not what I—"

I kiss her, hard on the mouth, biting her lip with my teeth. When I pull away, she is rigid. "Is that what you wanted?" I demand. "Are you happy now?"

Her fingers go to her lip. It's bleeding.

"Do you want me to do it again? Is that what all of this is about?"

The fury in her eyes is searing. "I hate you, you bitch. You'll pay for that." She spins around and runs back into the party.

That's when Ollie had shown up. That's why I listened to him. Because I'd been too stunned to move.

"I should have stopped," Kate had said. Did she run me over? And then retrieve the friendship ring to put on my finger so no one would know we'd had a fight? And when she told David to leave me alone, was that so he wouldn't ask any more questions and stir up my memory?

"You'll pay for that," Kate had said. And she'd had every right to be angry, I realized. At the beach, last summer, I'd used her. I'd thought I was going along with what she wanted, but it wasn't that simple. I was taking what I needed. Love. A sense of being important to someone. I thought it was okay—it was her idea after all. But it wasn't okay. Because I'd known it meant more to her than it did to me and I took it anyway. I owed her an apology.

If I lived.

The hospital phone on the table was ringing. Without thinking, I reached for it. "Hello?"

"Does she haunt you?"

"Who?"

"Bonnie, of course. The girl you killed."

"I didn't kill her."

"Would she be dead if it wasn't for you?"

No one except the people who had been in my room with me the night before could have known about that.

"It's time for you to pay for what you've done, Jane. Or what you didn't do."

And me. I knew.

Which meant I had to be hallucinating. This was all in my head. It was all—

"I hope you're ready to die."

I slammed the receiver down.

No.

It wasn't possible. I didn't want to die. It wasn't a hallucination—

Was it?

—which meant someone was on their way to kill me.

But no one could have found you. No one except Scott and Loretta even knew where you were.

I didn't make this up. I didn't—

Are you sure?

—want to die.

Stop!

I put my hands over my ears to stop all the voices. It was too hard; I couldn't take any more. I picked up the phone and started pushing buttons wildly until Loretta's voice said, "What are you doing, sweetheart?" next to me.

"Oh, thank God." I put the phone down. "How did you get here?"

"Scott came up to your room to tell me you'd had a bit of a falling-out, but he was worried about leaving you down here alone, so—"

If Scott had been with Loretta, then he couldn't have been the caller.

If there was a caller.

"We have to get out of here, Loretta." I used my arms to move the chair toward the door, but I got stuck between the dining table and the wall. "Get this furniture out of my way."

"Calm down, sweetheart."

I gripped her wrist. "He called again, Loretta. The killer."

She put a hand on my forehead. "You're feverish."

I ducked my head away. "That doesn't matter. Someone is coming to kill me. I have to get out of here. Loretta, you have to help me."

"Of course, sweetheart."

I turned myself toward the edge of the table. If she wasn't going to help, I'd find a way out myself. Palms pressed on the surface, I tried to stand. "There was no face. In the bathroom mirror I had no face. There were just hands."

"Sit down, angel."

My arms were shaking with the effort. "Don't you see what that means, Loretta? Just an empty place. I know what they did."

"Let's get you back into the chair."

"Kate. Kate said I would pay for what I've done. And David's car hit a post."

"Sit, sweetheart."

"I'm not crazy. I'm not hallucinating. There's no time. This is it. That's what the killer said. It's time to die."

"Okay, sweetheart."

"We have to leave. The killer is coming for me. No place is safe. I didn't drink anything, but I got drugged anyway. Don't touch anything. Anything could be poison. Don't you see?"

"I see. Sit down and I'll wheel you out of here."

A wave of relief swept over me. I'd gotten through to her. "Yes. Thank you." I collapsed into the chair, so happy I was sobbing. "Thank you, Loretta."

Out of the corner of my eye I was vaguely aware of her doing something with her hand, and then I heard her voice into the phone, "This is Loretta Bonner in the West Executive dining room. I have a code four."

"No." I tried to hang up the phone. "He'll find us first. We have to go."

She pushed my hand aside. "Get me security and Dr. Tan stat."

She didn't believe me. Because of the medicine. She thought the medicine was making me hallucinate.

That's when I saw what had been the solution to all of this, all the uncertainty all along. I could know! I could know if I was mad or not. I started clawing at the IV in my arm. "Take this out. Then we can be sure."

"What are you doing?"

"Making sure. Don't you see? We can know." I was so excited to have thought of it I was laughing.

"Know what?"

"If the calls are real or if it's just this, this poison, that's been going into my veins." I smiled at her and kept pulling on the IV. "It's so obvious."

She wrapped a strong hand around my wrist to stop me. "You need to calm down, sweetheart."

"No. This is what I need to do. Help me, Loretta. I want to know what's real and what isn't. Get it out of me."

Loretta was leaning over me holding my arms down. "Stay still, sweetheart."

"It's got to go. It's got to end. It's time for this to end." If she was going to hold my hands down, I'd bite the IV out. "I'm done. I want it to go." I twisted my neck to get it near my arm.

Loretta pushed my head back. "You have to stop this, sweetheart. Stop it and it will all be okay."

"You're lying!" I twisted away from her grip, my hand suddenly strong, and tried to raise myself out of my chair. "You're against me. You're all against me."

I didn't see the needle until she'd already plunged it into my arm.

Chapter 32

Whatever Loretta gave me knocked me out cold. Opening my eyes, I didn't recognize anything around me. I was in a completely different room. There were no windows, so instead of resting on the windowsill all my tokens of popularity had been moved from room 403 and placed on a shelf across from my bed. My face itched and when I went to scratch it, I couldn't move my arms. At first I thought I was paralyzed again, but then I realized it was worse. I was in restraints.

I tugged at them, but they held. "Hello?" I called out. The door to my room was closed and the window had louvers on the outside. "Is anyone there? Hello?"

A key turned in a lock and my mother and Dr. Tan came in.

"Oh, Jane." My mother was weeping openly. The entire pretense of perfection was gone. "Oh, darling, baby. What is going on tell me what to do I'm so sorry we didn't come this morning first thing Annie was sick oh darling just—"

"Mrs. Freeman, if you wouldn't mind." Dr. Tan tried to step in front of her, but she shot him a look.

"In a moment, doctor. Right now I need to talk to my daughter." She turned back to me. "Baby, I am so sorry. I feel like I failed you."

She put her arms around me and hugged me tight. I had the sensation of falling I'd had before, but this time it was good. Great. "Mommy," I said, trying to lift my arms to hug her back.

She pulled away. Her face was so full of love and trust and kindness for me. I wanted to brush the tears away. "Don't cry, Mommy."

"I love you so much, Jane."

"I love you too." I tried to move my arms again. "Where am I? Why am I tied down?"

Her smile was still there, but it faltered for a moment. She brushed hair off my forehead and rested her hand on my cheek. "We had you moved to the eighth floor."

"I'm in the psych ward? Why? I'm not crazy."

Dr. Tan came and stood next to her now. "If you'll allow me, Mrs. Freeman?" he said, and she moved slightly but didn't let go of my hand. She squeezed it, and I squeezed hers back. We were in this together. I was so happy I almost didn't pay attention when Dr. Tan said, "You had a rather severe psychotic episode, Jane. You tried to pull out your IVs and started talking about ending it all."

"No." I shook my head. My mother's hand in mine soothed me. I smiled at her. This was going to be fine, I just needed to explain. "You have it all wrong. I wanted to stop the medication so I could prove to all of you I wasn't hallucinating, that someone was trying to kill me. Or to prove to myself that they were hallucinations." I kept my voice even, rational. "One way or another, removing the medicine would clear it up. That's what I wanted to stop, the medicine. The poison. I want my mind back, my life back."

"And we're here to help you with that," Dr. Tan assured me.

"Good," I said. "Then can we start with removing the arm restraints?"

"Maybe in a little while."

Hadn't he been listening? I tried again. "But if I'm right and someone is trying to kill me"—I said, pronouncing each word carefully—"having me strapped in place will make it very easy for them."

Dr. Tan's eyes burrowed into mine. "Who is trying to kill you? Can you tell us someone specific?"

I looked at my mother, but her eyes were on the psychologist, not me. That was when I realized this wasn't going how I expected. "I don't know. We've been over this. I think it must be a friend of mine. Someone very close."

Dr. Tan patted my arm. "Until you figure it out, you'll be safe in here. There are guards on your door now and no one can get in or out without appropriate authorization."

"That won't stop this killer. I have to get out of here." I was trying to wriggle out of the leather cuff around the hand my mother wasn't holding. If I could just get that free—

"Why would someone want to kill you?" Dr. Tan asked in his maddeningly even voice.

"I. Don't. Know," I said, gritting my teeth. We were wasting time. "But this must all be part of their master plan."

"They're omnipotent?"

I didn't even have to see his face to know how insane that sounded. "Yes. No. God." I started to cry.

He addressed my mother. "This is normal after a psychic strain. The best thing we can do right now is let her rest."

She nodded and gave me a smile. The same smile as before, filled with love. Only this time she said, "This is a good place for you,

Jane. No one can hurt you in here. And you can't hurt—anyone."

"I don't want to hurt anyone," I said, but I realized that hadn't been what she meant. She meant hurt myself.

"I wasn't trying to kill myself, Mommy," I said, pleading with her. "You have to believe me."

She looked at me with the saddest face I'd ever seen. "Dr. Tan says that dredging up everything about Bonnie yesterday might have—" Tears rolled down her face. She bent down and held my hand against her cheek. "Oh, Janey, I'm so sorry we weren't here this morning. I'm not leaving, not going anywhere until you're better. Sweetheart, you have so much to live for. So many people who love you."

"Please have them move me back to my room. I don't like it here."

"It's just for a little while, darling. Until—until we're sure you're past this."

"Don't leave me. Please."

"I won't."

"Mrs. Freeman, I really recommend—" Dr. Tan began, but my mother shut him down.

She stood up, squared her shoulders and announced, "My daughter needs me and I'm going to stay with her."

They must have given me a strong sedative because I don't remember much after that. Falling asleep with my hand in my mother's, even if my wrist was manacled, was the most wonderful feeling in the world.

When I woke up again, she was gone, but the feeling of well-being persisted. This waking up was totally different than it had been four days ago.

God, had it really been only four days?

I thought about everything that had happened, the writing on

the mirror when no one was there, the paranoia about my room being bugged when there was no bug, the phone calls that no one but
me ever even heard ringing, the secret-admirer presents that everyone but me thought were nice. The weird looks and innuendos between my friends, which all seemed sinister but all had completely
innocuous explanations. The only thing wrong, the only thing that
made it weird in every example was me.

How did I get here? Four days ago I'd been a perfectly normal girl
and now—I stared at my wrist, held to the bed by a thick leather strap.
It looked like something out of a bad movie. My hands were fists and
as I unflexed them, I saw the friendship ring on my right hand.

There. That was one thing—the only thing—I could be sure I
hadn't made up. My ring. Not only had it moved, but at one point
it had vanished.

That sounded impossible, but it was true. And if that was true,
everything else could be true as well.

Which meant someone *was* coming to kill me.

*Don't worry, Jane, our destinies are linked. I'll take care of you
anywhere you go,* my secret admirer had said.

"Mom!" I shouted. "Mommy!"

No answer. Given the eerie silence in the room, I had to imagine it was completely soundproofed.

I pulled against the arm restraints, arching to get out of them,
but there was nothing I could do. I was looking around to see if there
was anything I could grab when I noticed the glassine envelope on
the table next to my bed. Looking closely, I saw that Officer Rowley
had come through with the crime-scene photo.

It was stark yet beautiful.

That was the first thing I noticed about it. It showed that moment just before dawn, when the world turned monochrome and

everything was subsumed under a blanket of blue-gray light. The streetlights had gone off, making the street a still gray ribbon scarred with two black marks trailing from the upper left of the picture to the lower right. In the background, blurry, large houses hunkered down, streaked dark from rain. In the foreground and slightly to the right, set in blue-gray grass, was a fantastic bush. It looked like something from a fairy tale, a witch cursed into an alternate form, gnarled fingers reaching for the sky. At the center lay a girl.

I looked at the photo as though it wasn't me, searching for clues. Shreds of tulle skirt were tangled among the branches blowing in the morning breeze like tiny flags. A ceramic rabbit, a mother duck followed by five tiny ducklings, and a squirrel playing the flute stood silent guard around the girl. One of her legs was bent up; the other jutted out of the bush dangling a Prada platform shoe. Her left hand was under her and the right one, with a friendship ring on the index finger, reached up as though to pluck the single deep-red rose that hung above her—the only spot of color in the image. There was dark hair feathering over half her face. Her body was covered with angry gashes and a magenta river of blood trickled from her head. Her lips were parted, as though she was about to say something, share a secret.

"Hello, princess," said a cheery voice from the door of my room. I raised my eyes to see an unfamiliar guy in scrubs walking in. I missed Loretta.

The new guy said, "I'm Ruben. And from the looks of this room, you're Little Miss Popular."

He fingered each of the bouquets that had been moved to the shelf opposite my bed, ending up with the two-dozen red roses. "This must have set someone back plenty. I wish I could find a boyfriend as generous."

"They're not from my boyfriend," I said.

"*Whoo-hoo*, then you're doing something right. What about this guy?" He picked up the teddy bear wearing a muscle shirt. "Not sure if that's from a friend or an enemy."

"Me either," I said.

The harder something is for you to handle, the more deeply it will be buried, Dr. Tan had told me. Looking at the photo, I felt like I was on the verge of it. The final secret.

Now Ruben was standing in front of the double-heart-shaped wreath. The doll Annie called Robert was propped against it and the ceramic figurine of the bunny stood to one side. Ruben squinted at the card next to the bunny. "'From your secret admirer,'" he read aloud. "So let me see—you've got a boyfriend, a *not* boyfriend, and a secret admirer." He shook his head at me. "Girl, no wonder someone tried to run you down." *The harder something is for you to handle…*

I stared at the face of the girl in the photo and thought about the mirror in the bathroom downstairs. The way it had steamed up, leaving only the blank outline between my palms where my face should have been. And the truth came rushing into my brain with the force of a rain-swollen river, inevitable, painful, leaving me gasping.

At once I knew everything. I knew how an invisible hand could write. How someone could call but never be heard. How a ring could vanish and reappear in the wrong place. I knew about the phone call. The drink. The car.

I knew I wasn't crazy and never had been.

"I'll be back to check on you in a tic, princess," Ruben said, but I barely heard.

I knew who my killer was. I'd known all along, but every part of my brain had sought another solution, another explanation. A way out.

There wasn't one. The last pieces of that night clicked into place. *I'm alone in the middle of the street. It's slick and shiny with rain.*

Don't stop, I tell myself. You have to keep running. Someone I trust wants to hurt me.

My heels clatter down the middle of the street, my ankle twists, and I fall.

Get up! Don't stop!

I want my mom, I think as I struggle back to my feet, want her with a longing so deep it resonates like a symphony through me. I want to be curled up next to her in the ratty old hammock under the elm tree in our backyard in Naperville, watching lazy bees flit from one flower to another and listening to Annie and my father's voices twining together into one of their made-up stories of princes and queens and hippos. I want to be back in our old station wagon making bets on how much longer it will be until the light turns green and marveling at my mother's ability to almost always get it just right. I want to be back in the kitchen with the yellow tile they never got around to renovating, eating blueberry pancakes with my father while Annie sings "Itsy-Bitsy Spider" in her high chair. I want to be in the new stone kitchen with my mother and Joe and Annie doing anything.

I want to be back before I knew so much, before I hurt so much. I want the pain to stop. What am I doing here, at another party, in another costume? Why didn't I stay home? Why didn't I always stay home? I'd been playing dress up for too long.

Move. Keep going.

Rivulets of water gush down the sides of the street, forcing me to walk toward the middle. It's deserted, with only the occasional discrete streetlight, like any fancy area. My ankle hurts and I'm limping and it's cold, but the rain is letting up.

My cell phone rings. I looked down at the caller ID and hesitate. Do I want to talk to Ollie? I need a ride.

I'm soaked and it takes me three attempts to get my trembling fingers to open the phone. A voice, not Ollie's, says, "Where are you? Let me come and get you."

"I'm at Peregrine Road."

"Turn right at the next corner and I'll be there."

"Okay, see you soon."

I turn and continue up the middle of the street, moving from darkness into pools of streetlight back into darkness. My phone vibrates and I fumble trying to answer it. It slides out of my wet hand onto the wet ground. My knees give out as I stoop to get it and I lie sprawled beneath a streetlight.

Up! You have to get up!

I've just gotten to my knees when I hear the sound of a car coming slowly up from the end of the block, but all I can see is darkness. Squinting, I make out the outline of a sedan with its headlights off coming toward me. It's David's car.

On my knees I wave.

It starts to accelerate.

It can't see me without headlights on, I realize.

"Stop!" I yell, trying to get upright. My feet slip wildly in the borrowed shoes and I flounder. It's nearly on me now, coming up fast. At the last possible moment the headlights flash on, pinning me in their glare. Now he'll stop, now—

The car speeds up. I make a final desperate lunge on my knees for the side of the road.

The car swerves toward me, hitting me head-on.

The impact lifts me off the ground. As I fly into the air, time stands still and I can see everything. I watch raindrops hang like shimmering diamonds in the air, power lines quiver with their current, the movement of the rubber on the car's windshield wipers. Then there is a horrible sound like bone being chewed and I am soaring, arching, *spinning around. I land with a crunching thud, my body exploding in a world of agony, sound and shape all combining into a cacophony of pain. Thousands of sharp points pierce my skin, grabbing my arms and legs and hair, holding me in their grip. I taste salt on my tongue.*

In the split second after the car hits me, in that moment of clarity, I see who is in the driver's seat. See the hands at ten and two, see the seat belt appropriately fastened, see the familiar face. The familiar smile.

"Bye, Jane," my killer says.

I looked up from the crime-scene photo, aware of footsteps in the corridor outside my room, aware that the last act of this play was about to start. A key turned and my door opened.

"Hi, Jane," Ollie said.

Chapter 33

I **should have known** about Ollie all along. He was the obvious choice.

"I didn't want to have to do this," he said. He kept the hypodermic needle by his side and his face looked genuinely conflicted. "You know, this wasn't anything I wanted. I tried to warn you. I tried to tell you to stop asking questions. Repeatedly. But you wouldn't listen."

"I know."

"And now—"

"You don't have to go through with it, Ollie," I said. "You can stop."

"I can't. I made a promise. I have to man up."

"You don't owe anyone anything. You're being used."

"No one uses me. I know exactly what I'm doing. This is my choice."

"Was it your idea to send the flowers? Really? Think back and tell me that someone else didn't suggest it. Your idea to lie about trying to kiss me? We both know you have no romantic interest in me."

"It was my idea. All of it. I did it to protect—"

A scream followed by the pounding of footsteps pierced the atmosphere of the room. The door exploded open and four burly security guards with guns and walkie-talkies came rushing in, followed by Langley screaming, "Stop him, you have to stop him. I told you he said he was coming here to kill her. Stop him!"

The lead security officer said, "Put the syringe down."

Ollie looked at it like he didn't know what it was. "This is just saline. It's not even anything."

"Put it down."

"I just wanted to scare Jane, not hurt her. Just get her to—"

The security guards surrounded Ollie, whose eyes bugged out. His whole body was vibrating, but he didn't seem to be seeing the men around him. He turned around and said, "Langley? What are you doing here?"

Langley ignored him, rushing over to me and cradling my head in her arms. "I told you. I told you he wanted to hurt her." She kissed me on the forehead. "Are you okay, jelly bean?"

"Yes," I said.

"Thank God we got here in time." She was weeping.

"Yes, thank God," I echoed.

Ollie was gazing around at the security guards now with his lips pulled back in a growl. "You all stay away from me." He got into a fighter's crouch but with his arm straight out holding the hypodermic needle. His breathing seemed labored.

The security detail was moving around him slowly. "Put the needle down," the lead officer said.

"Make me." Ollie lunged at him and missed. "I know how to fight. My father taught me before he died."

"Sir, please put the needle on the floor."

"You don't think I'm man enough to do this? No? Watch me," Ollie commanded. He was sweating and rubbing his free hand against the leg of his scrubs, but he seemed to be losing his focus, swaying back and forth. "I can—"

"He's got a knife!" Langley shrieked, and one of the security officers went in low and knocked Ollie off his feet to the floor.

Ollie tried to get to his hands and knees. "Stop it," he was saying, his eyes locked on Langley. "I—"

One of the security guards put a knee in his back and held him down. "Stay still," he said.

"But—" Ollie's voice was weak now, like the will had gone out of him.

"Shut up!"

The security team got busy on radios and cuffing Ollie and moving him out of my room. Before they could hustle him out the door, he turned to where Langley and I were and slurred, "I never had a knife. You know that. I hate knives. Knives…for cowards." And, eyes only half open, staggering over his own feet, he was gone.

"We have some routine questions for the two of you," the head of security said, coming over to stand by my bed. "Most of them can wait, but you, miss—" he looked at Langley, "—how did you get wind that Mr. Montero was going to assault your friend?"

"He came to my house today and he was acting—really strange. Finally he said he was going to protect me, that he loved me and he would take care of Jane. I had no idea what he meant, but apparently he'd formed some kind of delusion that I was responsible for Jane's accident." She shook her head ruefully and smiled down at me. "Can you believe that?"

The security guard couldn't.

"Anyway, I came straight here and tried to get in to warn Jane, but of course the ward is locked, so I just went up and down shouting at anyone I could find. Thank God it worked."

"Do you know how he got the uniform? Or the drugs in the syringe?"

Langley pressed her lips together. "I'm afraid those might be my fault. My grandfather is…not well and he has a private nursing staff. Ollie has been over helping my grandmother install a surveillance system in the sickroom and I suspect that it wouldn't have been hard for him to slip a few things away."

The officer nodded. "Thank you." He looked at me. "You're a very lucky girl to have such a resourceful friend."

"That she is," I said.

"Officer?" He paused and Langley threw herself at him, hugging him. "Thank you. Thank you for saving my friend."

He looked surprised and delighted. "You're welcome, miss." He went out blushing.

I looked at Langley, who was smiling down at me.

I said, "Why did you do that?"

"Do what?"

"Keep Ollie from killing me when you're planning to do it yourself? It would have been so much cleaner."

Her smile vanished and a crease appeared between her brows. "What are you talking about, jelly bean? I love you. I wouldn't hurt you."

Her voice sounded so sincere that for a moment I doubted everything. But then I looked in her eyes and I saw—nothing. Blankness.

I wasn't wrong. "I know all about it," I said. "I know it was you all along."

Her frown got deeper and she pursed her lips with confusion. "Me all along…?"

"Writing on the mirror. Calling. The secret-admirer gifts. Behind the wheel of the car. All you."

"How did I manage to pull all that off? I must be very clever."

I nodded. "You are."

There was a beat of silence. And then, as though she was unable to stop herself, she smiled. A smile so sunny that it made what came next more awful. "I am, aren't I?" She sighed complacently, then went on, musing aloud. "Wasn't Ollie so cute? Amazing how loyal people become when you figure out the right way to ride them. They're just like horses." Her tone was so casual she could have been chatting about the weather.

"But you couldn't let someone else have all the fun."

"No. I just needed a way to get through the battery of guards out front and dispose of all the security people. I wanted to be able to talk to my best friend for the last time in private." Her perfectly glossed lips were still curved into a smile. With one hand she tenderly brushed a lock of hair from my forehead. I didn't know then what she was doing with the other. "You understand, don't you, jelly bean?" Before I could answer—and what would I have said?—the furrow between her brows reappeared. She asked, "But if you knew, why didn't you say anything?"

I had an answer for that. "Because I wanted to find out how you did everything," I told her, but that wasn't the real reason. The real reason was that this was the only way it could end. If I'd accused her of trying to murder me, everyone would have assumed it just was me being insane. One of us *was* insane, but it wasn't me. This way, somehow, there would be proof.

"That's so flattering. But just in case you change your mind, I've taken precautions." I felt something sharp on my upper arm and looked down to see it was a syringe. I gasped. "I really want us to have a nice chat first, but if you start making things hard, I'll push this button and it will be bye-bye for you. So you'll be a good girl, right?"

My stomach lurched. *Stay calm*, I told myself. "Y-yes," I stammered.

Langley nodded to herself, her blonde hair falling forward to frame her angelic face, and reached out with the hand not holding the deadly syringe to touch my cheek. "You have such lovely skin, Jane. Did you know that's the first thing I noticed about you the day we met? Your skin. And the haunted look in your eyes. We were so much alike. We both had such heavy secrets. You needed me, I could tell. And I could help you. I did, didn't I?"

She leaned forward and her eyes glittered with anticipation like she was waiting on my answer.

I nodded.

She sighed and shook her head sadly. "It's really too bad it's come to this. But, you know, someone has to pay."

That was confusing. "What do you mean?"

She waved my question away, as though I'd insisted on covering half a lunch check and she wanted to treat. "Tell me from the beginning. How did you know it was me?"

"Lots of little things." I tried to sound confident, though my voice kept catching and the needle tip hurt my skin. Maybe if I could hold her attention, someone would come by and notice...something. It was the only chance I had.

"When I figured out how the writing on the mirror was done, that it didn't have to be someone in there while I was in the shower but could have been written by anyone previously when the mirror wasn't steamed up, the field narrowed," I explained. "And then I remembered the only thing Nicky, Sloan, and I had in common."

"Which was?"

"Lip gloss." At last I had a complete picture of what had happened. "The night of the party you drugged me with the lip gloss, but it wasn't acting fast enough—"

"I know! That bitch Nicky took it off when she kissed you. Freals, I could have killed that silly cow." Her voice was pleasant, happy, like this was just regular gossip.

"—so you summoned me upstairs to reapply it. After that I passed out somewhere and when I woke up, Kate dragged me to the room where David and Sloan were, to show me. I took my friendship ring off and threw it at her. I staggered out and ran into Elsa, who pushed me away."

Into someone. Into—

I'm in the hallway, desperate, and I see Langley. "Thank God. It's David. He was—"

"Come here, jelly bean," she says, pulling me into the bathroom.

I start telling Langley what happened. I say, "I can't take it anymore. It's over. I'm done, it's done. I just want to end it."

Langley examined her nails. "You went on and on and on and you were so boring, until finally you said, 'He's such an excrescence.' And that did it."

I'm sobbing with my head in my hands. I see something flash in the mirror in front of me and I look up. Langley is there, above me, her face pulled back into a terrifying grin. "Goodbye, Jane," she says, and smashes the cherub soap dish down on my head.

I wake up on the floor of the bathroom. It's dark and my eyes won't focus. I pull myself up to the counter and all I can see, reflected in the mirror, are eyes. Eyes filled with hate and disgust. My eyes. Glaring at myself for having been such a misguided fool.

I have to get out of there.

"Excrescence. I don't even think you used it right. So annoying."

"You knocked me over the head with a soap dish because I used a word you didn't like?"

"No no no. It was just so—so unsuitable. When you showed off that way, it wasn't who you really are. Who you should have been. I just wanted you to stop doing it." Something must have shown on my face because she said, "Stop looking at me like that," and jabbed the needle into my arm a little harder. "You weren't behaving nicely. But that has nothing to do with me. How did you know it was *me*?"

I racked my mind, fitting pieces together frantically like someone at a puzzle convention. "Elsa took a picture of me in the bathroom as I was waking up. After that I ran outside. Kate found me again to apologize, but I—I was horrible to her."

You're not the only one who got hurt tonight, she'd said. Now I understood. Sloan's *um, people* was Kate. Kate had been upset that David had hurt Sloan because *she* liked Sloan. Sloan and Kate were a couple. What I'd overheard her saying to David wasn't about me, wasn't *just stay away…alone*, she'd been talking about *Sloan*.

For a moment I felt a pang of envy. Not about them being together, but because Kate hadn't felt like she could tell me.

I would make amends for that later. If I lived.

"You're stalling," Langley said. "Talk about me. You and me."

"I ran down the street away from the house. And—" As I paused, a smile played over Langley's lips. Clearly I'd reached the part she wanted to hear. I said, "You. You called me on Ollie's phone. And then you made him pretend that it had been him with the police. That's why he got the details wrong. He was covering for you. That's why he sent the flowers too, to make the story of him trying to kiss me, like me, seem more credible. He thought he was doing you a favor."

"I wonder where he got that idea," she said with a happy smile.

Ruben poked his head in at that moment and asked, "Is everything okay in here, ladies?"

This was my chance, I thought. Then I felt the tip of the hypodermic press harder against my arm. Or not. "Yes," I said, my heart racing at panic level. *Think*, I told myself. *Be smart*. "Everything is fine."

"What happened to that boy they took out of here?" Langley asked, wide eyed.

"They were going to have him arrested for assault, but he passed out. So now he's in triage under restraint until the police get here. You're a lucky girl, princess," Ruben said to me. "Your friend here saved your life."

"Yes, she did." I gave Langley a big grin.

She smoothed her hand over my hair and jabbed my arm harder. "I don't know what I'd do without Jane."

"Yes, I'm a regular conversational hit man."

"What does that mean?" Ruben asked.

"Ask Pete, he'll explain it."

Ruben smiled. "Seeing you two together makes my heart swell. All girls should be so lucky."

He left and Langley said, "You'd have to be crazy not to agree with him." She laughed. "Of course, by all accounts you are."

"That was masterfully done. Convincing everyone I was insane."

"It was so fun. Especially coming up with the secret-admirer gifts. Admit it, I had you believing it too."

"Until I realized how easy it would be for anyone who had a bug in the room." I looked at the Get Well Beary Soon bear. "It took me a while to figure out where it was."

"It's not just a bug, it's video, too. It connects to my iPhone. Although I have to say, a lot of the time you were really boring. But it was fun freaking you out with things you thought were only in your head. Want to see how it works?"

"No."

She got the bear anyway and started moving it around while she talked, holding it at different angles and checking them on her iPhone. "My original plan wasn't to kill you. I just wanted to teach you a lesson about friendship. One for all and all for one. You'd started being so disloyal, jelly bean. Keeping secrets. Making friends with undesirables. Scott and Elsa and then, the worst, Nicky. I really couldn't have you wasting your time on her. Plus I wanted David single."

"You started the Licky Nicky rumors." I remembered how Nicky had attacked Ollie at the party. "No, you made Ollie start them."

"I didn't *make* him do anything. He wanted to. I just gave him direction. That boy was in such need of a maternal influence all I had to do was offer it to him and he was mine. I've been incredibly good for him. Now smile for the camera, jelly bean."

"The LAW cuff links he was wearing yesterday. I thought the other was ORDER. But it wasn't. They were your grandfather's. You must have given them to him. And that's why he has a collection of Agent Provocateur underwear. It's yours."

"We have a look-but-don't-touch policy."

"But what about Alex?" I started to say, then it hit me. I laughed. "There is no Alex, is there? There never has been."

"His photo came in the frames they sold at this one stationery store in London. The first time I saw him, I knew he'd be the perfect boyfriend. Handsome, invisible, and useful to make Ollie jealous and to make you and Kate sympathetic. So much more effective than a real boyfriend and without all that mess. But I was worried if you looked too closely, you'd see the picture was a fake."

That was it. The explanation. Ollie and I weren't any different. "You preyed on both Ollie's and my fear of being alone. It worked in different ways—he spied on people, I took pictures, but we were both outsiders. Like line drawings that you could fill in." And then I realized. "Only I started filling in myself. The tragic thing is, I was able to do that, to become a better person, because of you. Because of your friendship."

For a split second I could have sworn that a spark of confusion, maybe of fear, flickered in her eyes. But it was tamped out, like the last dying embers of a campfire, and her eyes were back to glossy and dark as she said, "Now you're pandering. See, you're not the only one who can use big words. And you're not so special just because your dad was a poet. My father was—anyway, as smart as yours."

"Your father was president of New Jersey Steel and Gas."

Her mouth fell open. "You don't know that."

I remembered the day of the equestrian meet, when she'd said, "He's more than a grandfather to me." There had been something speculative, amused in her tone that struck me. "Actually," I told her now, "I do."

"Well, it wasn't Popo's fault. My mother was a whore."

"Does your grandmother know?"

"That doesn't matter. All that matters is that Popo knows and I know. And since he had his little accident six months ago, Popo knows the consequences of being unpleasant." She was moving the bear around. "Oh, that's a good shot."

"You did that? You pushed your grandfather down the stairs?"

"He wouldn't buy me a new car!"

I gasped in disbelief. "What about your mother? Why did you kill her?"

Langley's expression went blank, like a shutter coming down. She kept her eyes on something just above my shoulder and her voice was strange and flat. "Don't be silly. I was trying to help her. It was time for her to stop messing around and get back to her parents. It was simply irresponsible of her to raise a child the way she was. There was liquor. And parties. And I had to wear clothes from the thrift store. All for no reason. She refused to go back, just because she felt dirty or something. Pure selfishness. Her parents were millionaires. So I did what had to be done to take care of myself. Just like she taught me. I set the trailer on fire." She shrugged one shoulder. "How was I supposed to know she'd be passed out inside?"

I stared at her in horror, but she didn't seem to notice.

"I saw her get up from the bed and stagger forward. She tried to get the door open, but it was stuck and she was trapped. I watched. I saw her face through the window." Now she looked me right in the eye. "You understand how it is when a person you love dies by accident, don't you, Jane? But even though it's an accident, someone has to pay."

I started to shiver. More terrifying than what she was saying was the cool calculation with which she said it. It was as though something had snapped inside of her. "You're nuts."

"Which of us is in the locked ward and which of us isn't?" she observed pleasantly. She put the bear down and heaved her shoulders up in a big sigh. "When I think of the wonderful obit you're going to get, I'm almost jealous. What I've done for you, raising your profile like this, is a gift. Freals, I've made your biography about a thousand times more interesting than it was when you were just Plain Jane. Or what is that your little friend Scott calls you? Just Jane? Well, you're not Just Jane anymore. When I think about what you did, I'm really not sure you deserve this kind of send-off."

"What do you mean, what I did?"

"You know."

"Let me see if I understand. You attacked your grandfather in order to get him to buy you a new car."

"To teach him a lesson," she corrected. "He needs to learn discipline."

"And you tried to kill me to get my boyfriend and because I use big words."

"No, no, no." She shook her head in a big arc from side to side. "That's not it at all. It wasn't until I saw you kneeling in the middle of the street, as if you were begging for forgiveness, that I knew what I had to do. It was all so clear. If I didn't stop you, you'd keep hurting people. And I knew you wouldn't want that. There you were, wearing my Prada platform shoes in the rain after I'd specifically asked you not to get them wet, it was like you were waiting for me to do it. So I stepped on the gas and off you went. At the last minute you decided to move, but I compensated. BAM!" She smiled.

"You tried to kill me because I ruined your shoes?"

She closed her eyes and took a deep breath. When she opened them and spoke, her voice was the voice of a disappointed parent. "You still don't understand. Those were just little things. Someone has to pay when a person they love gets hurt. You understand that now, right?"

Her pupils had been getting bigger and bigger as she talked, and now her normally light blue eyes were nearly black. "That's not true," I said, one last effort to calm her. "I didn't want to die. And no one has to pay for anything. You didn't do anything wrong."

"But you did." Her words sent a massive chill down my spine. "Leaving poor Bonnie like that. Never telling anyone what happened, keeping secrets. Pay pay pay. You watched her face through the window and didn't do a thing."

For a second it looked like Langley might cry. She was looking not at me but at the door. I wondered what she was seeing. I wondered if she was watching her own mother die, all over again.

"That's not true," I started to say. "That's you, not me. And it's not your fau—"

"Blah blah blah." She shook her head as though to clear it and moved her fingers at me to make it look like they were quacking like a duck. "We should probably wrap things up. You were a lot of work, you know. And know what was annoying? Somehow you managed to look so perfect even when you were supposed to be dead. Landing like a goddamned fairy-tale heroine in that rosebush. I would have taken you out and made you look more mangled if I could, but there wasn't time. David would notice his car was missing eventually."

She shook herself out of her reverie and smiled. It was the only moment I'd ever seen her look anything but beautiful. It was terrifying.

"This time, it's going to hurt a bit, so maybe you'll look ugly. You certainly did during the rehearsal."

"Rehearsal?"

She leaned in, animated, like she was describing a new dress. "You start to hallucinate again, and you think I'm Bonnie, trying to pull you down, and you struggle against your restraints trying to reach me. Or strangle me. I haven't decided. In the tussle your IV comes out, your blood pressure skyrockets, and you have trouble breathing."

"But that will bring all the nurses in. The way it did the other day." I understood it. "At the rehearsal." I felt like I was being smothered, pulled down by panic. *Fight it*, I told myself. *You have to stay focused.*

"Exactly. And they'll do what they did the other day, give you a shot of this." She nodded toward a syringe on the table. "Only this time you'll go into cardiac arrest and die."

"That's not what happened the other day."

"I made a few modifications."

"You tampered with the syringe."

She smiled. Elsa was right. There wasn't anything behind Langley's eyes. She was cold and conniving. And terrifying. A clammy sweat crept over my body.

"The beauty of this plan is that once it's set in motion, it can't be stopped and it looks like it's all the hospital's fault. I just stand back and let it tick away like clockwork." She tapped me on the nose. "If you do it right, I might consider telling them you were trying to *save*

Michele Jaffe

Bonnie in your hallucination. To make it that much more tragic for everyone."

"Don't," I pleaded, putting every ounce of emotion I had into it. "Please don't put my mother through that."

"You're going to beg for your mother but not for your life?"

"Yes."

For a second that spark reappeared in her eyes, the spark of something confused and almost pitiable. But again it was extinguished. "You can imagine how traumatic this is going to be for me. I think Popo will finally have to let me spend a year traveling around Europe to recover. He's been so stingy about that." It was getting harder to hear her over the sound of my panicked heart pounding in my ears. "And I anticipate David coming to visit for a month this summer. Maybe in Monaco. I think he'd look good there." She nodded to herself. "So, are you ready? I'm really excited. Any last words? No? Not even how sorry you are for killing your best friend?"

"I didn't." My voice came out rough but insistent.

"You did too. You did and now you're going to pay for it."

My throat was sandpaper, my breathing shallow, but I tried to keep my voice calm. "Bonnie's death wasn't my fault," I said. "And your mother's death wasn't yours."

Her eyes stared at me fixed and unblinking. "Don't you dare talk about my mother."

"Langley, it doesn't have to be this way. You don't have to do this."

"Yes. I. Do." Her eyes sparkled and her fingers reached for my IV.

Suddenly a silver object flew through the air and hit her on the head, sending her reeling backward, taking my IV with it.

A wave of pain crashed over me and I felt something jab my arm and then it went black.

Chapter 34

I **stood on the** tip of the dock, marveling at the stillness. It was just after dawn, the moment when the trees around the lake looked like a silent purple wall against a sky streaked with pink and blue and lilac. The water was smooth and flat like a mirror.

There were weeds below it, long curling whips with a will of their own, I knew from my best friend Bonnie, but I thought I could deal with them.

A white bird flew across the sky, its wings pumping, and I dove into the lake, slicing through the silvery surface, delighted by the prickling of the cool water on my skin. The weeds below reached for me, some grabbing, some caressing, but I swam through them, powerful, sure strokes. I swam down, not up, down toward the bottom, down toward the face of a girl I recognized.

She smiled as she saw me and held out her hand. I reached to take it, but she shook her head. No, she seemed to be saying. Look. And I realized there was something in her palm, a silver chain with an object—a medallion? A coin? A key?—on it. Take it, she seemed to say.

I tried. I extended my hands toward her as far as they would go, but I couldn't quite reach. Each time I swam closer, she seemed to recede. I pursued her as far as I could, but my lungs began to strain, then to ache.

"I'll be back," I tried to say to her. "Wait for me."

I turned and began to make for the light above. Bubbles escaped my lips as I rose, sure and sleek, from the bottom. I was short on air, but I was strong, I could do this. I could see the top of the lake. I could make it.

With my last remaining breath I exploded through the surface of the water. I gulped air and felt the warmth of the sun on my skin and pushed the water from my face and saw eyes hovering over me.

Eyes full of love. Five sets of them. My mother, Joe, Annie, Loretta. And Pete.

"Welcome back, Jane," my mom said.

✦

"You really did play on the pro-Frisbee circuit," I said to Pete a little later, still surprised at this revelation. "I thought you made that up."

"You need to learn to trust me," Pete said. We were back in room 403, only now there was a huge security detail outside to keep the press away. Apparently two suburban teen girls trying to kill each other is big news.

But not news my mother was part of. She'd forgotten to put on lipstick and her hair was slightly tousled and she looked, in my opinion, completely gorgeous and about fifteen years younger. She was in my room, alternating coming over and hugging me and smiling and saying how much she loved me and collapsing into chairs and bursting into sobs.

"I'm so sorry I let them keep you in that locked ward," she said, holding on to me as though for dear life. "I—I was just so afraid I wasn't thinking straight. They said it was the best thing and even though I didn't agree, I thought, who am I to argue? But I know better now. I know my daughter better than any doctor. I should have listened to you."

"We can unknot anything if we work together," I said. There was a flash of recognition in her eyes.

"You remember that?"

"I remember everything, Mommy."

We hugged for a long time after that.

But when the heaviest of the emotional baggage had been unpacked, she was left without anything to run, and she didn't know what to do with herself. Finally, after she'd tried to reorganize the nursing station for the third time and Loretta had sent her back into my room with orders to keep her there Or Else, I gave up.

"Look, Mom, you have to stop pacing around like this. You're going to drive me crazy."

"At least this time we'll know it's genuine," she said. And started giggling.

Joe turned to me. "I think your mom just made a joke."

"I think you might be right."

"She might need a little practice, huh?" he asked, his eyes twinkling.

"She might need a remedial course."

"I thought it was good," Annie said.

The two largest members of the security detail were sitting outside my room now, one of them drinking Gatorade and the other Tab. Apparently Joe had decided to get some of his guys to watch my room even though my mother didn't take the threats seriously because, as he put it, "I love your mother, I do, but she was so scared of losing you, she wasn't thinking right. I saw everything she saw and I had to say, you didn't seem nuts to me."

"Thank you," I told him. I said it again when he introduced me to Bruno and Lou.

"Don't thank us, miss, we wouldn't have stopped that little number if we'd seen her coming at you. Useless is what we would've been."

"I'm still glad to know you were there."

It was true. No one would have thought Langley would turn out to be psychotic. I was pretty sure she wouldn't have a hard time talking herself out of the maximum-security psychiatric facility her grandparents had installed her in before the police could question her. No one would believe she was guilty. No one except Pete. Pete was the one who had pieced it all together in time to warn Loretta not to use the syringe in the room to revive me.

"Why did you believe me? That I wasn't crazy? No one else did," I pointed out. I had his hand in mine and was tracing one of the lines of his palm with my finger.

"Joe did."

"Okay. But why did you? I wasn't even sure I was sane."

There was no mockery, no irony, no sarcasm in his voice when he said, "Maybe I have more faith in you than you do."

Gulp.

He nudged his nose against mine so our foreheads were touching. "Plus I thought I'd take my chances since no one else was bothering. The way I saw it, if you were right, then one of your friends was out to get you and all we had to do was figure out which one. And then it was easy."

"Easy? How?"

He shrugged. "I just needed to figure out who was left handed."

I pulled away to stare at him. "Okay, Nancy Drew."

"It was what you kept saying about that ring. When we saw the picture in Elsa's room where you weren't wearing it, I realized that the killer had probably put it on you after you were hit. If you wore a ring and you were slipping an identical ring onto someone's hand, which finger would you be most likely to put it on?"

"Whatever finger *I* wore it on normally."

"Bingo."

"So it ended up on my right hand—"

"—because that's where the killer wore her ring. I just had to figure out who wore it on their right hand. I threw in the lefty part to make it sound more Sherlock Holmes."

I was incredulous. "But Mr. Holmes, you never even met my friends. How did you know who was a lefty?"

"Remember that first day, you told me to watch the DVD Kate and Langley made you so I would see how popular you were?"

I groaned. "Yes."

"I did." He raised his eyebrows. "Twice."

"I'm going to regret having told you to do that, aren't I?"

He nodded somberly. "Oh yes."

I laughed. "I can't wait. But really, you figured it all out because of the ring?"

"Mm-hmmm." He dragged the word out. "Okay, fine. That, and you gave me a pretty good hint when you had Ruben ask me about conversational hit men. Made me think you were trying to tell me that the first person in had just been a decoy to open the way for the real-kill shot." He smirked, coming clean now. "Especially when the DVD helped me identify Ollie and Langley as the two people I'd seen making out in the stairwell that day. I figured they had a lot of secrets and might be working together for all kinds of nefarious purposes."

"I guessed it was more complicated than a ring."

"That DVD came in really handy. It helped me solve the crime *and* stop the killer."

"Stop the—" That's when I got it. The silver disc that had flown through the air and hit Langley just before I passed out. "*That's* what you threw at her head!"

"I was on my way back from watching it in the lounge when I figured everything out, so it was the only thing I had in my hand. But it seems like perfect justice, doesn't it? Popularity can be a real headache."

"It certainly can."

I looked toward the window of my room. There were no flowers or cards or presents there anymore. I hadn't realized how much they'd been blocking the view.

In fact, I was aware that there was a lot I hadn't been seeing, blinded by my own insecurities and guilt. But not anymore. Now I was going to have my eyes wide open.

Suddenly I remembered the medallion from the dream I'd just woken from—remembered I'd seen it the night of Bonnie's death. It had been clutched in her hand. But it wasn't hers. There was more to that night than I'd realized. And I owed it to Bonnie's family to help them find the truth.

But right now, there were things right in front of me that deserved a long look.

My eyes went to Pete and he smiled, the one with the crinkles around his eyes and the lines next to his mouth. He looked like a happy little kid as he stretched out a hand to smooth my forehead.

"Stop fretting, beautiful."

"I'm not fretting." I reached out to toy with the pearl buttons on his shirt. "I just wish—I feel like I've been myopic. I should have figured this out before."

"You knew the answer all along if you had just trusted your instincts."

"Yeah. I need to work on that." My eyes moved from the buttons to his lips, then his nose, finally resting on his eyes. "Do you think you could be my teacher?"

"Oh no. Absolutely not."

That wasn't the answer I'd expected. "Why?"

"I don't want to teach. I'd rather *do*."

"Do what?"

"This."

This was not like anything I'd ever experienced before.

"Look, everyone, Jane is kissing Pete! That's the third boy she's kissed this week."

"Is that true?" Pete said, pulling away to look at me.

"Purely medicinal," I said solemnly.

"I think your sister just made a joke," he told Annie.

"She should take lessons from Mom."

I started walking again the next day.

Afterword

$\mathscr{T}$he image is a mess.

It's the time of day just before sunset, when colors are at their richest. The sky is a deep mellow blue, the sea below it indigo. A red-and-white-striped tent stands on a greensward extending toward the ocean. Beneath it long tables covered in brightly colored floral cloths hold the skeleton of what had been a feast. There are beleaguered-looking flowers and crumpled napkins and plates covered in rainbow frosting everywhere. The remains of a cake list perilously to one side next to a huge silver urn with condensation running down its sides and an open bottle of Dom Pérignon poking out the top. On the left a little girl is showing a boy a snail she's trapped in a peanut-butter jar. On the right four large men who have shed their jackets are playing poker and smoking cigars and drinking beer, although one of them has a bottle of Gatorade in front of him too. In the foreground Rosalind Freeman, in a blue sundress she would have sworn was too young for her but that her daughters made her buy, with her hair swept off her face, is gazing up at her new husband, Joe Garcetti, with an expression of wonder and joy.

Periodically the company is disturbed by a bubble of laughter erupting from under the apple tree. There's a hammock there, old and so often mended that it looks like the hunting net of a powerful witch. In it, as though trapped in a spell, lie a boy and a girl. He's wearing a button-down shirt with penguins embroidered on it and she has on a white eyelet dress that is probably last season. He's devastatingly handsome. Her hair looks like it was styled with a machete and she will probably always have a faint scar on her forehead from where doctors stitched her back together, but she doesn't care. They are facing each other, nose to nose, and grinning.

In its chaotic festivity it looks a lot like the photographs I'm taking these days, only it's not one. It's not a photo. It's real life.

And I'm in it.